First Printing, 2020

Cover art designed by Suspirialand:
https://www.instagram.com/suspirialand/
Internal illustration:
https://www.artstation.com/drake7018
Find more books by the author at:
https://www.davidironswriter.com/books

D1412248

PRAISE FOR GRAVEYARD BILLY:

"ONE OF THE BEST BOOKS I'VE READ. I HIGHLY RECOMMEND IT!" – ERICA FIELDS @WETZELFIELDS

"IT'S GOT EVERYTHING, INTRIGUE, HUMOUR, ADVENTURE, THE SUPERNATURAL AND A CUTE FELINE HERO!" – VERIFIED AMAZON REVIEW.

"IRONS WRITES HIS HEROIC FELINE PROTAGONIST AS ONLY SOMEONE WHO DEARLY LOVES CATS COULD HAVE; THIS WAS MY FAVOURITE BOOK OF 2020!" – HAYLA RICHARDS @BOOKLOVINGCATMOM

GRAVEYARD BILLY

DAVID IRONS

FOR BILLY BEAR – THE BEST FRIEND I'VE EVER HAD.

CHAPTER ONE

A wind as cold as a vampire's bite shot through the graveyard's iron gates; it wound past grey tombstones that were twisted with ivy; shifted leaves rusted with autumn's corrosion. There was perfect silence in the graveyard, the hiss of the wind as authoritative as a librarian's *'Shuusssshhhhhhh,'* as it tried to keep the space's morbid tranquillity.

Yellow feline eyes batted awake in hidden blackness, sensing something coming closer.

Ears – no more than fuzzy triangles – turned to listen; thirty-two individual muscles in each rotated, then pinpointed where the new sounds were coming from –where the voices were coming from.

Fangs were bared in a yawn: He was awake now; alert, creeping, peering, slinking in the undergrowth.

A black nose twitched whiskers – a new scent in the air.

He understood what the scent told him: Two old ladies sat on a wooden bench, faces as lined as splintered glass, expressions puckered with age.

He sat, still and silent, watched with eyes that constructed colours mutely with dichromatic vision; the old ladies' vivid clothes washed to pastels by his retinas.

'Well!' exclaimed the first old lady – Maude Parkes – dressed in a mauve outfit: hat, jacket and shoes all in perfect synchronization. 'Personally, I don't know what this town's coming to.'

'City.' Elsie Slater, the woman sitting next to Maude – dressed head to toe in an earthy green – corrected her. 'Brighton's a city.'

'Well ... whatever it is, me and Harold came here back in the sixties to get away from all the weirdos in London.'

Elise nodded.

'And now–' Maude added with disdain.

'–we're surrounded by them.' Both women said this in unison, their faces souring with their jinx.

'This place ...' Maude said. ' ... If my Harold could see it now.'

'Never got any better,' Elsie moaned, offering a hard-boiled sweet to the woman next to her.

Maude politely declined, clenching her dentures tight at the thought. 'Never got *any* better,' Maude said, shaking her head, eyeing the bunch of flowers she'd bought from the petrol station for Harold's grave.

'How long's it been now since your Harold's been gone?'
Elsie asked.

'Nearly three years.' Maude said, her expression not
changing.

'Three years,' Elsie pondered, both women falling to
silence, an unsaid thought shared between them that in another
three years – they might not be here, either.

A black hooded figure rushed past them, a feeling as if the
Reaper had come early: A boy rode past them on his mountain
bike.

Both old women gasped.

'This is the thing!' Maude exclaimed, *'No one cares
anymore!'* The words were projected after the boy. 'That's why all
this crime has been on the up-rise.'

'On the up-rise!' Elise spluttered as she gummed her
sweets. 'Did you hear about them girls, all of them turning up …
you know …' she crossed herself quickly, then pointed to the
nearest grave, not even wanting the word on her puckered lips.

'I *know!*' Maude said, tensing. 'Just young girls, all of their
life ahead of them; then, just like that – gone.'

'There's not just weirdos in Brighton these days,' Elise said
through sucking her sweet, 'There's maniacs.'

'There's maniacs,' Maude repeated, her eyes rounded with
the thought of all the weirdos that could be creeping nearby.
'How many has he had now? Seven – eight?'

'About that,' Elise replied with equal worry.

'They've all been young so far, but you mark my words –'

'I'll do just that!' Elise interrupted.

'–The old will be the next to get it, we always d –' Maude
paused, her face stretching in shock, her wrinkles de-creasing as
if de-aged with fear. In front of her, in the cavernous black of the
bushes, something moved.

'Did you …' Maude said, grabbing Elsie's arm, stopping her
from eating her next sweet. The fear was contagious; both ladies
froze like the gargoyles on the church roof that looked down on
them.

In front of them, the rustling sound emerged into the
limited light of the grey sky above. For a moment, it was as if a
slice of night had grown legs and a tail; the yellow eyes blinked
at the two women; the whiskers twitched: a perfectly black cat
slinked towards them. The rustle of Elsie's sweet wrapper was too
much for the creature, the promise of food too much of a draw.

'Aghhhhhhhhh!' the two women cooed together.

'Look at him,' Elise smiled, something that was almost
youthful blooming in her complexion.

'It was your packet he heard,' Maude said. 'That's what
brought him out: I know my animals, me.'

The cat blinked at them both, slowly and smoothly, in as friendly a way as he could.

'Always watching, they are, know everything you do. You know what they say about cats, nine senses and all that.' Maude grinned as the cat sat at her feet.

'Six senses and nine lives, you mean.' Elsie corrected.

'Same difference really, isn't it?' Maude said with a snap of her false teeth.

'You're a beautiful little man, aren't you!' Elsie smiled as Maude patted the cat's head.

The black cat blinked in reply.

'I bet you love it round here, in the graveyard, plenty of things you can hunt!' Maude said.

The black cat blinked in reply, again.

'He looks too domesticated to worry about hunting; he looks very well fed,' Elsie observed.

The black cat turned to Maude, then turned to Elsie and blinked at them both; they never noticed how he blinked in response – most humans never did.

A chilled breeze rattled past the two women, both feeling it beneath their thick winter coats; both of their old bones were rattled by it. Neither commented – they never did.

'Look at that, he's got a name on his collar,' Maude said; both women cocked their heads, almost turning them upside down so that their old eyes could squint to read the penned words on the cat's old white collar.

'Graveyard?' said Maude, perplexed.

'Billy?' said Elsie, just as confused.

'Graveyard Billy? What kind of name is that?' Maude said.

Graveyard Billy blinked once as if to say: 'Mine.'

The biting wind returned, both the old women clutching their coats for protection. Graveyard Billy's fur heckled with the chill.

Suddenly, the cat cocked his head, looked at the empty space on the bench next to Maude. Something that could be fear or timidity flared in his eyes.

Maude noticed this: 'There ain't nothing to be scared of here!'

'Come on,' Elsie said to the black cat, 'come up and say hello!'

Maude patted the empty spot next to her, 'Come on, you silly thing, and sit up here!'

Graveyard Billy didn't move, his fur hackling a plume along his back as he eyed the empty space next to the old ladies.

'My Harold, he was never fond of 'em, ya know.'

'What's that?' Elsie asked, popping in another hard-boiled sweet.

'Cats, he hated cats, despised them, he did. I went nearly

11

thirty years without having a pet after my Pixie went missing – under very suspicious circumstances, seeings how I just got married to Harold,'

'*Very suspicious,*' Elsie reiterated.

'Would he ever let me have another one?' Maude asked as Graveyard Billy looked at her inquisitively. 'Would he, hell!'

'Well, you could get one now,' Elsie said. 'He popped his clogs three years ago, didn't he?'

'*Well,*' Maude replied, 'It wouldn't seem right after all this time. Up and down filling their bowls and my knees the way they are.'

'Well, yes, your knees,' Elsie nodded.

'*Yes.*' Maude nodded with finality. 'I don't think Harold would like me to get another one.'

That cold breeze passed again; they both looked down at Graveyard Billy, who looked up at them, then stared with a glaring intensity at the empty seat, backing away slightly.

'Silly thing, we won't hurt, ya,' Elsie said.

'Yes, *not us* –' Maude said, giving the hooded boy a glare as he rode back past them on his bike. 'It's those *others* you have to worry about.'

'Well, come on, we better go; there's free cake down at the WI, I don't want to miss it,' Maude said, her dentures not that much of a problem for one of Mrs. Taylor's Cherry Bakewells.

'No! We better not miss it,' Elsie said. 'Let's go give your Harold his flowers and head down.'

They both tottered away, forgetting Graveyard Billy as they went, as most humans did.

As Graveyard Billy stared at the empty space on the bench, he wondered to himself why the old ladies would have to find Harold's grave to give him the flowers. His yellow eyes followed something only he could see as it shifted from the empty spot and moved behind the two women.

In the distance, in some cosmic consciousness, Maude said, 'Maybe Graveyard Billy can sense old Harold around, knows he don't like cats.'

Graveyard Billy blinked in response.

In Maude's eyes, there had been only two of them sitting on the bench; through Graveyard Billy's eyes, there were three.

A vivid spectral scintilla of light, more vibrant and alive than anything else his limited vision would normally allow, trailed behind Maude and Elsie. It was a light that the human eye couldn't see that the two old women couldn't see, but through Graveyard Billy's eyes, it formed the shape of a miserable old man trundling behind them.

If Maude's eyes worked as Graveyard Billy's did, she would have known the old man looked like Harold.

CHAPTER TWO

Woodvale Cemetery was where Graveyard Billy spent most of his time, lounging around lackadaisically as if each day were a Sunday. Sunning himself along the stretch of a tomb in the summer, curled in a circle of his own fur beneath the shrubbery of the willow trees in the winter: No matter the season, Graveyard Billy would be there somewhere.

Unlike most cats – nocturnal by nature – out at night as if patrolling the graveyard were their nine-to-five, Graveyard Billy would go back to his home as dark pulled in. He had his routine, his order of doing things: dashing across a succession of graves – *Keith Marsden, Sabrina Ruther,* and *Neil Anderson* engraved on their stones – a quick jump onto the side of a crypt, and a hurl to the wall beyond, climbing its ivy to the top where his own little ramp lay connecting to the window of the flats next door.

The ramp was made from a beam of old decking, pieces of a cut-up pallet screwed into it as rungs, then stained a dark oak. Graveyard Billy understood this was his ramp, and at its end, through the little cap flat cut into the window, was his home.

They say cats pick their people rather than people pick their cats; for Graveyard Billy, this was all too true. He started his life in Rectory Road in Hackney East London. His mum was a black Bengal pedigree; his dad ... well, let's just say a window was left open, and the local tom couldn't believe his luck.

Then, before her owners knew it, their one pedigree had multiplied to five as a whole new batch of black kittens arrived. And as unexpected as they were, they were equally unwanted.

The Bengal's owner found the solution: her two Swedish cleaners who lived near the station. With the payment of an extra thirty pounds each to their wages and the added incentive of five new cat beds, five new cat bowls, and five new cat trays – Maja and Nora became the new owners of five new kittens to use them. And after a few days of them being in their flat, they were five new kittens that were soon looking for five new owners.

One Sunday, Piper Herbert sat on the underground from Camden to Hackney.

She was twenty years old, with big blonde hair always in a messy top bun, an old black sweatshirt, and ripped blue jeans. Her head swayed with the rocking carriage as she nursed a hangover. Dark sunglasses shielded her eyes from the glaring fluorescents above, a bottle of water in hand to dilute the dizziness in her head.

'Piper, come on, spill the beans,' Charlie, her more sober

redheaded friend, demanded.

'What's to tell,' Piper replied, rubbing her hand across her forehead as if she could wipe the dreariness away.

'You've planned this for weeks, come all the way up here from Brighton to stay at this new guy's house, and for some reason, you've texted me so you can come back to my place? What's that all about? I thought you were supposed to meet ...'

There was no way to dodge the bullet of Charlie's questions anymore, to keep avoiding the same thing said in so many different ways.

'Adam –'

'Adam! That's his name! Charlie interrupted, losing interest in her phone as reality became more relevant. 'Come on, what's happened?'

'Piper sighed, 'Let's just say when we were texting, he was one thing ... but in person ... he was something else ...'

Charlie stared at the air as if some invisible equation hung there. Then a sudden revelation appeared on her face as if it had been solved.

'Hang on!' Charlie exclaimed, getting comfy, pulling her feet up under herself, sitting cross-legged. 'You told me you *had* met him before ... *right?*'

Piper winced, 'Well kind of, in a roundabout way ...'

They passed through a tunnel; she hoped Charlie's next question would stay left inside it.

'This, *Adam* –'

'Yeah,' Piper sighed. 'This, *Adam.*'

'He wasn't like – some kind of internet app date ...' Charlie said with slanted eyes.

The man sitting opposite let his newspaper fall, a pair of eyes quickly scanning the girls, snooping over the paper's edge.

Piper raised her sunglasses, stared back with an unimpressed glare, watched as the newspaper rose in retreat. 'Well,' Piper admitted, 'maybe he was.'

'You told me you had met him in person down on the coast!' Charlie exclaimed, the cat out of the bag.

'Did I?'

Light burst through the carriage as they moved above ground.

'Yeah, you told me that on Facebook!' Charlie gasped.

'Don't believe everything you read on Facebook.' Piper said nonchalantly.

'So it was a lie, then?' Charlie asked.

'No ... I just bent the truth ...'

Charlie gave her a look.

'Okay! I didn't want to look like a complete loser; that was the plan if we got serious ... *got serious!*' she cried.

More newspapers dropped to catch a glance of the girl

spilling her guts.

'We had spoken online for over a month; I was supposed to be meeting a twenty-seven-year-old graphic designer with his own flat. I suppose thirteen years ago he might have been that.'

'What?' Charlie's face contorted.

'He was a forty-year-old divorcee who lived in a bedsit in one of the tower blocks near the Lock.'

Charlie bit her lip, tried to be as good a friend as she could.

'I ended up doing a runner after we went to the second pub, and he started showing me pictures of him with his wife and two kids.'

Charlie couldn't help it; she let out a snort. Luckily it was infectious; Piper pulled her first smile of the day.

'I went and spent the night in the cinema watching some comedy starring a guy with a head like Frankenstein's monster.'

Charlie squinted. 'That new Vince Vaughn film.'

'Whatever, I spent all my money on a last-minute Airbnb and a bottle of vodka.'

'Well, it could be worse,' Charlie said.

'Could it?' Piper replied. 'In his picture, he had a full head of hair.'

'Was he a baldy, too?' Charlie laughed.

'Worse: comb-over.'

Charlie exploded.

Piper couldn't help it: Out loud, in the open, under the prying eyes of the snooping newspaper people, she finally found the disastrous date as funny as her friend did and began to laugh and laugh.

Piper's life had always been a herky-jerky thing. Everything she had done, she had done alone. Her parents had both passed away when she was a child; she'd been only three years old when it had happened. A patch of ice, a pump of the car's brakes, and everything was gone: Piper was the only one to survive. Then it had been the children's home, temporary adoption houses, then at sixteen and with no other choice to go on the council list for accommodation, she was offered a flat in Brighton. She had no job there, no friends, but she had one thing, a roof over her head – a roof that was her own – and a chance.

She worked in supermarkets, bars, anywhere she could and saved and saved.

Almost ten years later, officially a mature student – unofficially not that mature – she had enrolled at Brighton University on an art degree.

Piper was doing everything she wanted to do, had pulled all the strings of her life together, was almost about to bow them, but one final problem bit and frayed the edges of the life she had created – the loneliness.

She would often dream blurred visions of what she thought were memories, what she thought were echoes of the past, what could have been her parents. She tried to substitute these echoes with boyfriends – Adam was a prime example of how that turned out. Loneliness wasn't a real crack in her life: She had friends, acquaintances, and her neighbours had known her for so long they began to feel like distant family.

It was just the lack of companionship when she closed her front door, that bite of being alone, that irked her.

'Come on,' said Charlie as they walked down the steps at Hackney Downs station. 'I need to pop round my friend's place; I borrowed a tenner off her last week, and I need to pay her back.'

They walked to a tower block around the corner, Piper noticing how much cleaner her block was in Brighton and feeling privileged. Up three flights and along an open-plan balcony, Charlie knocked at a flat with a blue door – Number 14.

There was a shifting and scuffling the other side, shouting in Swedish. One sentence in English breaking through: *'Don't let them out!'*

Piper and Charlie shared a glance as more Swedish words were thrown between the two voices. Suddenly, a gap was pulled between door and jamb; a single blue eye and a lock of golden hair covering it peeked through. 'Hang on,' the partial face snapped.

The door shut again, more kerfuffle the other side, more indecipherable Swedish.

'Where have you bought me, Charl–' Piper was cut off.

The partial face was revealed fully, one half of the two Swedish girls' – Nora –glowering at them as behind her, the kerfuffling sound shifted deeper down the flats' long corridor.

'Antar att du inte vill ha en Katt?' she asked the two girls at her door in her native tongue.

Piper and Charlie shrugged, wide-eyed, as the girl laughed, waved her hand for them to come in. They did, Nora quickly stepping behind them and slamming the door with the importance of an airlock.

Nora frog-marched them down to the last door in the hallway, pulling it open and seeing them in.

Piper and Charlie's eyes almost popped. Maja stood with her hands on her head in the middle of the living room as five small black bodies explored its every inch like a pack of gremlins

17

looking for something new to destroy.

'Antar att du inte vill–' Maja yelled; she stopped herself, teeth snapping shut and biting the end of her words off. She rolled her eyes at her own mistake, this time yelling in English: 'Would you like a cat!'

Black kittens tried to climb the curtains; black kittens sat in the basket on the front of Nora's bike; black kittens knocked things from sideboards. Five cat boxes overflowed with clumped litter; five cat bowls held the dregs of their last meals; five cat beds sat un-slept in.

'I only came round to bring you that tenner,' Charlie said, quickly passing a note from her pocket.

Swedish chaos was suddenly added to the cat chaos; the two girls arguing amongst themselves as cats clawed the furniture, clawed the carpet and tried to climb the two women as if they were curtains.

'Owwwww!' Maja cried, pain apparently the same in Swedish and English as she plucked a kitten's claws from her thigh. 'Enough is enough!' she moaned, raising her hands over her head, leaving the room and slamming the door.

'We're going to go,' Charlie said with a faux smile.

'Yeah,' Piper said, 'Nice to meet yo–' She paused, seeing a small black head cocking over the top of the dining room table, its yellow eyes fixed on her.

An invisible connection formed in the air around them both as the small black kitten cried out at Piper.

That was the moment she met Graveyard Billy.

CHAPTER THREE

Yes, it was true: Cats pick their people; people don't pick their cats.

Maja had emerged from her bedroom smiling: one down – four to go.

'So, you have a litter tray, you have a bedding, you have a food bowl ...' Nora listed as Piper fought the small black kitten's claws from her jumper, nodding, trying to take in what Nora was saying.

It had been like this for the last fifteen minutes, from the moment the little black cat saw her. He bolted up and across the dining table, knocked over a glass of water, slid over some magazines as if they were a toboggan ride, and leapt straight up and onto Piper's shoulder. Eighteen puncture wounds from eighteen claws appearing in her flesh.

The black kitten wouldn't get off; he clung and clawed, screamed and purred, rubbing himself all over Piper.

'He likes you!' Charlie said.

'I know,' Piper said, not impressed, prising the cat from herself, placing it back on the table, where he leapt up and went through the routine of clinging and clawing all over again.

'I think you have a cat,' Nora said hopefully as the cat that was to be known as Graveyard Billy explored his human.

'Here,' Nora said, placing the kitten into a plastic pet carrier. 'You can borrow ours, but you have to post it back.' She even gave Piper the ten-pound note that Charlie had brought round to help cover the postage, a smile on her face that one-fifth of the cat problem infesting their flat was about to go.

Nora saw them out, the front door slamming with a distinct finality behind them like a judge's gavel.

'I guess you have a cat,' Charlie said.

'I guess I have a cat,' Piper replied.

They walked to the bottom of the flats, Piper making a decision. 'I think I better go back to Brighton; I can't lug him about all day.' The cat was suddenly silent as he was taken from his surroundings.

'Yeah, no worries,' said Charlie. 'Give me a text to let me know you get home all right.'

Piper headed back to Victoria on the train, changed there for Brighton. Peering into the pet carrier through its plastic bars, she stared at the small, quivering mound of cat, nervous of his surroundings.

'It's all right, mate,' she whispered, knowing the judging faces behind their shields of newspaper were staring at her again as she spoke to the plastic box.

Someone was playing their music too loud, sharing it with everyone else, while a one-way conversation was shouted down a mobile phone.

I hate the train. Why can't they just piss off?

And as if by some telepathic connection, the small black cat made it so.

There was a jetting, splashing, hosing sound inside the cat box; the unforgivable smell of cat urine hit the air, the confined train being the perfect place for it to permeate.

'Disgusting!' exclaimed one miserable old git who'd had his eye on her, getting up and leaving.

'You could have let it go before you brought it out,' said a sneering woman that wrestled her pushchair out of the carriage.

One by one, everyone around her filed out, the entire carriage now hers.

With a grin, she took the cat carrier to the carriage door, apologized to the scared kitten inside, then tipped the carrier sideways so the yellow liquid could escape to the floor, draining as much as possible.

Piper went back to her seat, put her feet up, and had the luxury of an empty train all the way back home, only the pungent pong from her new friend an annoyance.

At the station, she caught a cab back home, the Indian driver not noticing the aroma at first, then with a few sniffs as he drove out of town, exclaiming, 'Something smells like pis–'

'I know.' Piper said, cutting him off.

With a sigh of relief, Piper finally was home with the stench of ammonia all around her. She clicked the flat door behind her and went about doing everything she'd Googled on the train.

You had to keep a cat in for three months to get him used to his surroundings – that's what the Internet said.

He needed a trip to the vet for jabs and to be microchipped.

Staring into his scared green eyes, she knew all the years alone, looking after number one, had been good practice for looking after number two.

She had never had a pet before, never had any feelings either way to owning one, but in the last few hours, that haunting loneliness that travelled with her had suddenly subsided with the companionship of the cat.

She hadn't even thought about Captain Comb-over in Camden, the immediate past seeming distant now.

With the flat in lockdown, she let the kitten out; curious,

20

scared, he quickly acquainted himself with his surroundings. Piper laughed as she watched him study everything, all straightened tail and wide eyes.

'This is your place now!' she called.

He let out a *'Mow!'* in response.

Food, she remembered, checking where she'd put the pouches Maja had given her, realizing what that slap was as she exited the train doors. *'I dropped them,'* she sighed.

Fixing his litter tray in the kitchen and putting his bedding by the window, she called out to the kitten, 'I'm just going out!'

Locking the door behind her, taking the shortcut to the corner shop through Woodvale Cemetery next door, she could hear a chirping behind her. Turning around, looking up, there he was, clawing at the flat's window, all wide eyes of abandonment.

'I'll be right back!' she called out.

In the corner shop, Piper perused the small shelf of cat food: expensive stuff, affordable stuff, cheap stuff, stuff so cheap she wondered if it was even edible.

'What is it you are after?' the Brazilian owner asked.

'Cat food.' she called back.

'Aggghhhh,' he said, 'very picky.'

'Very picky,' she replied, not knowing how picky her new cat actually was.

Piper chose the affordable stuff, hoping the happy medium would suffice.

'New cat?' the man behind the till asked.

'Very much so,' she replied, 'I've got no idea what he likes.'

The man thought about this, went through the door behind him into the darkness of the storeroom. Within a minute, he came back though with a full white carrier bag.

'You can have this; it's no good for people, out of date by a day. Good for cat?' he shrugged in his thick accent.

Piper looked inside: The bag was full of thin-sliced ham, thin-sliced chicken, pre-packed sandwich filler.

'Nice one!' Piper exclaimed as the man rung up the cat food and placed it inside the bag.

'No problem.' The man grinned.

The kitten didn't like the cat food, didn't like chicken, wouldn't touch the ham, but there was something in the bag he went mad for, clawing the white carrier to get to it.

'This?' Piper said incredulously.

'*Mowwwwwwwwww!*' the black cat screamed with excitement.

Passing him the pressed slab of processed sandwich meat, she watched him chew his way through it with his small fangs.

'What is it?' she said, trying to make sense of the smiling face printed on the meat. She searched the carrier for its wrapper and squinted at its name: 'Billy Bear ham for kids?'

She could see it now, the factory-pressed bear face grinning out as the little black cat gnawed through it. It didn't take long before he'd had every slice, jumping up to stare out of the flat window to the graveyard below while he cleaned himself.

Piper walked back through the graveyard to the corner shop, the cat whining at the window as she went. 'I know, I know,' she said back to him.

'Do you have any more of this?' Piper asked, putting the Billy Bear wrapper on the counter.

The man laughed, walking to the fridge and taking out the last three packets.

'New cat – fussy cat,' the man grinned.

'Yep,' Piper said.

'He have a name?' the man asked, punching in the meat's price to his till.

'Nope, all I know is he likes two things: eating this,' she held up the Billy Bear wrapper, 'and watching out the window into the graveyard.'

The till cranked open with a loud 'Ding!' It sounded like an idea.

'Graveyard Billy,' the man said with his hand out for two–ninety–nine.

'What?' Piper said, reaching for her purse.

'His name: Graveyard Billy,'

Piper laughed, passed the man a five-pound note. 'What kind of person would name their cat Graveyard Billy!'

Apparently, she was that kind of person.

It just … *stuck*.

And so the black cat that ate processed meat and watched out into the graveyard become Graveyard Billy. That first night in the flat together, Piper woke on the sofa at three a.m. to see the silhouette of the kitten still sitting in the window. He was still staring down into the graveyard; his head bobbing and weaving, his night-time eyes watching something down there in its murk … *moving*.

'What can you see?' she asked groggily, falling back to sleep.

Graveyard Billy turned to look at her, transmitted his answer in the telepathic way cats can. 'Lots of things,' he said.

CHAPTER FOUR

After four months to get used to his new home, trips to the vet, and jabs that made him hiss and spit, Graveyard Billy had been finally allowed out to the one place he wanted to go – the graveyard.

Piper had made him the ramp extending from the flat window, had said to him, 'Don't go out there and get lost... *please*,' with worry in her voice.

Graveyard Billy stared at Piper, looked soulfully into her eyes, caught her attention and blinked once for 'Yes,' then add two more blinks in quick succession that meant: 'I'll be fine, I know where my home is!'

Unlike others, Piper had taken the time to do the one thing most humans don't do with a cat: listen to what he had to say.

Now, humans aren't always receptive to how other creatures talk. Yes, Graveyard Billy would whine for food or to be let out, and he purred when happy, all done to oblige his human in a base, vocal way. But when a cat really wants to talk to a human, they do so *their way*, and their way is to transmit.

Humans never normally pick up on the telepathic tendencies of the cat: They can sense instinctively it's there, knowing that buried deep within that hypnotic feline gaze, something more is being said. When a cat projects its secret language, if you become caught in that stare most humans can't decipher, then you know that the slow bat of blinking eyelids is the only way for a cat to reply.

And if that person is the cat's true owner, is the person the cat picked to be their human, sometimes – *sometimes* that hidden language can penetrate through.

Piper, with worry, undid the cat flap and let Graveyard Billy out; he looked back, gave her a blink for 'Thank you,' and then ventured into the overcast graveyard.

CHAPTER FIVE

It has been said the cat is cryptic and close to strange things that humans cannot see. His soul is that of ancient Aegyptus, heir to the secrets of Africa. The Sphinx is his cousin, and he remembers her language, which she has forgotten. Whether it was an inheritance from his Bengal mother, passed down by his alley cat father, or part of that ancient heritage, Graveyard Billy was more susceptible than most to the stirrings of the dead.

It's what he had sensed from the flat window, what he understood in a way he knew not. Slinking over earthen graves and winding around the cold stone of tombs, he could sense and *see* the spectral residents of the sacred ground.

The ectoplasmic workings of a ghost had a pattern: Some said such things were echoes of the past imprinted on the present; others said a ghost was a freethinking corporal entity, the vaporous soul of the living, now dead.

Both theories were *wrong* ... but in a way, both were *right*.

Graveyard Billy could sense spectral things around him, his vision as controlled as a photographer's camera, able to pull focus between what humans consider reality and what the dead did.

But how the dead were jumpstarted to the un-dead was a different thing altogether. It was a union of will between the dimension of the dead and the physical world of the living. A bridge made through emotion.

With a quick scarper through some ivy, a huge bound from the ground, he quickly clambered a wizened tree. Graveyard Billy ended on the top of an old grey mausoleum and watched down at a funeral in progress.

'We have come here today to bury the dearly departed Robert Seckler,' said the portly vicar as he stood at the edge of the freshly dug grave. People in black lined both of its edges, their tearstained faces the only matching idiosyncrasy apart from their dark clothes. As the vicar went on, as the tears flowed, as the funeral attendees' emotions peaked, that's when it started to happen.

If humans could use their minds to their fullest, could be as instinctively open as a creature such as Graveyard Billy, maybe they would be able to see it, too.

The reason for the dead's return as an undead entity was because of their conjuring. Because of human emotion opening that portal, creating a slice into that deep focus that a cat can so easily see.

Above the open grave, unseen by the humans, a crackling, sparking electrical storm brewed.

Graveyard Billy's eyes opened wide; golden rings with an

endless black centre.

Bursts of otherworldly light forked supernaturally around the attendees, feeding from their grief and the emotion of being wanted. From being missed – from the dead's desire to be returned to the living.

That's how spirits are created: by the unseen will of the human mind, resurrecting them with grief, giving them solidity with sorrow.

A scintilla of light formed, folding out of itself to create a nebulous manifestation, a palpable presence invisible to the humans below.

The vicar went on – 'As we stand here in the house of the Lord …'

As tears flowed, the collective consciousness of the funeral guests tore the fabric of what they understood as reality, and an otherworldly voice wisped into the graveyard. The muffled voice crept from the grave, speaking in a Liverpudlian accent: 'Hang on … what the *hell* is going on here?'

A spectral figure had formed, one that anyone at the funeral would have recognized as the spirit of Robert Seckler as he sat up in his open grave as casually as waking up on a Sunday morning in bed. Translucent ectoplasmic tendrils emanated from his vaporous body. 'What the hell are you lot doing up there?' he said, staring up as his entire family stared down.

'Uncle Jimmy? Aunt Jenny? Why ya staring at me in bed? Can't I get no priva –'

He looked around at the six-foot rectangular shaft he had sat up in, his bed's blanket not a feathered duvet but a pine box.

'Oh no!' he gasped, realizing where he was. 'I knew I should have sorted the brakes on me Fiesta!'

The vicar threw a handful of dirt down into the grave straight over where he sat. 'Ashes to ashes, dust to dust.'

Robert's spirit, overreacting, coughing and spluttering as if he could breathe, shouted up. 'Oi! Watch what ya doing with that, you disrespectful bastard!'

Looking up, he spotted the looming tombstone overhead – his tombstone.

Here Lies:
Bobby 'Bomb Head' Seckler

'Oh Mam, did you have to put me bloody nickname on me tombstone?'

'Amen,' said the vicar finally.

The ghost now forever known as Bobby 'Bomb Head' stood up in his grave now, understanding now that he was standing on and tiptoeing around his own corpse as if trying to avoid a puddle with new shoes. 'Oh no, *nooooo!*' he cried. 'Someone get me out of here! I'm not dea –'

Suddenly, he understood he was.

His family started to move away, retreating tearfully towards the line of black cars in the graveyard's car park. As they went, as they moved away from the grave and the spirit they had conjured with their emotions, the power they had given it started to fade.

Bobby "Bomb Head" stared at his already transparent hands as they became even more so. 'Oh *nooooo* … Mam! *Mam!*' he cried, clambering from his own grave, running after his family, still wearing his Adidas tracky with matching pumps that he'd crashed the Fiesta in, his vitality growing with the proximity of his family's grief.

That was how spirits worked, their presence on earth powered by the remembrance of others.

As he got closer to his mum, the woman who had provided for him up until his death – 'Don't leave me, Mam!' – instinctive ectoplasmic teleplasms weaved through the air, seeped around the woman as they became tethered together, entangled with her.

This was how it worked; the dead could stay on Earth, but only connected to a loved one or relative, attached with a wispy strand of supernatural essence.

There would be a period of learning acceptance for the bereaved to understand what had happened, a transitional period for the spirits until they were ready to pass on to … whatever was next …

Graveyard Billy watched on, understood in that way cats did the earthbound side of supernatural law … not knowing himself what was truly out there in the unseen ether.

CHAPTER SIX

This had been Graveyard Billy's life for the past two years: exploring the graveyard by day, inside with Piper at night. Watching her progress as an artist, watching how her sketches from Uni became vivid canvasses as she neared the end of her degree. He was her companion, her friend. The pair curled together at night in sleep. He was her family as much as she was his.

He wasn't the only cat in the graveyard, just as Bobby 'Bomb Head' wasn't the only ghost. There were few scraps with other cats over territory here, a few hissing fits there, but he always got on with the local foxes: they left him alone, and he left them.

Life was simple: He loved Piper, and she loved him.

But lately, something else had started to happen: A new scent had entered the graveyard, an odd, smoky smell he couldn't decipher: something heavy, dark, and sinister inside it.

It lingered at the far end of the graveyard near the iron gates, and then, day by day, it crawled nearer as if the smell itself was some kind of living thing. As if that dull heaviness in it was transforming to a slithering, living dread.

Something bit into the bones of Graveyard Billy, the one thing a cat with a routine took a strong dislike to.

Change was coming, a bleak, dark change.

CHAPTER SEVEN

Everything had been normal that day, just the same as all the other days they had spent together. It was a Saturday, and Piper was at home working on her final major project for Uni.

Perched on the windowsill Graveyard Billy watched her, his front paws crossed comfortably, eyes staring intently, ears listening to every noise she made as he wondered what exactly she was doing?

She had brought home the fake human – an old female store mannequin – and, piece by piece, chopped it to tiny shards, then reassembled it again on all fours with hollowed-out patches so you could see inside its vacuum-formed body. This gave its fibreglass skin the appearance of a cracked eggshell.

Then she added the finishing touch to the sculpture: an old smashed mobile phone glued to its right hand.

Piper stood back from her creation, put her gluey hands on the hips of her old dungarees, screwed up her face, and tried to eye it with an objective opinion.

'What do you think?' she said to Graveyard Billy. 'Do you think this is a good representation of the emptiness of a life connected to social media?'

Graveyard Billy stared at her, gave her two soft bats of his eyelids for no, not really knowing anything about the emptiness of a life connected to social media.

'You're right,' she said, throwing one of her old work rags over the thing's plastic face, covering its glazed dead eyes. 'It stinks.'

She bent down towards where he was sitting, kissed him in between his ears as he raised and pushed his fuzzy head into her face.

'I'm done with this today,' she said, walking to the bedroom. 'Catnap?' she asked, slapping her hand to her thigh.

Graveyard Billy made a quick, *'Bruuupppp,'* sound, jumped from the window ledge, padded across the flat's laminate flooring, ready for a well-deserved sleep after a hard day's sleeping.

Piper crashed out immediately, Graveyard Billy leaping up and flopping next to her on the old mattress, nudging his head into her shoulder and looking up at her with giant moon eyes.

She smiled down at him. 'I love you, you know.'

He blinked once for yes.

In no more than five minutes, they were both asleep: The evening sun dipped down; long shadows faded to the deep pitch of the night. Both drifted into the endless corridor of a dream, far away from the outside world, all earthbound worries vaporized behind heavy, tired lids.

There was a distant lull of bassline from music played in

one of the flats above, as repetitive as a metronome used to hypnotize.

Everything was calm; everything was silent.

Graveyard Billy jerked his head up, immediately awake, immediately sensing … *something*.

His small heart beat faster, hackles immediately growing down his spine.

It was that *thing* that he sensed in the graveyard; the thing that he knew had no name.

Instinctually, nearly everything in Billy's world was something based on its aroma: the sweet smell of cut flowers left on graves, the dull smell of turned earth after a burial; the stinging stench of old beer cans thrown in bushes that would make him wince if he sniffed their innards.

Everything was something he could understand through its scent … apart from this. This was … *something else.* Something old, something smoky, something he *knew* didn't belong here in his deep, catlike way.

Slowly he stalked from the bed, his soft footsteps padding the duvet as gently as walking in clouds. He dropped to the floor and stealthily rushed up to the open window, staring down into the graveyard.

Wind rustled through the trees; leaves clapped like tiny hands applauding; the moon held full and fat like a single observing eye.

Graveyard Billy sat watching down, his own unmoving stare penetrating the graveyard's sea of black. His senses were on full alert, knowing *something* was there, still and waiting to show itself.

Seconds ticked past on the wall clock behind him, each beat of its moving hand-making his whiskers twitch.

Then it came and hit his senses like an anvil.

That sulphurous, smoky stench closer now than it had ever been.

Graveyard Billy let out a guttural growl, something that, when translated from cat tongue to human language, would have said, 'Keep away.'

It, something, that *thing* was down there.

A bush to his right rustled, a twig snapped – it was here.

Graveyard Billy glided out the window with long strides and slinked down his ramp, his gaze never leaving that intense black patch of bushes the movement came from. His nocturnal eyes never revealed anything but what had been there before: the slush of blown leaves, the branches shifting as if they were reaching over the graveyard wall to claw the flat's windows.

But it was there.

It *was* there.

Graveyard Billy moved along the graveyard wall with that

inherited swagger of a puma. He was all tiger now, all lion – the king of the jungle, surveying his domain, his kingdom. An intruder was in his midst, a creature he had never experienced before.

A bolt from the bushes put him on edge; his body lowered to a pouncing position.

'What are you doing!' Graveyard Billy transmitted at a cowering fox, its usually bushy tail folded beneath itself in fear. Terror filled the fox's glowing eyes as it glanced back at him over its shoulder, its own transmission back to him short and simple: *'Run!'*

The fox's fear made Graveyard Billy's own swell: He opened his mouth as if to hiss, silently baring his fangs, sensing invisible horror all around him.

That's when the slam came from behind: It had come from the flat.

He bolted along the wall, made it to the ramp, and came face to face with glowing, wide eyes. He tensed, paused; his own reflection stared back at him in the window's closed glass.

He tried to push in the cat flap, but it was locked.

Why was it locked? Why was it …

A sound he never wanted to hear pricked his ears, an awful shriek that turned him inside out.

A scream: his friend's scream, his family's scream – *her* scream.

Piper.

He sensed it then, that thing, that *awful,* sulphurous thing.

Quickly he leapt to the window, clawing and biting at the frame, seeing inside his home, the bedroom lamp swaying indecipherable shadows around the hallway outside.

What was happening!

He couldn't get in, no matter how much he tried to prise the small window and cat flap open. It was all glass, plastic, and wood, impossible to penetrate with paws and no human hands.

He began to howl now as more screams came from inside.

Then he remembered – the door! The flats' main door: he had sat there once a year ago, and one of the other residents had let him in; maybe that would happen again.

He bolted from the window, slipping, staggering, spilling around to the front of the flats, climbing the iron staircase and making it to the huge wooden front door; clawing, jumping up and at the handle; at the intercom, trying to make the ridged buttons buzz; trying to get the attention of someone – anyone that could let him in, that could help her: his her, Piper.

Lights were popping on around him, the commotion heard by others.

He howled, screamed, *'Pleaaasseeeee!'* Heading off, back around towards the graveyard.

31

A car pulled into the road leading to the flats, the driver not seeing where he was going, Graveyard Billy not seeing where he was going, either.

The skid of brakes echoed; an oncoming blaze of headlights pushed towards him as he froze solid to the spot.

The mechanical monster moved closer and closer.

Graveyard Billy, running, bolting, narrowly avoided the oncoming car. A blare of horn, a voice shouting: 'You stupid bloody thing!'

Yes! More noise, more attention; she needs help! – Help! – *Help!*

He bounded back up his ramp, pressed tight against the flat's window, and stared inside to … *silence.*

A cold calm had come across the flat; the eerie chill of the night touched his fur.

It wasn't it there now. It had gone – he could sense it.

He could see the sculpture Piper had been making sprawled out in the hallway for some reason now, the phone in its hand, its dead eyes planted straight on him.

They were *her* dead eyes.

It wasn't the sculpture that lay motionless on the floor: It was Piper.

He could sense the thing that had attacked her was gone. In the heaviness of his heart, he knew she was gone, too.

Graveyard Billy stayed transfixed at the window. He didn't hear sirens, wasn't distracted by the flash of their lights.

All he felt was a cold stone of sorrow sink through his body.

His friend, his family, his Piper – was dead.

CHAPTER EIGHT

No one noticed Graveyard Billy perched outside, his fur as dark as night, framed within the flat's window. He watched men in black uniforms walking around his home, some dusting power around, some taking pictures with aluminous pops of light, some examining the shell of Piper that was once filled with life.

He stared into her wide-open eyes and blinked for a response – none came back.

An October chill as cold as an arctic breeze shivered through his small body as he listened to their words.

'Yeah, it's another one, Sarge,' said a man, examining the back of Piper's neck. 'Same markings as all the others.'

Graveyard Billy's eyes recorded what they were looking at: the awful sight that had ended his friend's life. A ragged hole lay open three inches below her hairline; it tunnelled deep beneath her skin. Around the wound were the bruised marks of eight extended lines that reached out like piercing arachnid legs, four symmetrically placed on each side of the gruesome gash.

'What do you think could have done that?' a female in black asked, a distinctive quiver to her question.

An older man shook his head, bit the inside of his cheek, and rubbed his stubbled chin. 'I don't know, but that's eight of them now, all of them the same as this. Hopefully, we can find something in here to help find the nutter responsible.'

Graveyard Billy closed his eyes: The man's words hurt him inside as they reduced the person he loved to a number.

Ignorance says animals don't feel emotions as humans do; the distinct tears that appeared at the corners of Graveyard Billy's eyes solidified the fact they do.

He watched silently as Piper's body was taken into one of the machines with flashing lights on top. The commotion had calmed now, everyone who had come to gawp retreating to their homes as heavy doors were slammed shut.

A sudden thought galvanized Graveyard Billy into action as the ambulance holding her body began to roll away – *She can come back!*

Just like all those others, he had watched in the graveyard: She would rise as a spirit and need someone to supernaturally tether to so she could stay alive after death. He had seen it so many times and knew he was that person! He was that cat!

He bolted down after the flashing lights that accelerated away – that took *her* away. He *had* to catch her, *had* to get to her so he could be there when she rose.

His small paws became sore on the road's rough tarmac, legs aching, every joint burning as it became impossible to keep up speed as the ambulance slowly disappeared into the distance. Horns blared, headlights flashed, and Graveyard Billy dashed to the side of the road to avoid Brighton's rush of traffic.

He couldn't catch her without being killed himself.

Slowly and solemnly, he turned and returned to the one place he knew – the graveyard.

CHAPTER NINE

Questions swirled in his mind: Why did this happen? Why would someone do this? What was next for him?

He climbed the ramp Piper had made for him and looked longingly into the home that was no longer his home, trapped forever on the outside, looking in. He transmitted in his mind for her to contact him, sent out a signal in that telepathic way cats can, asking where she was: There was no reply.

A black eclipse rose within him then, a dour, depressed understanding bled from it in cold rays: He was alone now, and he wasn't going to ever see the human girl he loved again.

Six words struck as dull as the church clock's bells at dawn: Piper ... is ... *dead ... now ... I'm ... alone.*

They were words that cemented everything into a harsh, cold reality.

CHAPTER TEN

October's orange hues faded into the steely greys of November; it had almost been a month since Graveyard Billy had lived alone in Woodvale Cemetery. He didn't want to leave, partly due to the warmer memories of the past, partly due to this being all he knew.

Cats are creatures of routine, always welcoming the expected rather than the possibility of the unexpected. Caution was part of their makeup, an instinctive wariness of change, as curiosity was known to kill cats.

His heavy heart still burdened him: That vivid image of the human he'd picked laying still with glassy eyes plagued the darkness beneath his lids.

He did not want to forget that which was important to him, so he stayed in the cemetery while all about him, everything changed.

Men in jumpsuits came and emptied their home, took all of Piper's belongings out and tossed them into the back of a van that smelt like the bins at the back of the flats.

He watched from the branch of an old oak tree hanging over the graveyard's wall as the mattress they'd shared was loaded into the vehicle's rear. Sensing Piper, he cocked his hanging head up, an excitement at feeling an echo of her as their old bed was thrown inside the van.

He leapt from the branch tore down to the van, a sudden excitement in his heart, a sudden hope that maybe, somehow, she was still there. Jumping in the van and on the mattress, he padded his paws up its length, hoping to reveal her hidden there.

Please ... please ... be here.

'*Oi!*' a voice behind him yelled, swiping out with an old worn broom to try and flush him from the van. Surprised and scared, he felt the harsh bristles of the broom spike his flank, flipping him out as if he wasn't even worthy of frequenting the rubbish inside.

'*Bloody thing!*' the man wielding the broom shouted, locking the van's back doors, taking the final remnants of the past away.

Graveyard Billy's ramp was dislodged from its position outside his old home's window; eventually, a different light illuminated its frame, new tenants who had no use for a cat.

'Come on,' the new girl who lived there would say, shifting him from the flat's front door with the toe of her shoe as she went. Not looking at him as she pushed him away, too concerned with the handheld device she stared into that occupied her time.

There was no chance of living with Woodvale's vicar: He too would storm towards Graveyard Billy with a face as thunderous as Pentecostal fire whenever he saw him, knowing the cat always used the freshly laid earth of a grave as a giant litter box.

Graveyard Billy couldn't stop nature from taking hold, and that grave dirt ... it was like a throne ready to be perched on.

Food was scarce. The shop's bins opposite the graveyard held some edible aromas; he had even found some meagre discards inside that would settle his empty belly. The shopkeeper who'd given Graveyard Billy his name chased him off if he was ever caught trying to feed there. It became clear: all you needed to do was add an 's' for a pet to become a pest.

He found a tight spot behind some old gravestones he could pack into at night, his own body heat the thing that kept him warm. Questions always rattled his dreams: Where is Piper's grave? Surely if he could find her grave, he could become tethered to her? Why wasn't she brought here? He had watched every funeral, eagle-eyed. And what was that ... *thing* that killed her? That smoky aroma was smudged into his mind, its lingering sulphurous stench as palpable as the ever-darkening nights of winter.

A feeling like revenge would take hold of him some days, wishing he knew what the smoky thing was that ended his life with the human he had picked.

He used that angry feeling; it pushed him forward when hunger bit to starvation, when birds he would only ever stare at with pie eyes before became meals to be hunted.

As his feral lifestyle became everyday survival, he would often transmit to the other animals that frequented the graveyard, wanting answers.

Pomped pets he used to see off – or would see him off – passed with pampered relish. 'Look, I know we've had our differences,' he transmitted, 'but were you in here the night–'

'Well, well, well,' a rather plump tabby interrupted as it weaselled through the long grass. 'Look who's come down a few pegs, not so feisty now, are you? You're looking a bit worse for wear, a bit rough around the edges, a bit thinner around the midsection, a bit –'

With a howling hiss, Graveyard Billy saw off the feline and its snide tongue.

He visited the largest of a family of hedgehogs that lived beneath an overgrown tomb at the graveyard's east side.

'You always seem to be around here,' Graveyard Billy transmitted to the hedgehog that stared back with trepidation. 'Where is another graveyard? One where my owner might be?'

'It's no use trying find anywhere else like this, cat,' he replied. 'You and I are different, but we share the same enemy: the metal-wheeled ones they call cars. There are long rows of those moving menaces to do us in out there.' The hedgehog pointed its snout towards the graveyard's iron gates. 'You're better off in here.'

Graveyard Billy blinked once for Yes, pacifying the creature that his idea of doing nothing was the best.

It was the fox he sought next, the one that had transmitted psychically, 'Run!' whose nocturnal eyes burned with fear.

He remembered the fox, its coat a dirtied grey, its tailless bulky due to mange. Skittish were the foxes and often impossible to track, stealthier at times than the cat.

It was by chance on a foggy night he saw the creature in question perched on the old stone wall that cut off the graveyard's north side with the busy road beyond. Making his body as flat as possible, stalking towards the creature as not to scare it off, Graveyard Billy slowly crept closer.

The fox turned its head, eyes alert, ears as pricked as a bat's.

'Please don't run!' Graveyard Billy exclaimed as the fox poised to bolt. 'You remember that night when we met before? When you sensed something in here, when you told me to run, when ...' the words still hurt ... 'when the girl, the human girl, died in the flats?'

The fox never eased, just replied with a timid, 'Why, what's it to you?'

'Well,' fumbled Graveyard Billy, 'you told me to run, but you never said what from? I need to know, what was in the graveyard?'

The fox stared untrustingly. 'My senses are keener than yours, cat. I have to be on my toes. I'm not welcome in their houses as you are, not fed portions of meat. I have to find mine by any means necessary.'

Graveyard Billy understood this creature in a way he hadn't before.

'I can see a wider spectrum of the dead,' the fox went on. 'We foxes can see deeper into that other place which is right before your eyes.'

'But ... what was it?' Graveyard Billy asked, needing an answer.

'There are things that roam around places such as these that are no good; things that are neither alive like us nor dead like the ones they bury. There are *things* that just are, and we don't mess with them as we don't mess with the humans. Some of these *things* are friendly, some ... not so much.'

'But that night,' Graveyard Billy desperately cried. 'What was that thing I should have been scared of, the thing you told me to run from?'

The fox thought about this question and went to answer; a group of humans who had scaled the fence walked through the graveyard, laughing and drinking from cans. The fox disappeared as quickly as evaporating smoke, dropping to the other side of the fence and mixing his grey fur into the foggy night.

More nights alone passed until a time when great bursts of light peppered the sky, explosions that would jolt Graveyard Billy's heart, particles of colour spitting to the ground. It was the part of the year when Piper used to keep him inside, the part called Guy Fawkes Night.

Piper had warned him you couldn't trust all humans, a knowing glint of their behaviour in her eye. A sliver of their meanness she had experienced. Soon, he found out what she'd meant firsthand.

'Get him!' shouted a snarling voice as three teenagers chased him through the graveyard, lighting small sparking sticks that exploded when thrown in his direction.

'No one likes black cats; it's a fact,' panted one of them. 'We'll be doing it a favour if we catch it.'

'Yeah,' the chubby one at the rear of the group added. 'They ain't even worth wasting our bangers on!'

They laughed like devils as the explosions echoed out.

Graveyard Billy could climb, winding himself around a tall tree to escape.

The hedgehog family had no such luxury, a heavy sadness entering Graveyard Billy when he found their bodies the next day.

You could get no peace living as a stray, the world around you always prodding at you like a pointed stick to move on.

Sitting in silence alone, snuggled behind the gravestones at the back of the graveyard – a place that had become his home – a snarling, snapping hum buzzed like an oversized bumblebee, coming nearer and nearer.

A smell overpowered his senses: grass, weeds, and flowers churned to compost pulp. Peeking around the gravestone, he could see a flock of men with buzzing strimmers slicing away at the overgrown grass – coming closer and closer to him.

Eyeing where to run and what to do, he saw the face of the man, a snarling menace drawing into his features. His lips folded back to reveal his bone-white teeth, eyes squinting to vile slits: his face something from a nightmare. He was coming straight towards Graveyard Billy, the spinning strimmer hovering nearer.

Billy made a mad dash across the graveyard, bounding over tombs and graves to a safe spot on its farthest side.

'What are you doing, Issac?' another man with a strimmer nearby shouted.

'Well, the boss did say cut everything.' Issac replied the awful expression on his face lost as he smiled at his overweight workmate.

'There's something wrong with you,' the portly man

replied, shaking his head and moving off in the opposite direction to cut the grass.

The vile smile stretched back across Issac's face as he glared in the direction Graveyard Billy had run.

'There's nothing wrong with me,' he leered to himself.

The bursts of firework light in the sky passed; pure, cold darkness returned as December settled to a grey, cast-iron cold.

There were no answers here in Woodvale. No way to find out where to go in the future or what had happened in the past. Only the sadness that anchored Graveyard Billy here was reliable: The old life filled with companionship was gone now, and that was something he had to accept.

He remembered the year before, the previous December, the time he would be more in than out of his and Piper's old flat due to the bitter cold – that choice now also only a memory. Behind his closed lids, tucked into the warmth of his own fur, a voice of reason told him he had to leave the graveyard, had to forget the past he clung to so dearly if he was to survive.

He could have never predicted that soon – very soon – something was about to cling to him for survival.

CHAPTER ELEVEN

It was the week leading up to Christmas. Snow had been threatening for the past few nights. All the other creatures in the graveyard had found their patches to hibernate, and Graveyard Billy sat looking out over the graveyard wall to the busy road outside.

If he was going to venture out, he had to be careful; he had to have his wits about him in this unknown place. Mystery lingered in the air, as palpable as the streams of hot breath that huffed from his small black nose. All he had to do was remember where the scent of Woodvale Cemetery was. If all else failed, if everything he found beyond its stone walls was worse than what was here, he could return.

A new worry entered him: What if I never find the graveyard again? It wasn't much ... but in a way, it was all he had that resembled a home.

Two long, slick, black limousines and a hearse rumbled up the stone pathway into the graveyard, a popping, snapping sound coming from beneath their tyres. Graveyard Billy pitched his head round and watched as the three vehicles pulled into the graveyard's small car park and stopped.

Humans started to step out, gathered around in noir outfits that matched the hearses' gloss paint. A coffin was carried into the church, four men on each side; the shuddering weeping of bereavement like a backing track to the organ music played from inside.

Graveyard Billy suddenly understood. *This was what the open grave on the graveyard's far side was for; there was a funeral taking place today.*

A gleam of hope fluffed his black fur – was this Piper's funeral?

He leapt, darted like a black missile between tombstones, scrabbled up the church's wall, and perched on the window ledge to stare inside.

The coffin was open now, the girl inside exposed.

He stared with huge eyes that began to dim: Piper had white skin; the girl in the coffin was black, as was all her grieving family.

A deep sigh passed Graveyard Billy's lips: a sigh for himself as it wasn't Piper, a sigh for the poor departed girl inside of her box. He wondered if anyone had gone to Piper's funeral? If she'd had as many people as this girl here did? Maybe Piper was tethered to one of her family he had never met? Maybe she had already crossed over?

Eventually, the coffin was brought back outside, the same men who had carried it in now carrying it out, taking it to the open maw of the grave.

Graveyard Billy secretly followed, tried to keep out of sight, watched as the girl's body was slowly lowered into the waiting hole.

'We have come here today to bury the dearly departed Kelly Minter,' said the vicar, as he took his place at the edge of the freshly dug grave.

Tears began to fall as everyone crowded around the grave, that palpable air of solemnity growing as the conjuring began.

Graveyard Billy leapt up onto a tombstone and made himself comfortable.

The crackling, sparking, electrical storm unfolded from a tear in reality and brewed overhead. Kinetic forked lightning struck around the mourners, feeding on their grief.

It was happening – just as it always did.

A nebulous manifestation spewed from the void overhead and rushed into the grave below.

The vicar's usual words continued, 'As we stand here in the house of the Lord ...'

The usual tears flowed as an otherworldly voice wisped into the graveyard. '*Oh-my-god!*' it whined. 'How much did I drink last night?'

With a stretch and a yawn, the dead girl stood up in her grave, a pale blue spectre of her former self.

She began to rub her face, her eyes still closed, 'Will you lot keep down the racket? Do you know what time I got in?' she moaned.

Graveyard Billy stared at the spirit's attire: What was she wearing? Her hair was curled out and up in a huge sparkling golden bush, her almost non-existent dress shimmering with tacky gold material; bangles jangled as if they were the plastic equivalent of chains from a Dickens' novel, and her jacket sparkled with purple sequins. Her makeup was exaggerated, bright blue eyes shadow clashing with enormous red lips.

'What the bloody hell are you watching on the telly? I thought *Songs of Praise* was on in the evening? Sounds like a right load of old –' She stared up, eyes fixing disbelievingly on her mourning family all staring down.

The vicar said his final words. 'And may the soul of Kelly Minter rest in peace.'

'*What – the – hell!*' she gawked, looking down at her ankles protruding wispily through the pine coffin that lay beneath her.

Quickly, she turned to her family above her. 'What is this, some kind of *laugh?*' she screamed, watching as her family slowly walked away from her grave. 'Hey!' she yelled at the attendees. '*Hey!* I'm not *dead*! Why am I down this hole?'

Awkwardly she clambered out of the grave, rolling onto

the cold winter grass, her feet pressed inside golden high heels that matched the rest of her gaudy outfit. 'Oi! Why are you lot ignoring me?' she cried, staggering after her family, almost upon them, then running through them, passing through each one as if she wasn't even there –, *but she was!* – stumbling and slamming face-first onto the ground.

The girl rolled over and began to cry. 'Why are you all ignoring me? Whose idea was it to dump me down there? I can't help it if I got *too* drunk again; it's not *my* fault!'

A thought hit her that opened her mouth into a perfect circle: *'Oh no!* I didn't think your wardrobe was the toilet again, did I, mum! You said you would teach me a lesson if I did!'

Her relatives said nothing.

'I'm sorry! *I'm sorry!*' she cried back to her family as they loaded into the limousines.

Graveyard Billy squinted his eyes: Was something wrong? Normally, the dead tethered with their family before moving on; the dead girl's spirit should have automatically conjoined with the living like the others.

Her spectral form was somehow different; her translucent body was a muted outline of spectral blue with something … missing.

Then, limp ectoplasmic tentacles fired out from her ghostly aura, tried to connect with her family, but as they went to wrap around her mum, they withered and failed.

That wasn't supposed to happen …

'Why can't you hear me!' the girl was shouting as the last limo pulled from the cemetery gates. The girl ghost now alone in the graveyard, breaking down to a weeping wreck.

Graveyard Billy moved closer.

This wasn't right … she should have attached to them.
'That's so odd!' he transmitted to himself.

The girl spun around, staring at the tombstones that surrounded her.

'Who said that?' she said, wide-eyed terror, filling her face. Scanning the graveyard, trying to find where the voice had com – a black cat sat staring straight at her.

'You can see me!' she said with importance, staggering in her high heels across stony graves.

'Oh no!' Graveyard Billy cried, slowly backing away, looking at different ways to escape.

'And *you* can hear *me*!' she grinned, getting closer.

'No, I can't!' he lied.

'Yes, you can! And I can hear you!' she shouted.

Graveyard Billy puffed up his fur, eyes wide with shock.

'No, you can't.' Graveyard Billy thought.

'Yeah, *I can!*' the girl shouted, on top of him now, staring down into his small face. 'This is *mental!*' she grinned. 'I've had

43

some dreams after a night boozing, but this one takes the cake!'

'You can hear me?' Graveyard Billy said, backing away farther, curious about their connection.

A pang went off in his head, knowing what curiosity killed ... He should just run, should just get out of here, just –

'This is mad! I'm talking to a bloody cat!' she grinned, wiping the ectoplasmic tears from her face.

'And I'm talking to a bloody ghost,' he replied evenly.

'You're talking to a wha –' She spun around, a chill emanating from her vaporous form as she stared at the tombstone that loomed over her grave. The legend engraved into its granite, her name: Kelly Minter. 'Oh, noooooooooo!' What is going on! Is this a bloody dream? It has to be!'

She felt around herself, grabbed at the tacky golden dress. 'Why am I still in this outfit? Danni's hen do was ...' She checked for her bag, wanted to find her phone, wanted to find out the date and time: There was nothing.

'That's what happened!' she cried. 'I was at Danni's hen do, and I left them, went outside for a –' she looked at the cat who stared at her, a sudden spurt of decorum painting her face – 'to find a toilet,' she nodded. 'Then ...' a blank expression appeared on her face. She checked herself again, reached around now, not for a phone, but for her pulse: There was nothing.

With terror in her eyes, she stared at her hands, felt her face; the cold of the grave had sunk into her features. She stared into Graveyard Billy's eyes, a rush of emotions filling her all at once: agitation, frustration, anger, and sadness.

'It's not supposed to be like this,' he said, trying to comfort her. 'I've seen this so many times. You're supposed to connect yourself to your family to share their energy until it's time to cross over.'

Something in his words made her instantly ball with tears. 'Maybe they don't want meeeeeeee!'

'No, no! I'm sure they do; didn't you see how upset they were! Of course, they want you. I just don't understand why –'

A curl of her big golden hair bounced down the centre of her face and touched the end of her nose. She went cross-eyed, tried to blow it away with an outstretched bottom lip. Growling in primal rage, she reached up at her hair and began to tug at it. 'Get off! Get off!'

'What are you doing?' Graveyard Billy cried.

'Look at the state of me; I never knew that the bloody clothes you died in were the clothes you would have to wear the rest of your life!'

'Afterlife,' Graveyard Billy corrected, instantly feeling guilt as she wailed harder at his words.

'Stupid Danni's stupid hen do was come in eighties fancy dress.'

She began to cry as she pulled harder and harder at her now-obvious wig. 'It was my mum's idea for me to go as Tina Turner!'

Graveyard Billy just stared at the girl, not knowing what a Tina Turner was.

'Look at me!' she wept, 'hair like Tina Turner, clothes like Tina Turner – I'm an un-dead joke!'

She yanked at her hair so hard she fell straight back onto her bum. 'And do you know what's worst of all ...' she wailed, face screwed up as more tears came, '... I don't even *like* Tina Turner!'

'Well ...' Graveyard Billy said, 'I'm sure it's not that bad?'

Suddenly she shut up, tears all disappearing. 'Hang on ...how exactly did I die?' Death amnesia struck her; un-dead brains racked at the question of how she had become just that.

How did I die?

She looked at her hands; they were beginning to wisp into a transparent nothing. 'Oh god, now what's this?' she cried, her translucent form slowly fading from existence.

'You're going back to where you came from,' Graveyard Billy commented. 'There's no life force here for you to cling to, to feed off.'

'Where I came from? Where's that?' she cried.

'Somewhere between being living and ...well, you know,' Graveyard Billy said.

She turned to the cemetery gates, wailed again. 'Why is this happening to me ... I just want to see my mum again; there must be someone I can connect t –'

She spun around, her face filled with concentration.

Graveyard Billy's eyes popped wide. 'Oh no! Are you ...'

Kelly's spirit concentrated, started to splutter with supernatural sparks, wispy ghost tendrils stirring from her pale aura as she gritted her teeth.

'No! No! *No!*' Graveyard Billy cried, firing from the top of the tombstone, bolting as fast as he could across graveyard-cold grass.

Behind him, the girl began to wail, a strobing ethereal light ripping from around her body.

Graveyard Billy moved faster, paws pounding to escape. 'Not you! It shouldn't be you! It should be –'

A flashing spurt of light engulfed him, drew his paws to a stop. It was as if a length of supernatural twine had been threaded through and around him, a literal ghostly cat's cradle with him at the centre. He rolled over, tried to escape the wavering tail of teleplasm that connected to the girl behind him. Her tears were gone now, her life force replenished, now tethered to Graveyard Billy's vitality.

'Looks like you and I are friends now, mate!' she grinned

45

as her sequined jacket sparkled in her own ghostly glow.

Chapter Twelve

If anyone knows anything about cats, it's that they are autonomous creatures: They do what they want to do, go where they want to go, pick the humans they want to be with. So, caught in that supernatural cat's cradle, tethered to a ghost that he didn't know, Graveyard Billy did the one thing any cat in that situation would do – run.

He rushed between gravestones, weaved back and forth, bolted up a nearby oak tree, almost de-clawing himself in the process; anything to escape the ties that bind.

His small lungs wheezed; his eyes bulged. 'It shouldn't happen like this!' he transmitted to himself. Why was he stuck with this girl, this sparkly, whining, obnoxious girl? Why was this suddenly his lot in life? 'It can't be happening, it can't –'

'It is,' she grinned, appearing on the branch next to him.

Graveyard Billy jumped at her sight, spun on the branch, swung upside down like a jet-black koala bear, holding on for dear life. He stared down towards the ground, kicked off the branch with his legs, turned in the air to land on all fours, and started running.

'Oi!' the ghost of Kelly Minter yelled, 'Be careful! We're a team now, and cats don't really have nine lives!'

Graveyard Billy moved like a black streak, trying to push his small body faster now to escape the girl. His eyes rotated to every little nook and cranny he could hide in to try and make her grinning face a part of the past.

The old tomb near the cemetery gates – there was a crack in its side, a hole big enough to squeeze through – he could make it there, fit inside and wait for her to go, wait for her to burden someone else.

He was coming closer to it, bounding over long, unkempt grass to the secret spot that wasn't visible to the naked eye. Not stopping, thinking thin, he slotted himself through the ragged gap and stopped dead in his tracks as he came upon the tomb's old occupant: a dusty, decomposed corpse.

Graveyard Billy stayed as silent as the new company he kept, keeping away from the near-skeletal remains as he listened to the outside to see if she was near. There was nothing for a long time, the only sound in the tomb's small echo chamber that of his thumping heart.

Slowly he lowered himself to the ground, completely alert, poised and waiting. Could he escape her as simply as running? Who knows, but if that was all he had, it's exactly what he would do.

Then her voice rattled out, 'You can't just run! We're partner's now –'

She leant down, passed through the tomb's stone slab that

covered him, her grinning face quickly becoming a grimace as she came face to face with the tomb's rotten inhabitant that stared back at her with blackened, empty sockets. Her scream was deafening, her terror immense.

Graveyard Billy ran again, thinking thin as he squeezed out of the tomb, just as he had on the way in. He shot through the middle of two old people coming to pay their respects to a family member, both of them gasping in surprise, the old lady losing her dentures with the shock, the false maulers spat out onto the ground.

'Poxy cat!' the old man creaked with a raised fist.

'*Yerrrr poxvvyy cafftt,*' the toothless woman next to him garbled.

Graveyard Billy drew to a stop, panting, chest moving up and down at a rapid rate as he tried to think of somewhere to go, somewhere to hide.

'*Oh–my–days*!' Kelly exclaimed, her hand on her non-beating heart. 'I thought I was in one of them zombie movies!'

Graveyard Billy gave up, resigned to his connection with her, knowing it was useless to try and escape.

'Why did you attach yourself to me?' he asked sadly.

'Mate, I was fading into nothing, disappearing before our eyes! You told me how it should work.' She pondered on this. 'In a way... I *knew* it worked that way; that's how I controlled it.' She looked suspicious of the knowledge of her new ability. 'I didn't want to just ... *fade away*. I need to know what's going on – what the answer to all this is.'

Graveyard Billy's problems surfaced within him: He, too, had to find answers to questions he didn't know how to ask.

'I'm dead,' Kelly pleaded. 'It's quite a big thing to have to take in ... I panicked, I ...' She shrugged and sighed.

Graveyard Billy nodded, looked at the ground. He understood.

'What's written on your collar?' she asked.

'It's my name,' he signalled.

'*Graveyard Billy?*' she read, face scrunched as if it were a lie.

'Yes,' he communicated.

'That's your *name*?' she asked, incredulous.

'Yes,' he replied evenly.

'That's the stupidest name I've ever heard,' she laughed. 'You're having me on.'

'That's my name!' he exclaimed, her bluntness grating against him.

'Well, who gave you a stupid name like that?' she asked, pulling a face.

'My owner,' he replied.

'Well where's she?' Kelly exclaimed a tinge of jealously in her voice.

'She's dead,' he said dully.

For the first time since meeting the ghostly girl, he saw a softer side, her eyes filling with emotion. 'I'm sorry, Bill,' she said with genuine sadness.

Graveyard Billy said nothing.

'What happened?' she asked.

'I used to live over there in those flats.' He nodded in their direction. 'Then, one day, *something* turned up in here, and ... took her ...'

'Took her? Like, killed her?'

Graveyard Billy snorted with sadness.

She stared, open-mouthed. 'Shut up, that's just freaky! What do you mean *something* turned up? Like a ghost?'

'Like something,' he replied. 'Something that I couldn't figure out, something that I didn't know what it was. Not human or ghost. It just came in the window, and ...' He stayed quiet then, staring at the ground again, a visible misery shuddering through his body.

'I'm sorry, Bill,' she said again, the hurt in her voice as genuine as the first time she'd said it.

'So I have to live out here now; I ... haven't got a home. I was waiting to see if they would bring her here so I could connect with her again – like I have with you – so we could help each other. I could help her cross over ... and she to help me ...' He didn't have an answer for that.

'Well, if she's not in here, she must be buried local in one of the other graveyards. Did she have any family nearby?'

'No, just me,' he replied. 'I was going to leave here, try and find her out there. I don't think she's come back yet. If I can just find where she's buried, maybe like you've come back, she will, too.'

Kelly nodded, a breeze kicking up fallen leaves like a swarm of brown moths.

Graveyard Billy said, 'I've never been out past the graveyard before, never seen what's beyond it. I know it's dangerous with all the mechanical machines that move.'

She thought about this: 'The cars?'

'Yeah,' he replied. 'I just don't know where to go to start looking. I can't sense her, can't feel where she would be.'

'You better be careful out there,' she said. 'If you ain't streetwise, you're gonna get flattened, Bill.'

'Thanks,' he said, a gleam in his eyes like a raise of his eyebrows.

There was a silence between them, Kelly pulling her bottom lip and thinking.

'Look, we both want something: You want to find your old

owner's grave –' it made him cringe hearing those words out loud, '– and I want to go home and figure out what the hell happened to me.'

He nodded.

'It's easy,' she said with an instant grin on her face. 'Don't you see? Now we're connected, we can do this together! You help me, and I'll help you! Partners!'

Graveyard Billy stirred, the cold hackling his fur. 'I don't know …'

'You look like you haven't had a good feed for a while. We'll go back to my house – my Mum will love you! We can find out what's going on and then figure out a way to find your owner!'

'Well …' Graveyard Billy said, not really wanting to commit, knowing in a way he had no option.

'Partners!' she said again, giving him a double thumbs-up.

The wind picked up again, the trees rattling like old, dried bones with its draft.

'Partners,' he said with a blink, instantly regretting it as the word was transmitted.

Chapter Thirteen

'All right,' Kelly said, standing in the middle of the road opposite Woodvale Cemetery's wall, looking right and left, up and down the road, checking there weren't any cars coming.

Cautiously Graveyard, Billy looked left and right, then scampered across the road to the path opposite.

'See!' said Kelly. 'It's easy, Bill.'

'Can you please stop calling me Bill? It's not my name!' he said as he leapt up onto a small wall at the front of someone's garden.

'Well, I'm not going to keep calling you Graveyard Billy; that's just a mouthful.'

'How would you like it if I called you something other than your own name?' he said.

'Yeah, I bet you can think of a few,' she said sarcastically. 'Okay, I get the graveyard bit – *I think* – because you were always stalking around that graveyard,'

He nodded gently and blinked.

'But why Billy? Are you named after someone in particular?'

'Well, it was because ...' he thought of that processed meat face, its stubby factory-pressed ears, its dyed-red lips and nose. 'Never mind,' he said finally.

Graveyard Billy sniffed at the air. Aromas so far away before, now so close. Each of the little terraced houses that led along the road as vibrant in its own colour as it was in its own set of smells. 'So where do we go?' he asked.

'It's a bit of a fair old trek; it's about a forty-five-minute walk, mostly up hills.'

'Well, we don't have to go the roadway; we could cut through gardens and over fences,' he said.

'I can't jump over fences! What do you think I am, some kind of acrobat?' Kelly gasped.

'No, I think you're some kind of ghost,' Graveyard Billy replied.

She deliberated this for a second. 'I don't know; if we do cut through gardens, who's to say that there might be some dog you could get into a scarper with. I won't be any use then. I can't do a thing.'

Graveyard Billy, wary of his new surroundings, understood. This was all new to him, all a huge step out of his comfort zone of Woodvale Cemetery, hopefully, a step towards finding Piper.

They walked together up Bear Road. Graveyard Billy strolled along the old houses' front stone walls, Kelly's ghost next to him on the pavement.

'Bill?' she said.

'Yes,' he replied, navigating around a green recycling bin, sniffing in its direction to see if a morsel of food was inside – sadly, there wasn't.

'How come I can understand you when you talk? How come you talk human?' she asked.

'How come when you talk, you talk cat?' he replied.

'*Yeah*, but I'm not!' she exclaimed.

'Well,' Graveyard Billy pondered. 'When you talk, you move your lips; when animals talk, we use our minds. I think when humans die –'

She interrupted him: 'Don't remind me.'

'When humans die,' he reiterated, 'I think the missing link between how we can communicate is somehow … connected.'

'I didn't know cats could be so smart,' she said, genuinely interested in what he was saying.

'How would you; you've never bothered talking to one before.'

'*Ha-Ha,*' she said sarcastically. 'Do you ever think some people hear what you say, though? You know,' she said awkwardly, spitting the words from her mouth as quickly as possible, 'live ones.'

'I think Piper could,' Graveyard Billy replied. 'I think she knew what I was saying to her at times even if she didn't realize it. You do know that cats communicate with their eyes? We do it so humans can understand us physically – not that many of them pay attention, though – but we do. You ask us a question directly, we'll blink in reply – if we want to, that is.'

A few doors along, loud barking could be heard coming from inside a house; the squinted eyes of a Staffordshire bull terrier pressed against a window, glaring straight at them. '*Whoof, whoof, whoof!*' the huge, meaty, white creature repeated over and over.

Graveyard Billy froze dead in his tracks, not moving a single step as the dog's eyes made contact with him.

'You're all right; he's not getting out.' Kelly said as Graveyard Billy uneasily stalked along the house's front garden. 'Bill, if you can see me … can other animals see me, too?'

Graveyard Billy thought about this. 'I think so,' he replied.

'Hang on,' she said. 'Let me just try something.' With a huge levitating leap, she bounced off the ground, floated towards the window where the dog constantly barked – '*Whoof, whoof, whoof!*' – her astral blue glow streaking through the air behind her as she went. Landing down near where the dog was, Kelly screamed, '*Shuttttttt–upppppppp!*'

Her voice was so loud it even made Graveyard Billy wince.

Suddenly, the dog shot away from the window, no more barking coming from its huge mouth, just the high-pitched whimpering of retreat. '*Yeeeep! – Yeeeep!*'

The window's net curtains got caught on its front paws, yanking them down around it like a cheap ghost costume on Halloween as it escaped, blindly ploughing through a Christmas tree in an explosion of cheap tinsel and baubles on its way to the back door.

A loud voice roared; in came the beast's slobbish owner in a pair of dirty jogging bottoms and a soiled white vest. He screamed the fleeing creature's name, seeing the destruction it had caused: '*Satan! What have you done, you bastard!*' he bellowed.

'*Haaaaaaa!*' Kelly laughed, wisping back towards Billy. 'Well, I guess that proves they can see ghosts.'

'I guess it does,' Graveyard Billy agreed.

'Did you have to learn how to talk?' she asked. 'Like – talk to people?'

'No, it's just instinctive. I say the things that make sense in my mind, and they transmit to how you understand them in yours.'

'*Ohhhhhh,*' she said.

'It's like when you were alive – '

She visibly tensed at being reminded of her death.

'– you couldn't shift through solid things or move through the air or use your supernatural ability to tether to someone. But in death –'

She visibly tensed again.

'– It's just instinctive to what you have become; it's just part of you.'

'*Agghhhhh*, Mum!' A little girl wrapped in a thick winter coat, her face poking through the hole in her hood, pointed up at Graveyard Billy on the stone wall as they walked past him down the hill. 'Can I stroke him, please!' she asked her mum, who was as equally wrapped up, trying to fend off the winter chill.

Her mother – a woman who shared her daughter's deep brown eyes, reached out and stroked Graveyard Billy's back, testing to see if he was friendly. A slight shock jolted through his body as the woman's warm touch, a deep purr instantly bursting from within him. 'Yes,' she said, 'he's a very friendly boy, aren't you!'

She smiled; Graveyard Billy blinked in response.

Kelly impatiently rolled her eyes, held her hands to her hips.

The woman picked the little girl up, held her nearer to the wall; she reached out and rubbed his head with her mitted hands. Graveyard Billy rotated his head, so her small fingers dug in

53

behind his ears. A deeper purr, as if he was incubating a hive of bees, escaped from within him.

'Milk it much?' Kelly said, watching as Graveyard Billy's eyes turned dreamy from the attention.

'I wonder if I can scare people off,' Kelly said aloud, leaping next to the little girl's face, hands held high, mouth open wide as she wailed like a banshee: Her roar had no effect, though.

'Come on, Kelly,' Graveyard Billy said, rolling his own eyes.

'We have to go now,' the little girl's mum said, her arms becoming tired of holding her up. 'Say goodbye to Mr. Cat.'

'Goodbye, Mr. Cat,' the little girl giggled as she was let down to the ground.

'Why can't they see me if that stupid dog did?' Kelly asked.

'Why can't they hear me like you can,' Graveyard Billy replied. 'That part of them is just … switched off. You know, it's not all that great being alive,' he said. 'Being dead does have its perks.'

She quivered all over, 'Do you have to keep saying that! Come on, you've had your jollies for the day. Let's get moving.'

She was an odd human, Graveyard Billy thought to himself. Ex-*human* – he smiled.

CHAPTER FOURTEEN

Slowly they travelled along Bevendean Road, turned right to Meadowview, and then made it to Kelly's house on Dawlish Close. As they drew nearer, Kelly did something she had not done since she had returned from the grave: she stayed quiet.

As they walked to the end of the close, Kelly suddenly stopped, turned sheepishly, stared at a three-bedroom house with a large willow tree in the garden.

'Is that it?' Graveyard Billy asked.

The girl just nodded quickly, little strands of ectoplasmic whispers moving like stray hairs around her as she did. 'Look at that, all the cars parked outside; they're all my Aunties and Uncles.'

The pressing winter cold cut deep; a gust of snow ruffled Graveyard Billy's fur. 'So ... what shall we do?' he asked, thinking of her promise of a feed. 'I don't know how we can get in?'

'Well, I'm all right ... it's just you.' she said, thinking, 'I ...' she stopped herself, took her eyes off her house and looked down Graveyard Billy. 'I need you to come in, Bill. I... don't know what I'm going to do.' A genuine fear gravelled her voice.

'Well ... what did you want to come here for?' he asked.

'I wanted to see them, wanted to connect to them – tether to them like you said I should! And I ...' she swallowed, sighed, clenched her fist's quickly. 'I want to know what happened, why I'm ...'

She expected him to say the 'D' word again: He didn't, and she appreciated it.

'You're a good mate, Bill; I can tell that,' she said evenly, looking back at the house. 'On the back door,' she said, 'there's a cat flap; it's been there ever since I was a kid. You can get in.'

The winter wind bristled against him again; his expression changed with its touch.

'Come on, let's go in.' she gulped.

Chapter Fifteen

Graveyard Billy leapt from the ground to the top of the six-foot fence that enclosed the back garden; meekly, Kelly stepped through the fence next to where he dropped.

'Ready?' he asked her.

She nodded in response.

He stepped up two concrete steps to the back door, and as she had promised, a cat flap was cut into the old wooden door. He arched his neck round, gave her a single blink for 'Yes.'

Learning the way of the cat instinctively, she gave a single blink back.

Graveyard Billy stepped inside.

He was in the kitchen, and an abundance of smells hit his senses: the natural aromas of each individual person inside, remnants of cooked food, remnants of food uncooked, and, more importantly, the dull smell of the artificial heat given off by radiators. A memory blinked in his mind; that warm radiator smell reminded him of being in his own home during the winter. He sighed.

Slowly he made his way along to the adjacent door and poked his head warily around the corner. In the front room, people all in black sat on the three-piece suite – with extra chairs taken from the dining-room table – in a huge circle.

Kelly peeked around the corner. There was no image on the T.V. – which used to be constantly on – no sound from her brother's bedroom upstairs – which used to be constantly blaring music – just a morose tone the family shared.

Graveyard Billy looked up. The sequined shimmer of Kelly's outfit breezed silently past him to the centre of the room. She stood under the old chandeliered light fixture above and listened.

'Do you remember when she got her first bike without stabilizers?' her brother said, dressed in a black suit – the smartest she had ever seen him – 'what she did when she fell off?' he smiled.

'Fell off, Kevin?' her mum said, shaking her head. 'You poked a stick through the front spokes and sent her over the handlebars!'

A flicker of a smile spread over Kelly's face. *They're talking about me; they're remembering things about me!*

'But she made you pay for it,' her father smiled. 'She got right back up and beat you with that stick all the way back up to your bedroom!'

Her brother laughed; it was quickly tainted by sadness.

'That girl always had a hardness to her,' her Aunty Vicky said. 'She knew her own mind.'

Kelly looked around, pirouetted in the middle of the room:

56

her Aunty Debbie, Debbie's three kids, Vickie's two kids, her cousins; even old Uncle Frank had come down from Brixton, him always arguing with someone in the family. She had always liked Frank – even when others said different – he was the definition of a character.

'She was a good girl,' Uncle Frank said in his Caribbean accent – one her dad had accused him of putting on at her tenth birthday party – 'she deserved better than what happened to her.' His words drained any joy from the room.

'What happened to me?' Kelly cried, *What happened!'*
Graveyard Billy saw her frustration.

'I'm here! I'm all right! I'm right in front of you!' she screamed.

'Kelly!' Graveyard Billy transmitted. 'They can't hear you; you have to try and be calm!'

'Be calm, be calm, what can I do – nothing! I'm useless; I might as well just be dead!' she cried.

'You are!' he replied. 'We just have to listen and learn, find things out as they go along.' As he looked around the room, the tension palpable, he had an idea. 'Hang on,' he said, quickly grooming himself. 'Who here likes animals?' he asked Kelly.

'Aunt Vicky isn't too keen, Mum does, and Uncle Frank has had cats all his life.'

'Which one's Uncle Frank?' Graveyard Billy asked.

Kelly pointed to the older man who sat in an armchair by the window.

'Got it,' he replied with a wink.

Graveyard Billy, straightening his posture, tail held high like an exclamation point, wandered around the kitchen doorway and scampered into the middle of the room with an alert, *'Brappp brappp brarawww!'* sound.

Everyone in the room let out an, *'Agghhhh!'* at the sight of the cat.

'I didn't know you had a cat?' Aunt Vicky said to Kelly's mum.

'We don't,' she replied.

All the kids rushed to Graveyard Billy; to save himself from their pawing hands, he leapt up to Uncle Frank's lap. The man let out a laugh, instantly petting him in the right places to make Graveyard Billy purr, his experienced hands telling all that he was indeed a cat owner.

The kids all came over, and Uncle Frank held them all away. 'You can pet him one at a time, or you'll scare him off.' Each of them listened to his deep, echoing words.

'I wonder where he came from?' Kelly's dad said.

'That cat flap,' her mum replied.

'It's a good omen having a black cat cross your path,' Uncle Frank said.

'I thought it was bad luck,' Aunt Vicky said, a slight sneer on her face.

Kevin dropped down to the floor with the kids and started to pet Graveyard Billy. 'Stop being so superstitious, you lot,' he said. 'He's all right.'

'Kevin, be a good boy and go and get some of those salmon slices your mum cut up. I can feel his bones through his skin.' Uncle Frank said.

'Oh, you're doing all right, aren't you,' Kelly sulked as Graveyard Billy purred louder.

'Just be calm. The longer we're in here, the more chance we have of finding out what happened,' Graveyard Billy transmitted.

Kevin came back with a plate of salmon, the pink fish piled high.

'Oh, that's too much,' Aunt Vicky said. 'What a waste.'

'Here you go, brother.' Uncle Frank said, holding the china plate in his hand, smiling as Graveyard Billy, not looking a gift meal in the mouth, began to tuck in.

'We should put him outside after that,' Aunt Vicky said. 'Who knows where he came from?'

'He's all right,' Uncle Frank replied with a grin. 'He's got an owner; he has a name on his collar.' Uncle Frank read the name and said it with a laugh, 'Graveyard Billy! That's a good name, my old mate!'

Graveyard Billy stopped his chewing for a moment, looked up at Kelly, and gave her a wink.

'Yeah, shows how much he knows,' Kelly said, nodding at Uncle Frank.

'I reckon he must be lost,' Uncle Frank said.

'Or hungry,' Kelly's dad said, unimpressed.

'*Hmmmmmm,*' Aunt Vicky hummed in agitation, eyeing the cat up and down.

'Are you all right, little fella?' Uncle Frank asked.

Graveyard Billy blinked once at him for Yes.

'Good,' Uncle Frank smiled.

'Hang on a minute,' said Kelly. 'Did he …'

'If you take the time to listen, you can understand anyone.' Graveyard Billy transmitted through the last mouthful of salmon.

Uncle Frank stroked Graveyard Billy's back and asked him another question. 'You want some more to fill ya belly?' Graveyard Billy blinked, and Uncle Frank said, 'Go fetch him another piece of the salmon.'

Kevin ran to the kitchen and brought a slice back.

A slight smile broke on Kelly's face, an idea forming in her mind.

'Come on, Frank, you can't keep feeding him everything,'

Kelly's mum moaned.

Kelly hissed towards her mum as she might if she were still alive: 'Mum, keep it down, will ya!'

'Do you have an owner?' Uncle Frank asked.

'Two blinks for no!' Kelly said to Graveyard Billy.

Graveyard Billy gave the man two blinks.

'Be nice to the cat,' Uncle Frank said, 'He don't have no place to go.'

'*Oh-my-god!*' Kelly cried. 'This is it!'

'Come on, time to put him out,' her dad said, calculating the cat had already eaten nearly three pounds and sixty-six-pence's worth of salmon.

'Oh, Dad!' Kelly cried. 'Just keep your nose out for once!'

'I'll take him outside,' Uncle Frank said, getting up from his chair, holding Graveyard Billy in his arms.

'Good,' Aunt Vicky huffed under her breath.

'You were always such a miserable old cow, Aunt Vicky!' Kelly exclaimed.

With Graveyard Billy cradled in his arms, Uncle Frank walked to the front door, opened the latch, and walked outside.

'Touch his face with a paw,' Kelly exclaimed excitedly.

Graveyard Billy did.

'You're a friendly little fellow,' Uncle Frank grinned.

Graveyard Billy blinked once for Yes.

'You know, showing up today, it's like you are a good omen to tell us something,' Uncle Frank said.

Kelly squealed with delight, 'Yes–Yes–*YES!* Uncle Frank believes in all kinds of weird stuff – mysticism, spirits, all that mumbo jumbo! He doesn't know it, but we all call him "Uncle Frank the Crank" behind his back! Blink again, Bill, do something!'

Graveyard Billy blinked, pushed himself into the man's warm arms with an enormous purr.

Making sure he was out of earshot of the others, Uncle Frank placed Graveyard Billy on the top of his worn-out Escort – how it made it here from Brixton even the spirits couldn't answer – and asked him another question. 'Do you know what happened to our Kelly?' he whispered to the cat.

Graveyard Billy blinked once for Yes.

Then inquisitively, Uncle Frank squinted his eyes and asked, 'Do you have a message for us from her? From our Kelly?'

'Bill, make it good, mate! Make it good!'

A tear had welled at Uncle Frank's right eye; it fell down his cheek.

With a blink for Yes, Graveyard Billy put out his left paw and dabbed the tear away.

Kelly jumped up and down, squealing, 'You milked it proper! You milked it proper, Bill!'

'Trust me,' Graveyard Billy transmitted to her with an air of cockiness.

'You're a special cat, aren't you?' Uncle Frank asked.

Graveyard Billy winked in response.

'You want to help me ... talk to Kelly?' Uncle Frank bit his lip, looked back at the house once more. 'I've got an idea, Graveyard Billy,' he grinned.

CHAPTER SIXTEEN

'Did you put him outside?' Kelly's mum shouted from the living room as Uncle Frank clicked the front door back in place.

'Yeah, he's gone,' Uncle Frank replied, whispering, *'Be quiet now, boy,'* into Graveyard Billy's ear as he held him tight.

'Samantha?' Uncle Frank called out, his tone that of a needy child.

'Yes,' Kelly's mum replied, like a put-upon mother.

'Is it all right if I go up to the spare bedroom and lay down? It's all been a bit much for me today.'

A long pause stretched to infinity; then her reply came: 'Yes, of course, Frank.'

Uncle Frank smiled, then quietly padded up the stairs.

'Told 'ya we called him Frank the Crank – it's because of all this,' Kelly said, watching as Uncle Frank lit stubby candles and arranged them around the bedroom, adding an old battered Ouija board that he placed in the middle of the room.

'This is why him and Mum fell out in the past: When we were kids, he heard about that Enfield Poltergeist story in East London. He got the train up there to visit that house on Green Street, knocked on the door, and bought the bloke that lived there a Big Mac meal to let him look around,' Kelly said.

'That doesn't sound so bad,' Graveyard Billy said, sitting on the floor sniffing at the Ouija board.

'Yeah, but he was babysitting Kevin and me at the time. When Mum found out, we had our Happy Meals in the most haunted house in Britain, she did her crust; when Dad found out, he planted one on Uncle Frank and told him *he'd* turn *him* into a ghost if he didn't stop prating around.'

Uncle Frank lit the last candle, drew the curtains, so the room glowed orange with the exposed flames. 'Now we are ready,' he grinned.

'Good to see he learnt his lesson,' Kelly said with a roll of her eyes.

'Now, my small friend, I'm going to try and use your perception to contact the other side, to see if we contact our dear Kelly.'

Kelly grinned. 'I knew I could count on you, Uncle Frank!'

'Graveyard Billy,' said Uncle Frank.

The small cat looked at the man and blinked; Uncle Frank's smile grew wider. 'I want you to put your paw on this.' Uncle Frank touched the board's planchette. 'Then let the power of the spirit world flow through us for answers.'

'Put your paw on it like he did, Bill,' Kelly said.

Graveyard Billy did and then took his paw away. Uncle Frank let out a small chuckle.

'Kelly,' Graveyard Billy transmitted. 'You do know these things don't work.'

'What?' she said, her face slackening to an unimpressed stare.

'Well, ghosts can't actually interact with the living or touch physical objects; I think people just make up what they want to hear from these things,' he replied.

'I thought I could just … move it… with my mind or something?' Kelly said, unable to find the words she needed to describe the act.

'No,' Graveyard Billy said, feeling the heat from the candlelit room growing.

'Right,' Kelly said, 'this is how we're going to do it. I'll tell you what letters to point the thing to, and you move it.'

'We might be able to talk the same language with transmitting,' Graveyard Billy said. 'But I can't understand all these words.'

'Fine, look, I'll point to where it has to go; you push it.' Kelly said.

Uncle Frank had his eyes closed now, hands held out in front of him, palms down as if energizing the board with his low chant.

'Will he believe that?' Graveyard Billy said.

'*Bill,* look at him! He'll believe anything because he wants to believe something!'

'*All right!*' Graveyard Billy snapped back.

Uncle Frank finished his chanting. 'Now we are ready.'

Graveyard Billy sat to the left of the board, Uncle Frank to the right. Kelly darted around them, sat forming a triangle in the same cross-legged position as Uncle Frank. Uncle Frank placed a finger on the planchette. 'Now you do the same, my friend, and keep your paw there this time,' he said to Graveyard Billy.

'Do it, Bill.' Kelly said.

Graveyard Billy placed a paw on the side of the planchette.

'Good,' Uncle Frank said. 'Spirit, if you are there, come forth, and –'

The bedroom door burst open. 'Uncle Frank! Aunty Samantha said do you want a cup of te–'

Maxwell and Rona, Aunty Vicky's kids, stood at the door with wide-open mouths; Uncle Frank and the cat he had just put 'outside' gave them the same face back.

'*Oh my days,*' Kelly moaned, her head falling into her hands.

CHAPTER SEVENTEEN

'Now, you have to keep this a secret,' Uncle Frank said to the two kids who were now sitting around the Ouija board cross-legged. 'This is … just a game … a special game that we can't tell ya, Mum, about. We got that?'

Maxwell and Rona nodded back.

'It's no wonder Dad clumped him,' Kelly said.

'Come on,' Graveyard Billy said, feeling the pressure. 'We have to concentrate.'

'Now, everyone place their fingers on the planchette.' The two children followed Uncle Frank's lead, giggling as Graveyard Billy did the same.

'Quiet now!' Uncle Frank hissed. 'Don't mock the dead.'

Kelly blew air through her lips and shook her head.

'Is anybody there?' Uncle Frank asked.

'Right, point it down to this,' Kelly said, showing the cat the printed 'YES' that sat inside an engraved skull. Graveyard Billy put pressure on his footpads and pushed the planchette, so its end pointed to 'YES.'

'You are magic, Bill!' Kelly grinned.

'Good,' Uncle Frank grinned. 'Who is talking to us from the world of the spirits?'

'Right, follow my finger, Bill,' Kelly said.

Graveyard Billy spelt K–E–L–L–Y.

'It said her name!' exclaimed Rona.

'Quiet!' Uncle Frank snapped at the girl.

'How do we know you aren't some demon from hell?' Uncle Frank asked.

'Here we go, how do we know you're not off ya rocker, ya silly old –'

'Kelly, just listen to him!' Graveyard Billy transmitted, his multidirectional hearing picking up something behind him.

'What age are you?' Uncle Frank said.

'Point here and here, Bill,' Kelly said, pointing to the numbers two and one.

Graveyard Billy pointed the planchette to the two and the one.

'It's her!' Maxwell said.

'One more thing!' said Uncle Frank. 'What was your nickname as a child?'

'Oh, for God's sake,' Kelly said, shaking her head.

'What do I do?' transmitted Graveyard Billy.

Kelly said nothing, just huffed like a petulant child. 'Trust him to bring that up.'

'I repeat,' said Uncle Frank. 'What was your nickname as a child?'

'Kelly, *tell me!*' Graveyard Billy said.

'Is it not her?' asked Rona.

'Be quiet, child!' Uncle Frank said. 'You don't want to upset it if it's a demon.'

A splash of fear hit both the children's faces.

'I repeat!' boomed Uncle Frank.

'Kelly!' Graveyard Billy transmitted.

'Is it a demon?' Maxwell said with a quivering lip.

'What was your nickname as a child?' Uncle Frank demanded.

'Kell –'

'All right!' Kelly cried and pointed out the letters: C–O–M–B–I–N–E–K–E–L–L–Y

'It is you, Combine Kelly!' Uncle Frank exclaimed.

The two children giggled.

'You are such a plank, Uncle Frank,' Kelly sneered with a disgruntled face.

'Combine Kelly?' Graveyard Bill asked.

'Graveyard Billy?' she sarcastically blurted back.

Graveyard Billy titled his eyelids, so they looked like a smile.

'Pshhh,' she replied.

'Now you are here, you have to tell us what we need to know, girl; we need to see that justice is done,' Uncle Frank said. 'We need you to tell us what happened to you the night you were taken from us.'

'What?' Kelly said.

Maxwell and Rona stopped giggling; stared seriously at the board.

'They don't even know what happened to me!' Kelly gasped. 'Bill! What happened to me!'

'What do I say?' Graveyard Billy asked.

'Tell him I don't know!'

'How?'

Kelly quickly pointed her fingers around the board: D–O–N–T–K–N–O–W.

'You must try and remember, Kelly,' Uncle Frank said. 'Justice has to be done, girl! What happened the night you were taken from us?'

'I don't know!' Kelly cried. 'Ask him what he knows, Bill!'

'How do I do that?'

'Kelly pulled at her Tina Turner wig, made fists with her hands, whispered *'Think, think, think,'* over and over. 'Right! Follow my finger, Bill!'

Graveyard Billy spelt: T–E–L–L–M–E–W–H–A–T–Y–O–U–K–N–O–W.

'She cannot remember,' Uncle Frank said.

Maxwell and Rona looked chilled to the bone, their mother not telling them the details either, saying they were too young to hear such things.

Uncle Frank swallowed, then began: 'You were out that night with your friend Danni –'

'*Yeah,*' Kelly confirmed, bug-eyed.

'It was her hen do on the seafront –'

'*Yeah,*' Kelly agreed, leaning in closer.

'You went out dressed as Tina Turner –'

'Oh, don't remind me,' Kelly winced.

'Then you left the group, went outside of that night club you were in ...'

Kelly drew in closer.

'... You walked around the corner ...'

Maxwell and Rona moved in closer.

'... Walked up towards the lanes ...'

Graveyard Billy leaned in farther, listening to the man's words.

'Then you walked past The Pavillion ...'

'I did ...' Kelly said, remembrance flaring in her eyes. '*I did!*'

'And ...'

'Yeah ...' Kelly said, her ectoplasmic aura tingling.

'That's when ...you fell down the steps...'

'Oh no ...' Kelly cried. 'That's it ... I remember! These poxy shoes! They must have done me in!'

'And then ...' Uncle Frank went on.

'And then?' Kelly gasped. 'There's more?'

'And then?' the children both said in unison, faces scared witless.

'Then you –' Uncle Frank stopped as the bedroom door flew open.

'What are you two doing up here annoying your Uncle Frank when he's trying to get some slee –'

Aunty Vicky stood in the doorway, mouth gaped open, jaw hitting the floor. Here she was: aunty to Kelly, sister to Uncle Frank, mother to Maxwell and Rona, and the one member of the family who had taken an instant dislike to Graveyard Billy.

Everyone froze around the Ouija board.

'*What the hell are you all doing!*' Vicky screamed.

A succession of feet all ran up the stairs, Kelly's mum and sad piling into the doorway.

'*Oh noooooo,*' Kelly whined.

Her dad pushed his way into the room, shouting, 'Here he is, at it again, the bloody Ghostbuster is after more ghosts – on the day of our daughter's funeral – practising his bloody voodoo!'

'It's not voodoo –' was all Uncle Frank managed to get out. Kelly's dad's thick hands wrapped around Uncle Frank's neck as the two men started to roll around the room, bumping into everything: the bed, the wardrobe, the chest of drawers. A candle was knocked over, and the net curtains went up like a bonfire on Guy Fawkes Night.

'Oh no! My nets!' Kelly's mum cried out.

Rona and Maxwell began to cry. Graveyard Billy looked left to right, not knowing what to do as pandemonium broke out around him before a choice was made for him.

'And *you* shouldn't be in here!' Aunty Vicky grabbed Graveyard Billy by the scruff of the neck and hoisted him down the stairs.

'*Oi!*' Kelly yelled. 'You old bag, don't treat my mate like tha –' suddenly she was yanked along, too, the ghostly tendrils that attached her to Graveyard Billy becoming taut.

Vicky threw open the front door, tossed Graveyard Billy outside; he twisted through the air and landed on all fours, watching as Kelly flew over him and rolled head over heels to a stop in the street.

'Haven't learned your lesson yet, huh? Haven't learned when you're not wanted?' Vicky yelled, reaching for the hosepipe attached to the side of the house, turning its tap on and blasting a cold jet of water all over Graveyard Billy.

The cold water was like a shower of instant ice in the December air, a million frozen needle tips all puncturing his body at once. Graveyard Billy let out a '*Yowwwlllllll!*' and bolted towards the end of the cul-de-sac in retreat.

Kelly got to her feet, stomped up to her Aunty Vicky, a wispy finger pointed in her face. 'You know, I never liked you, ya miserable old bit – *Whoooaaaaaaaaaa!*' Kelly cried out, pulled through the air like an un-dead kite as Graveyard Billy took off.

Her house seemed to shrink as she was pulled away: The blazing nets in the bedroom window, her dad's bellows of 'Ghostbusters!' and 'Voodoo!', and Uncle Frank's anguished cries of pain, all slowly disappeared from view.

And, with all that, the mystery of Kelly's death was yet to be solved.

CHAPTER EIGHTEEN

'Now!' said Kelly, looking left and right.

Graveyard Billy stalked into the back door of the Sure-Fry Fish and Chip shop on Queens Park Road, looking left and right as his cat senses went into overdrive. The place was filled with a menagerie of new aromas: disinfectant, boiling oil, the sweat of the humans who worked there, and, most importantly – food.

'Up here Bill, up here!' Kelly said, pointing to one of the stainless-steel counters where an order was being wrapped up, the kitchen worker leaving the order, going to the walk-in fridge to fetch an extra can of Coke.

'Quick!' Kelly said, pushing her top half through the wall next to her, materializing inside the walk-in fridge to see the Asian man struggling to pull a can from a multipack.

Graveyard Billy leapt up and onto the counter, instantly coming face to face with a huge piece of battered cod lying next to some chips. Wasting no time, he sunk his fangs into the fried fish, ignoring its heat, immediately overwhelmed by its size as he dragged it over the edge of the counter with him, hanging on for dear life as he toddled with it to the open back door.

Kelly laughed to herself, watching Graveyard Billy slip into the cold black of night. She laughed again as the Asian man walked back to the counter, put down the can of Coke, paused, realizing what was missing; swearing in his native tongue as he started searching the floor for the missing piece of fish.

'Your takeaway just got took, mate!' she said, disappearing after Graveyard Billy.

They sat on top of the chip shop's roof looking out, over the view of Brighton: Car headlights flickered like mini lighthouses as they circulated roundabouts; rows of fairy lights winked in the breeze as if they knew Christmas was almost there; in the distance, the pier's amusements glowed in neon.

The kitchen's flue sat nearby; pale vapours spewed into the air from its opening, its heat creating a round circle in the frost that had settled on the tiled roof; a warm spot where Graveyard Billy could enjoy his dinner and dry out.

'You deserve that, Bill,' Kelly said, staring into the distance.

A silence grew between them – thinking time – only the sound of Graveyard Billy tucking into the soft, white meat in the air.

'I'm sorry,' Kelly said, 'for dragging you into this, for everything I've done.'

Graveyard Billy swallowed his mouthful and replied, 'You don't have to apologize.'

'Yeah, I do. None of this is your problem; I've made it your problem by being selfish.'

'I don't know why you think what you did was that bad. You panicked; everyone who comes back from the dea –' Graveyard Billy stopped himself. 'Everyone who comes back panics; it just doesn't make sense why you couldn't attach yourself to your family? Honestly, that's how it works; I've seen it in the graveyard so many times. Sometimes people stay here on earth when they are with their family; sometimes they move on, but they always have the power to tether to them – always.'

'I suppose I'm just the odd one out,' Kelly said, looking down at her ghostly blue aura. 'I don't feel … you know… the "D" word. I mean, it was a shock, but it just feels like I could go back home, walk in, and everything would be normal.'

'I wouldn't recommend trying that again,' Graveyard Billy said, fluffing his fur up at the thought of another burst from the freezing-cold hose.

'I'm sorry about that, Bill,' Kelly shrugged. 'I miss them all, though. I thought they were so annoying when I was aliv …' suddenly the 'A' word became as hard to say as the 'D' word. '… when I was about, I couldn't wait to get out of the house and have a night on the town with my mates, but now … I miss them.'

Graveyard Billy sighed, started to eat his fish again.

'It's so ridiculous,' she said, becoming annoyed with herself. 'The living are supposed to grieve the dead, not the other way around!'

'I know,' Graveyard Billy said, a distinct heaviness in his voice she picked up on.

'I'm sorry, Bill, I'm just being selfish. I forgot about our deal … I forgot about your owner.'

'That's all right,' he said. 'It was nice being inside a house with people; it took my mind off things. Honestly, it's probably the first time in a while I haven't had to think about my own worries, and I kind of liked your Uncle Frank.'

'Uncle Frank,' Kelly smiled. 'Yeah, he's always good for a laugh.'

'Does he really come from the Caribbean – is that his home originally? I mean, with that accent, it must be?'

'The closest Uncle Frank ever came to anything from the Caribbean was when he was caught nicking a Bob Marley L.P back in the nineties. We really don't call him Frank the Crank for nothing – all of it's a put-on.'

'I don't know. Even if he doesn't know it … I still think there's something in him that knew you were there. I think he had some kind of instinct in him to tell that something was going on he didn't quite understand.'

'I'm sure he understands what's going on now Dad's had hold of him,' Kelly chuckled.

'Yeah,' Graveyard Billy smirked. 'I'm sure your mum's net curtains understand, too.'

They laughed together. For a moment, everything was all right.

'I fell down a flight of steps,' she sighed, 'what a way to go. I can remember it now, you know, head over heels ... I think I was near an underpass ... can you believe it? Drunk on a hen do, and I fell down a flight of stairs.'

'You won't do that again,' Graveyard Billy said.

'Well, I should think not!' Kelly exclaimed.

Graveyard Billy gave her a wink.

'You're a good man, Bill,' Kelly smiled.

'I'm an even better cat,' he said, getting comfy.

'Stupid,' she smiled. 'It's not too bad being with you, Bill.'

'It's not too bad being with you, either,' he replied, curling into a circle, staring at the lump of fish he had left for breakfast.

'I'm true to my word, Bill. How about tomorrow we go round some of the other graveyards in Brighton, try and find your owner's grave. Maybe, if we find her, she could help me get back to my family.'

Graveyard Billy looked up at her. 'Thank you,' he said with sleepy eyes.

She smiled. 'You get some rest, mate, then we'll set off in the morning.'

There was silence for a moment, only the distant sound of the sea in the air.

'*Bill,*' Kelly whispered.

'Yeah,' he replied, not opening his eyes.

'Can ghosts sleep?'

'Lay down and close your eyes,' he whispered back.

She shifted down into position; fortunately, her ghostly body could not feel the frost creeping across the roof.

A minute passed, then she spoke again: '*Bill,* I don't think it's working.'

'*Shhhhhh,*' he transmitted. 'Be quiet. It will.'

Another minute passed. 'But, Bill, I –'

'*Kelly,*' he said in as much as a whining tone as she, 'Why is your nickname "Combine Kelly"?

There was pure silence before she said, 'Night, Bill.'

'Night, Kelly,' he smiled.

CHAPTER NINETEEN

Samantha Isherwood stood at the bus stop outside Hove Cemetery. Her arms were loaded with foil-wrapped Christmas presents, each shimmering under the streetlight next to her. The huge faux fur coat she was wearing did little against the night chill that wrapped around her like an ice-cold python.

She buried her face into the huge scarf wrapped around her neck, breathed into its thick wool, and relished the heat it held around her features. Thick winter boots, two pairs of jeans, and a woollen hat: none of it was enough to make her feel warm.

She bit into the frayed ends of her brunette hair that hung around her face. It was a bad habit as much as the gnawed nails on each of her fingers. *'Come on,'* she whispered to herself. *'Where are you?'*

The 700 bus was supposed to be here every twenty minutes; she had been waiting for … shifting the pile of presents in her arms, she squinted at her wristwatch – 'Forty minutes! *Come on!'* she moaned.

She was only doing this as a favour, helping her friend Charlotte get all the presents she had bought her boyfriend into their flat without him knowing. 'I'll take him out for a meal, take him to the cinema – keep him occupied – then you can take everything I've bought him into the flat and hide it in the loft,' Charlotte had said as they wrapped the presents she had stockpiled in Samantha's flat.

'Oh, can I,' Samantha had replied. Charlotte not picking up on any on the sarcastic tone in her voice.

'He's going to love all this,' Charlotte beamed. 'I've spent so much on him.'

'That's good,' Samantha smiled, glad the pile of designer clothes and video games was finally going to be removed from her small studio apartment.

'Are you sure you don't mind taking all these round there?' Charlotte said, suddenly seeing past her own selfish bubble.

'No, it's all right,' Samantha smiled dully. 'This is what friends are for, right?'

'Of course, they are,' Charlotte grinned. 'If you found yourself a man, I'd do the same for you.'

Samantha nodded, knowing full well that when Charlotte had been single – and she had been for the past year – anyone else who had a boyfriend was frowned upon: 'God, I don't know why she keeps him around; men are such losers.'

'Come on, girls, we don't need a man around to have a good time!'

'It's us, girls! Will always be us girls!' she would say as they walked home from the pub.

'Always us girls' had soon become 'none of you girls' when

Charlotte had met Dan at the gym. Tall, well built, good looking in a slack-jawed kind of way, his conversations as vapid and foamy as the sea spume on Brighton beach.

'It's *us*, girls – always *us* girls,' Samantha would say snidely to herself, looking at the pile of Christmas presents for Dan in the corner of her flat.

One rule for herself, one rule for other people, and nobody ever pulled Charlotte up on it. With her big dopey grin and big dopey giggle, she got away with everything.

'*Awwww!* Thanks for taking all this to his flat! I don't know how I would have got it all there secretly!' Charlotte grinned. 'It's good having a *single* friend like you!'

'*A single friend like me,*' Samantha said through gritted teeth, peering up the road for the bus. *This is how she gets away with it because mugs like me let her.*

She checked her watch again – forty-seven minutes late. With a sigh, she stepped back to the railed fence behind her and leant against it. The night chill thickened as she looked over her shoulder to the black silhouettes of the tombstones inside Hove Cemetery.

There was an odd, palpably creepy atmosphere in the Victorian-era cemetery, the frost-covered grass emitting a rolling mist that lay a few feet off the ground. Even though it was almost Christmas, it was pure Halloween in the cemetery grounds.

'*Got one for me!*' a voice screamed in front of her, as a stoned-looking teenager in a beanie hat reached out for one of the presents.

'Keep out of it!' she said, kicking out as the teen laughed and pulled off into the night on his B.M.X. His two equally stoned-looking friends followed on their own bikes, laughing.

'Sharing is caring!' one of them yelled back towards her.

Samantha leant back on the cemetery's iron railings, a smile appearing on her face as, in the distance, the illuminated windows of a double-decker bus came nearer.

'About time,' she said with a shiver, the cold suddenly feeling more arctic with its bite, a new scent mingling in the atmosphere attacking her nostrils.

Her face wrinkled as the sticky, smoky smell filled her senses, covered her body like a layer of slime. She gasped loudly, presents exploding from her arms all over the sidewalk.

Something cold and lifeless clamped around the back of her neck; it felt like the legs of a huge, frozen tarantula.

The gothic imagery of Hove Cemetery flashed in her mind – the shadowed tombstones, the inky mausoleums, the thin forms of leafless winter trees – as what felt like the chilled fangs of a vampire bit into her neck.

She was unable to scream, unable to do anything as she was lifted up and over the railings into the cemetery's pitch, dropping the presents on the path as she disappeared as if she had never existed into that thin veil of fog that lingered there.

The 700-bus driver changed gears and sped past Hove Cemetery's bus stop, not knowing he was one passenger down. Not noticing as Samantha's thick scarf was tossed back over the cemetery railings next to the bus stop with a foul bloody splat.

Chapter Twenty

A screech filled the air; a loud mechanical hiss escaped the big, red, opening maw. People filed on one by one, willingly queuing to disappear inside the great beast.

'Are you sure this will get us there?' Graveyard Billy asked.

'Yeah, of course, I used to get this bus every day to work.' Kelly answered.

Bus, Graveyard Billy thought, his mind caught in the three letters humans used to name the contraption.

Kelly walked in through the big sliding doors to the middle of the bus, looked left and right. 'There's space down the back. If you hide under the seats, no one will see you, and I can tell you where to get off.'

Graveyard Billy gave her a wink, slinking down to the ground and stalking forward, cautiously, still unsure of the bus.

'Come on, Bill! Quick!' Kelly said, waving her hand to coax him inside; everyone on the bus too busy staring at his or her phone to notice him pad to where Kelly was pointing at the bus's rear.

Graveyard Billy skulked under the seat; white dots of dried chewing gum prodded overhead. The bus cranked to life, the doors letting out a spitting hiss that put him instantly on edge.

'Don't worry, we'll be all right on here,' Kelly said.

They had been travelling around all morning, had already visited the Brighton and Preston cemeteries trying to find Piper's grave. They had looked at every stone, monument, and cross in search of her name. Graveyard Billy, with his senses, turned up to their peak, couldn't sense the girl; couldn't feel her presence anywhere nearby. It was Kelly's idea to start a search pattern: 'We'll go to Hove and work our way back to Kemptown – trust me, it makes sense, Bill,' she had said.

He just nodded and trusted her.

'Where did you use to work?' asked Graveyard Billy as the bus chugged on.

'What?' Kelly said, sitting in the seat adjacent to him, forgetting for a moment where she was, the old routine of her life among the living echoing back.

'Where did you work?' Graveyard Billy asked uneasily, his eyes like saucers every time the bus braked.

'Where we're going now – Hove. I worked as the receptionist at one of the hairdressers. It was perfect, really.' A modicum of whimsy appeared in her voice. 'All I had to do was sit there and answer the phone.' She mimicked picking a phone up and placing it to her ear. 'Hello, Hove Styles, can I help you?' She smiled. 'That's all I had to say, all day long ... oh, and make the tea, it was perfect ...' a dreamy look glazed her eyes.

'Sounds riveting.' Graveyard Billy said.

'All right, it wasn't rocket science, but at least I wasn't just sitting around doing nothing.' A moment of self-realization hit her, knowing at that moment that's exactly what she was doing there.

The bus pulled to a stop, the doors letting that bestial hiss from their hydraulics again.

'I did plan on doing more, to be honest,' Kelly said. 'You want to know a secret?' she asked Graveyard Billy as she watched more passengers shuffle on. 'I applied to uni before I ... well, you know.'

Graveyard Billy did know and winked once to acknowledge the fact.

'I wanted to study digital design. I could have been good at that; I always had a good eye for laying things out. I used to do it for the school magazine, you know.'

Graveyard Billy didn't know, but he winked politely.

'I didn't tell any of my friends, though; they would have just laughed if they thought I was going to do something like that. They always said, *"Everyone changes when they go to uni."* Not they knew anyone who went to uni.'

'Piper used to go to uni,' Graveyard Billy said.

'Really,' Kelly said, a visible peak in her interest.

'Yeah, she used to paint and make sculptures,' he replied.

'Art and design?' Kelly asked.

'Yes, I think that's it,' Graveyard Billy said.

'Do you think me and Piper would have got on?'

Graveyard Billy thought about this, 'I think you're very different people, but I can't see why you wouldn't have.'

'Yeah, I can get on with most people, me,' she said. 'I think it's one of my life skills to be fair, I'm a bit of a people perso –' She stopped dead in her words, mouth open as if someone had muted and paused her, stuck frozen in a past second.

Graveyard Billy stared at her, sensing something was wrong; he spun his gaze around the bus floor, seeing only shoes and ankles and bags. 'What's wrong wit –'

'Bill,' she said quietly, becoming unglued from her solid-state.

'What!' he gasped, crawling up and onto the seat opposite, his eye line matching hers.

'Bill, is that what I think it is?' she whispered, her face never breaking her shocked gaze.

Graveyard Billy looked and understood what had seized her up with fright. There, a few rows down, a spotty-looking teenager in glasses and an old cardigan stared back at Kelly, his hair slicked over to one side, his face pale and transparent, his eyes as big as hers in joy rather than in fear. 'Hi!' he said, waving a ghostly blue hand towards her.

74

'Is he ...'

'Yeah,' said Graveyard Billy nonchalantly. 'He's a ghost.'

'Bill,' she gasped, 'I've never seen a ghost before.'

'Well, you should try and look in a mirror.' Graveyard Billy said sarcastically.

'Have you only just passed over?' the boy asked.

'Bill, he can see me.' Kelly said, still in shock.

'Yeah, well, that happens at times with spirits; different plains of existence are all layered up on one another, and it's like potluck where you might fall into them. But for cats, it's like a dark spectrum of colour. If you shift your eyes, you can pass through the plains and see things that others can't, and sometimes other ghosts can –'

'– see other ghosts too.' Kelly finished.

'Can you see me?' the boy said. 'I like your cat!'

'Thanks,' said Graveyard Billy.

'Hey! You talk!'

The boy put his thumb up geekily at Graveyard Billy and grinned a strained smile. 'That's all right, mate! My names Kelvin,' he grinned at Kelly, 'and this is my mum.' He thumbed over at the living grey-haired woman sitting next to him, who stared out the window as he talked, seemingly neither seeing nor hearing him.

'I haven't had the heart to pass over yet,' he said. 'I know she needs me around; she lives alone, you see. At least this way, I can keep an eye on her, make sure she's all right, you know. Anyway,' he stumbled, 'I'm being rude, what's your name?'

Kelly said nothing.

'Can she see me?' Kelvin said.

'Yes,' Graveyard Billy replied.

'No, I can't.' Kelly said.

'Kelly, just talk to him,' Graveyard Billy frowned.

'Kelly,' Kelly said, something that resembled a smile curling at the corner of her mouth.

'Kelvin and Kelly! It's like a pair of names you would see on a sun-strip on a Mini's windscreen, you know what I mean!' Kelvin enthused.

Kelly said nothing.

'Like back in the seventies, when everyone had their names on the top of the windscreen. You know, when everyone used to have leopard-print seat cove –'

'Yeah, I get it.' Kelly said finally.

'Sorry if I seem a bit keen,' Kelvin said, getting up and moving to the back of the bus.

'Oh my God, he's coming closer.' Kelly said as a grin pulled over Graveyard Billy's face.

'It's just that – I never normally get to talk to many people these days,' Kelvin explained, pushing a lank strand of hair to one side.

'I bet,' Kelly said evenly.

'Especially girls, good-looking ones like you, I never spoke to many of them when I was alive.'

'Never would have guessed,' Kelly said, even more sarcastically than she had before.

'How long ago was it when you were alive?' asked Graveyard Billy.

'Oh, let me see now ...' the ghostly teenager picked at his ectoplasmic chin; bit his vaporous lip. 'Oh, it was nineteen-seventy-nine,' he grinned.

'What!' Kelly yelled. 'You've been mooching about with her –' she nodded to the grey-haired woman, ' – for *forty* years!'

'Well ... she's my mum, and she doesn't have anyone else. You know, between you and me, I think she knows I'm there, talking to me when she's talking to herself, you know.'

Graveyard Billy gave him a blink with both eyes; he did know what Kelvin was talking about.

'Mate, I ain't being funny,' Kelly said, 'but I'd be out of here at the thought of spending forty years hanging about with my old girl, you get me?'

'Yeah, I do,' Kelvin replied. 'So why don't you get out of here?'

She went to reply, the words catching in her throat.

'Well, that's one of the things we're trying to work out,' Graveyard Billy said. 'For some reason, Kelly here –'

'That is a nice name,' he interrupted.

'Shut up,' Kelly said sullenly.

'Okay,' Kelvin replied, never losing his grin.

Graveyard Billy raised his voice. 'Kelly here wasn't able to connect with her family; she couldn't become tethered like other ghosts do with her families. She only had enough power to connect with me.'

'Lucky boy!' Kelvin said with a wink.

'Mate, don't even go there,' Kelly said, holding her open palms out to him as if to deflect the unwanted interest.

Graveyard Billy studied the ghostly teen, asked, 'I was just wondering if you had seen or heard of anything like that before?'

Seriousness settled in Kelvin's eyes; he looked around as if he wanted no one to hear his words, 'Do you want to know something?' he gulped, 'It's funny you say that little fella because I have ... only recently, mind you.'

'What do you mean?' Graveyard Billy asked.

'Well, you know what it's like. I know cats are aware of, shall we say, "unearthly" goings-on. Every spirit you see has a connection to someone in the living, right?'

'Yeah,' Graveyard Billy said, drawing nearer to Kelvin.

'Me and Mum are always out and about, on the bus

76

pottering around; that's when I started meeting them …'

'Who?' asked Graveyard Billy.

'Lost souls …' Kelvin replied.

'What are you on about?' Kelly said.

'Spirits, ghosts like you and I that aren't, you know – like us,' Kelvin said.

Kelly sat forward in her seat, becoming mesmerized by his words.

'Lost souls that haven't tethered or connected to the living; wispy-looking folk they are: pale, almost gone from existence but not … they can't communicate or find their way to their loved ones like the rest of us do. They're just kind of trapped between … un-dead and dead-dead. If you know what I mean.'

Both Kelly and Graveyard Billy nodded.

'One of them found their way on here a few weeks back, a girl, her face all twisted in pain.'

Graveyard Billy's heart jumped.

'A red-headed girl, in a smart suit like she worked in an office or something.'

A slight relief passed through Graveyard Billy; he was glad it wasn't Piper.

'All she kept doing was howling and moaning, trying to figure out what had happened to her. I tried to talk to her, but it was no use. She screamed the place down, just repeating, *'Where am I! Where am I!'* before she just – "poof!" – vanished.'

Kelvin pushed that lank piece of hair from his brow again. 'You never forget a lost soul … *never…*'

A loud hiss exploded like a dragon's breath; Graveyard Billy leapt three feet straight up in the air in shock. Kelly slumped back in her seat, hands-on a heart that didn't beat, a reflex of fright from the bus's opening doors.

Kelvin's mum shuffled down the front of the bus, Kelvin's teleplasmic tendrils becoming visibly taut as distance was made between them. 'It's our stop; better go,' he said, being pulled away. 'Just remember: If you see one of those lost souls, best to keep away. Seeing one of them … it's like your grave being walked over.' He shivered as the tendrils between him and his mum yanked him from the bus's doors.

CHAPTER TWENTY ONE

The day never brightened beyond a dull industrial grey, everything as monochrome as an old strip of film. Winter chill held suspended in the air; an unmoving sugar puff of freezing fog lay in between the gravestones of Hove Cemetery. Two figures walked along the gravesides: one whose forward progress broke through the white covering, the other gliding through it as if it didn't exist.

'We're nearly at the end of the west side,' Kelly said. 'Where do you want to go now? Back up towards the north?'

Graveyard Billy stopped for a second, then leapt up onto the corner of an old stone tomb and licked his cold footpads for warmth. 'Hang on a second,' he said. 'I know I'm the one with the fur coat, but it's freezing out here today.'

'I guess being ... well, you know ... does have its advantages. I can't feel a thing,' Kelly shrugged.

'Good for you; trust me, you're not missing much,' he replied, scratching the backs of his ears with his hind paws, a rubbery flexing sound coming from them with each bat of his footpads. 'Where shall we stay tonight?' he asked. 'That fish and chip shop wasn't bad.'

'Can't hit the same place up twice in two nights, Bill. Trust me, it will look proper suss.'

He blinked to show her he understood.

'There's a kebab shop down near the seafront; you're bound to be able to grab something from there. We better be careful with that one, though; I don't know how friendly some of those Turkish guys will be if they see you robbing the place, especially if they have one of those machetes they use to cut the meat.'

Graveyard Billy stopped his cleaning and stared at Kelly. 'Yeah, I think maybe we should give that one a miss. I think having you attached is draining me,' Graveyard Billy said with a yawn. 'I seem to be hungry all the time.'

'Don't blame me!' she said, shaking her head. 'You're a cat; that's all your lot do, innit? Eat and sleep.'

Seagulls darted overhead, their shrieking cries putting both cat and ghost on edge.

'I don't think she's here,' Graveyard Billy said with a sigh, looking at the other gravestones, barely visible through the fog.

'Well, we don't know that yet,' Kelly said. 'We should check all of them; we don't know she's not buried here, do we?'

Graveyard Billy squinted his eyes to get a better look through the veil of white that covered the graves. 'I don't know,' he said. 'Everything we've seen and heard is wrong ... just *wrong*.'

'What do you mean?' Kelly asked.

'I've seen how it works so many times when you pass over – like clockwork – but if Kelvin was right, and people are just staying put and not even attempting to cross over after death … something is wrong.'

Off into the fog to their left, something caught Graveyard Billy's attention. Something glowing strangely, something … that walked. 'What was –' Graveyard Billy said.

'– that?' Kelly finished.

They went down towards the phantom flickers of light with trepidation and moved closer until they could see where they were emanating from. A spectral figure strolled slowly through the graveyard, plodding slowly between graves.

'Is she another …' Kelly asked.

'Well, I don't think she has a glowing blue tint to her for nothing,' Graveyard Billy replied.

'Excuse me, I was wondering if you might know where someone, in particular, is buried here?' Kelly called out in a put-on posh voice – her receptionist's voice.

The figure stayed silent, seeped farther into the foggy mists, becoming almost invisible.

Kelly nodded to Graveyard Billy and started to follow the girl, who wore a faux fur coat and a black woolly hat.

'*Oi!*' Kelly called. 'I'm talking to you! My mate and me are looking for a grave in particular and wondered if …'

A horrible, low, gurgling moan came from the girl as, step by step, she moved away, completely ignoring the words called to her, never turning around.

'Cor, she's not as keen as old Kelvin, is she?' Kelly said.

'What I'm wondering is …' Graveyard Billy pondered, '… if she's a ghost … who is she tethered to?'

He and Kelly stopped in their tracks, aware of another sound coming from behind them: a crackling, static-filled voice that came from the front of the graveyard. A pulse of blue light beat through the day's miserable fog.

'What's that?' Kelly asked.

'I don't know,' said Graveyard Billy, slinking down low and stalking towards the mystery light. 'Come on,' he transmitted back to Kelly. She – out of earthly instinct – crouched down behind a line of tombstones as she moved forward.

Slowly, they came closer to the new blue light that swirled through the fog, its intense power highlighting a congregation of figures that shifted from left and right, in and out of the banks of white mist.

'What is that?' Graveyard Billy said.

'Cop car.' Kelly said, squinting at the outline of two vehicles. 'Looks like there's an ambulance, too.'

'What are they doing here?' Graveyard Billy said.

Kelly shushed him as they hunkered down together, stared

at the scene before them as two officers drew closer.

'This fog isn't making our job any easier, Sarge', said a voice.

'I know,' said the silhouette of the man he was talking to.

'Yeah, it's the Old Bill,' Kelly said.

'The who Bill?' Graveyard Billy asked, perplexed.

Kelly rolled her eyes, 'The police.'

'We're doing our best to scour the area for evidence,' said a tall male officer, 'but the lads can't even see their hands in front of their faces.'

The other man sighed.

'What do you want to do, Sarge? Shall we keep this place locked down and hope this fog burns off?

'Weather said it's staying put for the next three days, Palmer. There's not much chance of it shifting, I'm afraid.'

'It's all pretty much cut and shut, isn't it, Sarge? Same as the other ones?'

The Sergeant let out a sigh. 'Yeah, this is becoming a joke. Nine of them now... *nine,* and not a single thing to go on.'

Something sparked in Graveyard Billy; he shot big full-moon eyes up at Kelly. 'They said Piper was eight!'

'What?'

'When Piper was killed in our flat, men dressed like them, who spoke like them, said she was *eight!*'

'Oh my God,' she swallowed.

'We have to get over there and have a look, find out what happened. Whatever happened here must be the same thing that happened to Piper – it must be!' He went to run over to where the two men stood.

'*Bill!*' she yelled, 'Stay here, 'I'll go.'

'But –'

'There ain't no buts; none of them can see me. I can –' she gulped, '– get closer.'

'Give me some slack if I need it,' she said, pointing to the wispy ectoplasmic tendrils that joined them.

Graveyard Billy huffed, nodded, eager to bolt over towards the two men and flashing lights to try to find answers. Kelly slowly began to walk towards them, worried that somehow they might see her, that suddenly she would burst back into their vision of reality as plain as day.

She walked through the fluttering blue and white police line, shifted between the officers who searched the ground back and forth. Carefully, she drew nearer to the ambulance. She looked inside as a body was being examined: Two paramedics talked as they worked.

'Have you seen the hole on the back of her neck?'

'Yeah, what the hell could have done it?'

The second paramedic turned the corpse on its side for a

moment. Kelly moved closer, winced at the ragged hole pierced through the back of the girl's neck before the paramedic gently placed the corpse face-up again.

Graveyard Billy watched Kelly, cocked his head from side to side to try and enhance his vision. Suddenly, he became aware of something behind him, something that held its eyes fixed on him as he held his eyes fixed on Kelly.

Slowly he turned, looked up to a gaunt, drained face, the face of the phantom figure that had gurgled and wandered away when he and Kelly had approached it a moment ago. Her eyes were as sunken as a carved pumpkin's; face gurned to a rictus of agony.

'You can see *meeeee* ...' she groaned, reaching down to Graveyard Billy with fingers as withered as the skeletal trees of winter.

Kelly moved in on the ambulance as the paramedics positioned the corpse face up; she stared down at the murdered girl, her eyes widening as she stared into the drained visage.

Something like a shudder of terror forced its way through her body, rippling up the tethered ghostly line that connected her to Graveyard Billy.

She turned back to him as shock ate through her like shark's teeth.

She had never seen a real dead person before; for a second, she wasn't sure she just had.

For there, looming over Graveyard Billy, was the same drained corpse's face that lay before her in the ambulance, only upright and animated.

It was staring down at Graveyard Billy like a nightmare that had stepped from the deep recess of dream invading reality.

'You can help *meeeee* ...' the lost soul of Samantha Isherwood said. 'We could be *together* ...' Her withered blue aura sparked; ghostly tendrils reached to connect to Graveyard Billy, who, scared to stiffness, could only watch.

Kelly gasped, 'Oh no! Bill!'

Chapter Twenty Two

Samantha Isherwood's ragged lips peeled back, her teeth looking paler and more lifeless than the rows of tombstones around them.

Graveyard Billy backed up, his tail swishing against the grass anxiously as he reversed from the corona of supernatural light that began to spark around the ghostly girl.

'*Pleasseeee,*' she hissed, 'You must help *meeee ... we can connecttttt ...*'

'No! No! No! *No! No!*' Kelly murmured, seeing this happen from the ambulance, quickly running towards the spot where Graveyard Billy continued to back away. She ran straight through a female police officer who straightened and shivered, sensing *something* going on around her, even though she could not see or sense it.

The ghostly girl reached out with a shaking hand to Graveyard Billy, who was too scared to run or try and hide in case he triggered those capturing tendrils that connected the dead with the living.

'*No!*' Kelly squealed, jumping between Graveyard Billy and the shimmering spectre. Samantha Isherwood backed up, raised her hands to her face as if she were a vampire, faced with the correct religious iconography to ward her away.

'What are you doing, messing about with my mate?' Kelly cried.

'*Heeee cannn hellppp meeeee,*' the girl answered.

'Yeah, well, he's helping me, so bugger off!' Kelly cried.

Graveyard Billy stalked away, putting distance between him and the girl.

'But I must deliver the presents ... the *Christmassss* presents,' the spirit wheezed. 'I have to get them there before –' Samantha Isherwood stopped, grabbed at her vaporous head as if trying to remember – 'before ... *before* ...'

'What happened to you?' Kelly asked, 'How come you ended up out here like this, alone?'

Samantha Isherwood stared at Kelly with a bewildered gaze, 'I ... I ... was waiting for the *busss* ... the *busss,*' she repeated, eyes glazed to a memory of the past. 'And it grabbed me ... something dragged me into the graveyard ...' she looked over to where her corpse lay in the back of the ambulance. 'Something ... *smokey* ...'

Graveyard Billy's eyes grew so big they looked fit to burst. 'Kelly!' he exclaimed. 'In my graveyard – in Woodvale, the night Piper died. I sensed something then, something that was smoke, but living: It has to be the same thing!'

'I have to find my way back,' said the girl, 'I have to ...

deliver the presents ...'

'What was it, what was it that attacked you?' Kelly cried.

'The presents! *The pressennnttssss!*' Samantha Isherwood said, her face contorting to anger, the otherworldly aura around her growing again as she moved towards Graveyard Billy.

'Bill!' Kelly cried. 'Can ghosts touch each other?'

'I don't know, why?' he asked, backing away again.

'Let's find out!' Kelly cried, reeling back her right fist and planting it straight into the ghost girl's face. An odd, supernatural splitting sound erupted from the thrown fist. Samantha Isherwood reeled backwards, stumbled head over heels to the ground with an un-dead groan.

'Run!' Kelly cried, and both her and Graveyard Billy ran blindly through the foggy graveyard, never looking back, only looking forward as the lost soul of Samantha Isherwood cried out, 'The presents! I have to deliver the *presseeennttssss!*'

Graveyard Billy hid under a dense holly bush, eyes peeking from side to side from the shelter of the dark leaves.

'Don't worry, Bill, I can't see her anywhere,' Kelly said, peering into the bleak fog.

'I can't have her attaching to me,' Graveyard Billy said. 'It's bad enough –'

'Bad enough, with what with me?'

'No! I didn't say that!'

'That's what you were thinking,' Kelly sulked.

'You have no idea what I was thinking. We need to find out exactly what's going on around here, why there've been nine people killed and what links them to one another. If that girl out there is wandering around like a lost soul, and she died exactly the same way as Piper did, then maybe Piper's ...' he paused, '... lost, too.'

Kelly snorted. 'But it doesn't make sense! Why aren't people crossing over properly, and why are they coming back like ...' She nodded towards the graveyard where Samantha Isherwood wandered.

'How come you came back the way you did?' Graveyard Billy said. 'How come you aren't able to connect to your family?'

'Well, I ain't exactly like her, am I!' Kelly grunted, nose put out of joint. 'I wasn't killed; I fell down a flight of steps, didn't I!'

'I know,' replied Graveyard Billy, 'but there is something odd going on. Why are some ghosts unable to move on? There's some kind of connection here, and I can't put –'

The bushes juddered with a sudden movement. Something struck out and hit the ground in front of Graveyard Billy with a rattling clatter; a figure pulled itself from the fern bush adjacent to them.

'Well, well, well! So you're the culprit whose been digging into the graves, are you?' a man's voice snarled, the face accompanying it one Graveyard Billy recognized. 'I thought it could be foxes, but it's probably a little bugger like you!' A snarling menace drew into the man's features, his lips folded back, revealing bone-white teeth, his evil eyes squinting to vile slits.

He was the one from Woodvale with the strimmer, the one his pudgy friend had called 'Issac.'

He yanked up the garden rake he had planted into the ground in front of Graveyard Billy, held it over his head. 'Council gave us the contract for all of these graveyards,' he grinned, 'told us to deal with any pests.'

Graveyard Billy bolted as the man in the blue overalls jetted off behind him; Kelly yanked along behind them both before she found her footing and started to run, too.

'Who the hell is this?' Kelly called.

'Some kind of sadist from Woodvale. I think he was the maintenance man there,' Graveyard Billy huffed, 'For some reason, he's always had it in for me!'

'Come here, you!' Issac screeched, brandishing the rake like a weapon.

'Run, Bill, *run*!' Kelly shouted, 'Head for those trees! He can't get you up there!'

Graveyard Billy headed towards a great oak standing out from the copse in front of him; he pounded the frosty grass harder with his paws, leapt through the air, clung to the tree's bark, and began to scramble upwards. A loud, jarring *'Thwack!'* reverberated below him, the rake embedding its prongs into the tree's bark, barely missing his swishing tail.

'You lot are all the same,' the man frothed as Graveyard Billy clambered onto a low branch. 'I know what filth like you do, desecrating these graves, doing your business all over the freshly dug earth.'

Kelly wisped up to sit next to him, saying, 'Oh, Bill, you don't – do you?'

Graveyard Billy gave her a meek look before turning his attention to the man below.

'I've seen you before roaming round in that white collar. I've nearly had you in the past, haven't I,' he sneered. He began twisting the rake's wooden handle, a creaking, popping sound coming from his leathery hands as if it were a neck he was throttling. 'Come down here, mate,' he grinned. 'Come and see what I've got for you –'

'Issac!' A loud, burly voice bellowed behind them. An old transit van rolled along the foggy road that wound through the graveyard, an older man hanging from its open driver's side window. 'You've been warned about messing about with animals when we're out here doing this job! These are people's pets, man,' the bald-headed driver said.

'Yeah, I know,' Issac replied. 'The boss doesn't get it, though; it's *his* kind that ruin all the work we do, ' he pointed to Graveyard Billy. 'You think of all those hours we put in, just to let the likes of *him* use the graves as a toilet!'

'You're letting this job get too serious,' the bald man said. 'Come on, let's go. The grounds are solid from this cold; we can't do much here today.'

Issac glowered up at Graveyard Billy. 'You get a pass today, *mate.*' he grinned, walking back to the transit, throwing the rake in the back before loading in.

Kelly let out a sigh of relief as the van trundled away. 'Never a dull minute is there, Bill,' she said as they watched the Transit's rear taillights glow like demonic red eyes as the vehicle exited the cemetery.

'I think we should leave here,' Graveyard Billy said, clambering down the tree, pushing off, and landing with a thud on the ground. 'I don't think Piper's here; surely I would feel something if she was around. We need to find out what exactly is going on, what the story is behind the deaths … why there were nine of the –'

A pair of hands reached out from the foggy depths, a grinning, cragged face behind them. Fingers grasped around Graveyard Billy's midsection and lifted him in the air. 'Gotcha!' an ecstatic voice exclaimed.

Chapter Twenty Three

Graveyard Billy's ears went flat back on his head, his eyes widened to the popping point as an old lady drew his face up to hers. 'Look at *you!*' she said, grinning, vivid blotches of makeup brushed on to make her face look like an abstract canvas of colour.

'Oh God, now what?' Kelly groaned, watching the woman mollycoddle him.

'I've never seen you around here before, are you new?' the old woman grinned, her yellowed teeth contrasted to her powder-white face.

She worked her fingers around Graveyard Billy's fur, under his neck, around his chin, her nails hitting the spot behind his ear that made an audible purr erupt.

'Look at him – loving it,' Kelly said with a roll of her eyes.

'I saw what that man did, awful it was, disgusting.' Working for the council, too, you would think they would hire better than just common thugs.' She began to walk away with Graveyard Billy, shifting through the fog towards the cemetery's small car park.

'Oi! *Oi!*' Kelly cried, the tethering supernatural tendril between her and the small black cat becoming tight and forcing her forward.

'Graveyard Billy, well that's a funny name, *isn't* it,' the old woman over-emoted. 'Would you like some food?' she asked, looking down at his collar.

'You have to get used to this,' Graveyard Billy said to Kelly, 'Old people love cats, and I'm not exactly in the position to say no to a feed.'

'Say no to a feed! I'll sort you out, won't I!' Kelly cried.

'Look, after everything that's happened in here, at least with her –'

The old lady rubbed his head and back as she held him, then made a sound like, 'Oh-*chuckem-nuckens!*'

'– we can get out of here safely. It's been like a madhouse since we turned up.' he finished.

'Have some dignity, Bill,' Kelly said, shaking her head.

The old woman opened the door to an old purple V.W. Polo, plopped Graveyard Billy on the back seat, and quickly shut the door behind him, whipping quickly to the driver's seat.

Graveyard Billy panicked, not expecting to be confined inside the perfume-smelling car, jumping up to the windows and looking out with a tinge of terror.

'What is this, now!' Kelly cried as the car's engine started and its headlights burned through the clinging white mists. She quickly stepped through the car's bodywork and materialized in the back seat next to Graveyard Billy, the old lady singing an off-tune song as she reversed around and started to leave the graveyard.

'Get out of here safely, he said; now where are we going?' Kelly moaned.

'I don't know,' Graveyard Billy said worriedly.

'It was all fine a minute ago, wasn't it, when you thought you were getting a free feed. Now, look at us, stuck in the back here with Driving Miss Daisy, with no idea where we're going – beautiful, absolutely beautiful.'

'Driving who?' Graveyard Billy asked.

'Oh, don't worry about it,' Kelly moaned. 'Your belly is bigger than your brain! You forget I have to go everywhere you go!'

'I'm sorry, I didn't think,' Graveyard Billy said, staring out the car window as it shot like a bullet through the foggy streets of Brighton.

Kelly sighed, something she did a lot of lately. 'Look, first chance we see to do one, we take it,' she said.

'Do one?' Graveyard Billy said, rocking back and forth, unable to gain balance in the speeding car.

'Yeah, get out of here, away from her. We need to figure out what's going on here, why I can't cross over, why that girl back there is ... the way she is .... You said yourself it's odd – it's not normal.'

'It's not,' Graveyard Billy said. 'I can just sense something is wrong. Of all the time I lived next to Woodvale, I've never seen ghosts act like this. I just don't understand it.'

'Do you know what I think?' Kelly said. 'I think we need to get out of here and go back to what we were doing! What if Piper is out there like that girl we saw? You said the dead girl at Hove Cemetery was somehow connected to what happened to Piper.'

'It's what the police said; Piper was the eighth, and that girl ... was nine.' Graveyard Billy knew he'd let his belly get the better of him; he *should* be out there looking for Piper.

'Look, it's simple, isn't it! Whatever happened to that girl back there happened to Piper; we need to figure it out! Find where Piper is! Then maybe we can figure out how I can cross over. If she's wandering around like that, like some brainless zombie, then we have to hel –'

Kelly stopped; understood the sad look in Graveyard Billy's eyes. 'Oh ... I'm sorry, Bill ... I –'

'I know you're right. I should have thought about the bigger picture rather than about food. It's just ... you don't feel this cold like me, and ...'

'Bill, mate,' Kelly said sadly, 'I was selfish. I shouldn't have said that. I'm as scared as you. We're in this together; you're my lifeline – literally!' She ran a transparent hand through the breezy, glowing tendril that attached them. 'I'm sorry, Bill. I'll help you find Piper, just like you tried to get me home.'

Graveyard Billy blinked at her, and Kelly tried to run a hand over him, her palm passing straight through the small creature. 'Mates?' she said.

'Mates,' he transmitted back.

They stayed staring at each other, Kelly grinning with her mouth, Graveyard Billy blinking his eyes in response.

'Nearly there,' the old lady in the driver's seat said. 'That will be nice, won't it.'

'Oh, shut up! Why did you have to ruin the moment!' Kelly snapped with a sour face.

The Polo pulled into a driveway of an old three-story Victorian house in Richmond Road, just up from Brighton's city centre.

'Thank God she didn't drive us for miles,' Kelly said as the car's engine died.

'Where are we?' Graveyard Billy asked.

'Woodvale is about a half-an-hour walk back that way,' Kelly replied, pointing out the car's rear window.

'Well, that's not too bad,' Graveyard Billy said. 'At least we can –'

A long deep *'Rowwwlllllll'* came from his vocal cords as the old lady's hand reached into the back seat and plucked him from the car by the scruff of his neck.

'What does she think she's doing?' Kelly gasped, clambering out of the car after her.

The old lady staggered up to the house, opening the front door and quickly depositing Graveyard Billy inside. 'There you go,' the old lady grinned as she dropped Graveyard Billy onto the cold tiled floor. 'All safe now.'

She slammed the door shut behind her and toddled off to the kitchen. 'Let me get you some food, just like your old Aunt Coral promised you.'

'Aunt Coral,' Kelly sneered as she stepped through the front door into the house. 'Please.'

Everything was tidy in the house; everything had its place. Dust motes travelled through the disturbed air like unwanted invaders; every surface was covered in doilies and frilly coverings; floral patterns dominated walls and furniture as if they had somehow taken root and were growing.

'Look at it,' Kelly said. 'I can't even use my nose, but I know it stinks of old people. What does it smell like, Bill?'

'It's kind of like, soap, earth, something sweet like sugar, and ...' Graveyard Billy wrinkled his nose, ' ... perfume, lots and lots of perfume.'

'Yeah, old people stink.'

'That's really rude,' Graveyard Billy said.

'Yeah, so is kidnapping you and bringing you back to the retirement home.'

'There you go, just like Aunt Coral promised,' said the old lady, putting a piece of newspaper on the floor, then placing a perfectly white china dish filled with cat food on top of the paper.

Graveyard Billy dove straight in, waffling the food down his neck.

'There you go, Bill, your fill from old Aunt Barnacle.' Kelly said.

Graveyard Billy stopped, gave Kelly a look, then carried on.

She laughed to herself. 'Just enjoy it, mate.'

Aunt Coral began to stroke Billy's back as he ate. 'There's a good lad, such a good boy! Now make sure you don't leave a mess or spill it on the newspaper ... that's not acceptable, spilling it on the newspaper. Good boys don't do things like that, do they!' she grinned.

Graveyard Billy wolfed the food down, licked the plate clean so not a smidge of the food's brown gravel was visible. He sat licking his lips. Aunt Coral stroked him. 'Good boy, such a *good boy!*'

Kelly looked around the front room: the collection of rags and cans of polish lined up on almost every window sill, ready for action; the remote controls for the T.V. precisely arranged side-by-side on the couch, plastic walkways placed on the carpet; everything positioned perfectly, clinically; nothing out of place. 'Come on, Bill, let's go. This place is giving me the creeps.'

'Okay,' he said, and, backing away from the bowl with a little chirp, he reached up and placed his front paws on the front door, letting out a low *'Woooooooow!'*

'You want to go out?' Aunt Coral grinned, her lips slowly quivering at the edges, eyes glazing with dull menace. *'No,'* she growled. 'You're a good boy now, and good boys *never* go out.'

CHAPTER TWENTY FOUR

'*Errrmmm*, Bill,' Kelly warned as she watched Aunt Coral rise from her haunches, reaching to the windowsill by the front door, picking up a newspaper and rolling it into a tight tube.

'I said – *GOOD BOYS DON'T GO OUT!*' she screamed, bringing down the newspaper at Graveyard Billy.

'*BILL!*' Kelly screamed as Graveyard Billy used his agility to kick off from the floor and flip backwards, avoiding the whack of the newspaper as it was slammed into the door. He ran into the living room, leapt up onto the back of the sofa, and spun around to see where the old woman was.

'*Dirty feet!*' she cried. 'On my nice clean settee!' Trundling towards him with the newspaper raised, she yelled again. 'This is what the plastic is for – dirty paws! *DIRTY PAWS!*'

'She's absolutely bonkers!' Kelly cried as the old woman stomped forwards, the rolled newspaper slashing the air.

Graveyard Billy jumped down to the floor, using the plastic pathway like a circuit as he bolted around the sofa, then doubled back to the hallway door.

'There must be a window or something open!' he yelled, looking up at all the bolted frames that blurred past as he made it to the kitchen.

'She's coming, Bill! She's coming!' Kelly cried as the slow lumbering thumps of Aunt Coral's podgy legs plodded behind him. Graveyard Billy leapt up onto the worktop, winding his way between plates and utensils, constantly searching for any pane of glass that might have been left ajar: there was none.

'On the worktop now, I see,' Aunt Coral bellowed. '*AN EVEN NAUGHTIER BOY THAT I THOUGHT!*'

Graveyard Billy hit the tiled floor, squeezed past the old woman so quickly it took her a moment to register that the black cat had shot past her and headed up the stairs.

'Go, Bill! *Go!*' Kelly cried, quickly following him as he made it to the first floor and searched his options: The bathroom door was open – the window closed; an airing cupboard to his right; a spare bedroom he could sense no draft coming from.

Heavy feet thumped up the stairs behind him; Aunt Coral's croaky old voice gurgling, 'I got you! I got you! I GOT *YOOUUU!*'

'In here, Bill, in here!' Kelly shouted, already in the main bedroom's doorway, waving him in with as much fright in her eyes as his.

Graveyard Billy sped towards her. 'On the windowsill, look – *LOOK!*' Kelly cried. 'There, it's open!' she was pointing to the last of the bedroom's French windows. Behind heavy drapes, a three-inch gap was left open on a latch.

Graveyard Billy leapt up towards it, navigated his head in-between the gap, tried pushing his small furry head into the refreshing cold winter air.

'Think thin, Bill! *Think thin!*' Kelly cheered as he tried to squeeze his midsection through the gap, regretting the meal he had just scoffed minutes before.

He looked below, the long drop down to the gravelled driveway, the purple car an option to lessen the fall.

He was just about to pull his rump through, just about to make that split-second decision of either cold car roof or jagged gravel to leap upon when a scream came from Kelly's un-dead lips.

'*BIIIIIILLLLLLLLLLLLLLLLLLL!*'

A wrinkled hand seized his tail and yanked him backwards, the opportunity of escape shrinking as his body was pulled and tossed carelessly back into the house. He hit the bed, spun around, tail aching, and watched as Aunt Coral gleefully slammed the window shut with such force it was a surprise no glass was shattered from the frame.

'We almost had an escapee!' she snarled. 'His first day in, and he nearly got out. I'll have to keep an eye on you, won't I!'

The old woman lunged forward; Graveyard Billy, exhausted and aching from being pulled backwards, was slow to move as her outstretched fingers reached for him. He tried to move, tried to escape, but a cold bony finger hooked inside his collar; a moment of strangulation contorted his face as the collar tightened around his neck, a distinct cough escaping his black lips.

'You old bag!' Kelly shouted as Graveyard Billy managed to slip himself free of his collar, darting around and under the bed.

'You don't need that!' Aunt Coral cackled. 'What kind of a stupid name is "Graveyard Billy," anyway?'

Graveyard Billy curled into the darkness under the bed, huddling against himself in fear as he defiantly thought: *My name.*

Aunt Coral took the collar and tossed it onto the top of the old cream wardrobe that stood in the corner of the room. 'That's enough of that name,' she said, dropping down to the floor, one old blue eye peering beneath the draped bedspread, trying to find the cat she was terrorizing.

A distinct click popped from inside Aunt Coral. 'See what you did; you've put my back out,' she grimaced. 'No matter, you'll be out at some point; maybe then you can understand what it's like to be a good boy! We have rules here – rules good boys have to follow!'

'You all right, Bill!' Kelly called under from the opposite side of the bed.

'Yeah, I'm okay,' he called back.

'This old bag's off her rocker!' Kelly said.

'I know,' he replied. 'We're going to have to be careful with her. I'm quick, but she's just as cunning, even for an old woman.'

'Trust me, mate, she wouldn't get a day older if I could get my hands on her!' Kelly said.

'Blackie!' shouted Aunt Coral, as if hit with an epiphany. 'Your new name is going to be Blackie!'

'Original,' Kelly said sarcastically. 'Don't worry, we've already given *you* a new name – Barnacle.'

Aunt Coral let out a loud *'Phewww!'* her scrunched up face of menace slackening to the expression of the harmless old lady she'd seemed to be in Hove Cemetery. 'It's all-new, I know Blackie, but you'll get used to it.' A grin as welcoming as cancer spread over her wrinkled face. 'I'll set you up a bed – that you *have* to sleep on. A bowl and some water – but *don't* spill it. Oh, and a cat box – aim for the litter, *not* the edges.'

The meanness in her voice blossomed out like a split personality emerging. The juxtaposition of the sweet old lady and scowling matriarch came and went like the up-down motion of a yo-yo.

A crease of fear folded in Kelly's features, a genuine realization escaping her mouth: 'She *is* mad.'

'I'll let you calm down, Blackie; then we can be friends – *if you can behave.*' She snarled slightly as she got up and trundled from the room, clumping back downstairs.

'We need to get out of here, Bill,' Kelly said, worry in her eyes.

'We're just going to have to wait for an opportunity to escape,' Graveyard Billy sighed. 'If I play her game, it will come. What did she do with my collar?' he asked.

'Threw it on top of the wardrobe,' Kelly said.

Graveyard Billy sighed, the stale smell of dust under the bed filling his nostrils.

'See you soon, *Blackie,*' the old woman called from the bottom of the stairs.

The trembling black cat thought of the collar Piper had given him, thought of his name she had penned with her own hands. 'It's *Graveyard Billy,*' he said angrily.

CHAPTER TWENTY FIVE

Graveyard Billy sat under the bed for three hours until nature took its course, the plate of cat foot working through him until he couldn't hold it in anymore. Kelly sat with her back against the radiator opposite, hands on her knees, picking every now and then at the cheap Tina Turner outfit she was doomed to wear for eternity.

Slowly Graveyard Billy crawled out from beneath the musty bed, looked at Kelly, who stared solemnly back. 'I need to ... well, go and do ...'

Kelly clapped her hands against her thighs. 'I can't help you, Bill; I can't do anything: I'm useless.'

'That's not true,' he said. 'We're a team. You can be my eyes and ears to help us escape.'

'We can't end up stuck in here forever,' she said. 'Old people's houses do my head in; they're like being trapped in a morgue.'

'I know,' Graveyard Billy said, climbing out and extending his tail with a stretch, the underside of the bed reminding him of the tomb he had clambered in the day the pair first met. 'We have to make her think everything is fine; we have to make her let her guard down: It's the only way we can escape. I have to go down and ... well, you know. I can't do it up here.'

'You *should* be doing it up here,' Kelly said. 'Right there in the middle of her bed.'

Graveyard Billy blinked at Kelly; as loud and obnoxious as she was, he did like her attitude. 'Come on,' he said. 'I need to go.'

He stalked down the stairs, his soft footpads making no sound as he moved forward with trepidation. A TV was playing in the front room; he could hear applause on a shoddy game show, canned laughter and jingles that burrowed into your mind like a drill.

He poked his head into the living room, Kelly behind him, peeking around the door, the tyrannical attitude of Aunt Coral infecting her too.

'The old bag's on the sofa; looks like she's eating chocolates or something,' Kelly said. 'The cat box is in the far corner over there,' she pointed to the far wall beyond the T.V.

'Here we go,' Graveyard Billy said.

'Make sure you stick to the plastic; we don't to spark old Barnacle off for nothing,' Kelly said with a growl.

Graveyard Billy navigated around the plastic walkways behind the sofa, headed towards the spot Kelly pointed to. A loud, haggish cackle broke from the other side of the sofa; Graveyard Billy tensed to a halt as the old woman laughed at something on the screen.

He looked up at Kelly, whose eyes were burning daggers into the back of the old lady's purple rinse.

Meekly, Graveyard Billy moved around to where the cat box was, a white sheen of litter levelled perfectly in a bright red tray. With one paw after another, he moved cautiously towards it.

'*Ohhhh,* looks like Blackie's come down!' Aunt Coral squealed.

Graveyard Billy said nothing, glanced over his shoulder at her and climbed inside the tray, embarrassed. He looked up at Kelly, his eyes saying he wanted some privacy from her at least as the demented face of Aunt Coral stared at him with a fixed grin.

'That's a good boy!' she said as she watched him go, staring as he buried it in the litter. 'No spillage over the side!'

'*Pleaaassseee,*' Kelly hissed with her back turned.

'We really *need* to get out of here,' Graveyard Billy huffed.

'There's a good boy!' Aunt Coral said as he finished. 'You didn't spill a single bit. Maybe this time it will be different, maybe you, Blackie, won't be like *those* others ...'

Graveyard Billy and Kelly shared a knowing look; the sweetened menace in Aunt Coral's words when referring to 'those others' sent shivers down their spines.

They watched her fish Graveyard Billy's business from the cat tray with a plastic scooper as she hummed an upbeat little song to herself, walking to one of the French windows that surrounded the living room, opening it, and dumping the contents outside.

Graveyard Billy headed for the opening, aimed himself up to take flight towards it, but in a flash, Aunt Coral had already slammed it shut. 'That'll keep the flowers in bloom, won't it, Blackie,' she giggled childishly. Her laughter quickly dropped, her own cunning traits drawing attention to Graveyard Billy's posture. 'I hope you weren't thinking of making a leap of faith towards that window, Blackie,' she said, placing the plastic scooper next to the cat tray, bending down towards him. 'That would be a very *bad* idea.'

With reflexes that went beyond her old frail body, she quickly brought her right hand round and flicked Graveyard Billy straight in the middle of his small black nose. The pain was immense, his senses rattling and reeling with the sharp spiking pain, an instinctive hiss breaking from his fanged mouth. 'Looks like old Blackie's in a bad mood tonight!' she chuckled, shifting to the kitchen. 'Cup of tea,' she muttered to herself, 'time for a nice cup of tea.'

'I swear down, Bill, when that old bag passes over, I'll kill her again,' Kelly fumed.

'We just have to be careful,' Graveyard Billy replied,

rubbing his snout. 'There's something besides her I just don't trust; something in this house I can sense but can't put my paw on ...'

'I can't keep this up, Bill,' Kelly said, biting her lip and clenching her fists. 'I don't even want to look at the old cow's wrinkled-up face.'

Aunt Coral came back in the room, planted herself into the sofa, resuming position into the dip her rear end had worn into the cushions. 'Are you going to be a good boy and watch the television with your Aunt Coral?' the old woman asked. Graveyard Billy gave a look to Kelly and lowered himself solemnly to the plastic walkway around the room, sitting silently with closed eyes.

'That's a *very* good boy Blackie,' Aunt Coral smiled, feeding more chocolates into her mouth. 'There are rules, Blackie, simple rules to follow; that way everything will be perfect; that way everything will have its place just the way it's supposed to.' Something dreamy caught in her eyes, something that gave her pupils a lacquered, nightmarish look. *'Everything has its place,'* she grinned. *'And in its place, everything will be.'*

'Yeah, and if I could,' said Kelly angrily, 'your place would be with me pushing a pillow down on your face, love.'

Graveyard Billy gave Kelly a wink.

'I'm going to bed after my program's finished, Blackie; that's the routine – that's how we do things here. I'll show you where your bed is, then.'

The T.V. droned on: Faces grinned with unnatural pearlescent teeth; hands applauded like their owners were wound inside by clockwork. Eventually, credits rolled up the screen, and Aunt Coral shut the lid of the chocolate box. 'Time for beddy-byes,' the old woman grinned, quickly plucking Graveyard Billy from the floor, him visibly flinching with her touch as she carted him through to the kitchen.

Kelly plodded along behind them, giving a single finger salute to the old woman as they went. 'There's your bed, Blackie. Somewhere nice to keep you safe ... to keep you where *I want you*.'

The old woman opened the whining metal door of a three-by-three-foot cage on the kitchen floor and pushed Graveyard Billy inside.

'You have got to be kidding me.' Kelly seethed.

'There you go,' Aunt Coral beamed. 'There's a bowl of water in there, and I'll be down in the morning to let you out for breakfast.'

Graveyard Billy sighed held his head low in the small, confined prison: no blankets for comfort, only a shallow water dish.

Aunt Coral flicked off the kitchen lights. Only thick slithers of lunar light illuminated the French windows; a matrix of squares gridded the cold tiled floor.

Kelly followed Aunt Coral out through the kitchen door as far as their supernatural tether would allow, expletives coming from her mouth that made even Graveyard Billy's ears prick.

A moment later, Kelly returned, her face radiating anger. 'This isn't right, Bill; the sooner we get out of here, the better.'

Kelly pointed to the ceiling, her hand visibly shaking. 'We're gonna get her, Bill, somehow, someway, we're gonna get her, I–'

'Okay, calm down,' Graveyard Billy said. 'We have to keep level-headed.'

Kelly fell to the floor, sat cross-legged next to the cage, staring in at him. 'I'm so sorry, mate. If I could change this, I would, ya know.'

'I know,' he blinked back.

'Look, let's get some sleep,' he said, turning and rummaging up the newspaper in the cage to make a bed. 'Tomorrow, we can try and figure out a plan to escape. I know we can. I just–'

Graveyard Billy froze, his paw in mid-motion turning over the newspaper, eyes enlarging like the full moon outside.

'Bill! What's wrong!' Kelly cried.

'It's … *Piper* …' he gasped.

'What!' Kelly exclaimed.

Graveyard Billy pulled the paper back, folded it with his paws until the entire article was exposed. There, in black and white, was a picture of Piper – his Piper: his friend. Suddenly the confines of the cage didn't matter; a sparkle of freedom and happiness exploded in his heart at her face. 'This is *her*!' he cried. 'This is Piper! *My* Piper!'

Kelly shifted inside the cage, transposed her top half through the bars.

'Oh-my-God!' she gasped, reading the text beneath – '"Piper Herbert of Brighton."'

'What does it say?' asked Graveyard Billy anxiously. 'The words are all just symbols to me.'

'Oh yeah, I forgot,' said Kelly, shifting her head so she could read the article. 'The headline says: "Graveyard Killer Strikes Again."'

'Graveyard Killer?' Graveyard Billy said incredulously.

'Yeah … yeah … I remember something about this now. When I was working on reception, I remember someone talking about it. I don't pay much attention to the news; I mainly just read Instagram.'

Graveyard Billy had no idea what that meant but knew it sounded vacuous.

Kelly went on. 'The latest in a string of attacks that have

taken place around Sussex –mainly Brighton and Hove – continued last night. Twenty-year-old Piper Herbert of Tenantry Down Road, Brighton, was murdered at her council flat in the early hours of last week. Her body showed signs that she was a victim of the "Graveyard Killer", thus dubbed due to a series of rash murders with strange similarities. Eight small puncture marks and a larger wound have all been found at the back of the victims' necks –'

'That's right!' Graveyard Billy exclaimed. 'That's what Piper had on the back of her neck!'

'That's what was on that girl's body that tried to connect to you! The one in the back of the ambulance in the graveyard.' Kelly's eyes grew as big as Graveyard Billy's as they stared at one another before she went on.

'Piper was the eighth victim of the killer. The other victims: eighteen-year-old Zoe Spooner from Eastbourne, twenty-two-year-old Abi England from Hove, twenty-five-year-old Samantha Greenhill from Worthing, and ...'

Her eyes scanned through the list, her mouth falling open.

Graveyard Billy had never seen a ghost become so pale.

'The last victim ... *was me* ...' she gasped.

Kelly held a quivering hand up below her cheap wig, her face expressing complete fear. She turned around, lifted the synthetic hair, exposed what she had felt on the back of her neck to Graveyard Billy.

There it was: the same markings he had seen on Piper, the same markings she had seen on Samantha Isherwood's body in the back of the ambulance.

A memory hit her harder than the stairs; she *thought* she had died falling down.

'Bill,' she whispered. 'I was murdered by the Graveyard Killer.'

97

CHAPTER TWENTY SIX

'I remember,' Kelly said. *'I remember.'* Her eyes glazed back to the past, back to Danni's hen do, to the night she died. As the images accumulated in her mind, the words that described them fell from her lips.

'I was with my friends in a nightclub on the coast; we were all wearing these outfits.' Kelly grabbed blindly at the hem of her cheap golden dress. 'Kirsty was dressed as Madonna, Danni was dressed like Cyndi Lauper, and I –' her tone of wonder turned sour, '– was dressed like ... *Tina Turner.*'

Graveyard Billy locked onto her eyes, transmitting for her to go on.

'It was hot, too hot, and I'd had too much to drink. Everything was spinning and spinning ... I needed to go outside; I needed to get some air. It was cold, and the wind was cutting in from the sea.'

Graveyard Billy watched as the truth unfolded in her features.

'I'd had enough. I'd drunk too much and went for a walk, tried to sober up. Then I realised I'd been walking so long I was about halfway home, so I cut through the underpass on West Street. I got to the top where the railings are, and all of a sudden, I had a head rush: the cold, the drink; everything all came at once. I tried to walk, tried not to fall – I had my hands on the railings to keep balance. Yeah,' she smiled, the memory becoming more vivid. 'They were black railings, and the paint was chipping off, and there was red underneath – I remember!'

'And then?' Graveyard Billy said anxiously.

'And then ... the strap from my bag – that stupid costume bag – it was long and gold and kept falling from my shoulder ... it ... came off and got caught under my high heels ... somehow I tripped, went head over heels over the railing. I tumbled down over the edge into the underpass. All of a sudden, I was sober and could feel the pain as I hit the bottom. I was face down, knocked silly ... I...'

Kelly paused, the memory in the present becoming as fuzzy as it was in the past.

'I ... don't know how long I was lying there for ... but I heard footsteps echoing from the other end of the underpass ... someone was walking towards me.

'Could you see their face?' Graveyard Billy asked.

'No ... It's just a blur ... even as they came closer ... I ... held my hand out; I held it up to them and asked them to help me up.'

The words of the past echoed in her mind: *'Give me a hand, mate, I fell –'*

'But he didn't move ... just watched me ... then he reached into a bag, and –' A frisson of fear made Kelly shiver.

'– he took something from a bag ... I saw it under the underpass' lights ... it looked like ...' Horror clenched at the memory. '... a spider. A great, big grey or silver spider ... a big thing, bigger than your hand outstretched .... It was like a great big crab, all legs and bulbous body ... and something changed in the atmosphere like it was dark, but it suddenly became darker .... There was a smell ... a smoky smell.'

Graveyard Billy all but gasped. 'What happened?' he asked quickly, not wanting Kelly to lose momentum.

'And the figure spoke in a man's voice and said, *Always room for one more.*' And his voice somehow was like ... it was the smoke, and it was the darkness. I can't explain it!' she cried.

'Please try to!' Graveyard Billy pleaded desperately.

'Then ... he lowered himself down, put a knee on my spine, and the spider wrapped around the back of my neck. It was cold – ice cold – and then, it bit me hard, right here.' She placed a hand round to the back of her neck where the ragged hole still gaped now.

'And then it –' Kelly's teeth gritted; eyes winced in pain. '–it started to suck. It started to drink from me, and I was paralysed. I couldn't move, couldn't fight, couldn't do anything. Everything became black; everything started to disappear, and I heard footsteps coming closer from the other end of the underpass – he heard them too and took the spider thing from my neck – just yanked it out – and ran. As he did, I heard his voice ... *"Almost ... almos*t," Kelly hissed in a tenebrous impression of it. 'Then there was screaming as the footsteps approached me; then nothing ... and ... I was gone.'

She took a deep breath. A cold, ectoplasmic tear ran down her face.

'*Almost,*' Graveyard Billy said. 'That's why you aren't like the others, like a lost soul – whatever he was doing, he didn't finish it! That's why he said 'almost'! Whatever he was doing, whatever that spider thing was, he never finished what he intended to do.'

Kelly stared at Graveyard Billy and swallowed. 'But what the hell was that? Why did it happen?'

'I don't know, but this is the connection between you and the others. The only difference is you were the lucky one that got awa –' He stopped.

'Yeah,' she said, looking at her transparent hands. 'Real lucky.'

'But if he's done it before, he'll do it again, don't you see? That girl today we saw in Hove Cemetery, he must have got her last night. Whatever this spider thing is, it didn't finish what it was supposed to do to you; that has to be why you're still here –

weak, but still here. You're the only one who wasn't killed in a graveyard; maybe he just didn't expect to find you; maybe he just took the risk there and then because he couldn't find anyone else that night.'

'I just keep getting luckier, don't I,' she grinned sarcastically.

'What was the date of Danni's hen do?' Graveyard Billy asked.

'October the twenty-fifth, why?'

'And what date does this newspaper say?'

Kelly looked down into the cage that housed Graveyard Billy, squinted her eyes to make sense of the newspaper's date in the pale moonlight. 'October twenty-ninth.'

'This was why he came to Woodvale,' Graveyard Billy said. 'After what happened with you, he needed to find ...'

'Piper,' Kelly said flatly.

Graveyard Billy blinked at her and looked down at Piper's black and white image with a heavy heart. 'Somehow, we have to figure out why he's doing this and where he's going to strike next.'

'Easier said than done,' Kelly replied. 'What do we have to go on?'

'Not much,' Graveyard Billy said, looking at the bars around him with determined eyes, swishing his tail against the matrix of metal. 'But first, we have to get out of here.'

CHAPTER TWENTY SEVEN

It sat in darkness, captured in the thick smell of earth. The soft-touch of a moist chill peeled a smile on its face; the constant dead glaze in its eyes drawn forward as it stared at nothing.

It could hear everything in the room, could sense each and every single creature moving no matter its size: worms squelched in the walls, a woodlouse glided beneath the old wooden bench in the corner, a moth battered its delicate wings around the single unshaded bulb that hung from the room's centre ... and its favourite – the spider – pulled the silky strings of its web in a far corner.

Its cracked lips pulled back farther at the thought of the spider: those encompassing legs, those beady black eyes, and those long, delicious fangs. *'All the better to eat you with,'* it said in a broken voice as ragged as a sheet left to deteriorate in the elements.

Nine; that's how many it had collected – nine. It was becoming whole, more so than the first time it had tried to become one with reality. Its last host – the one that had brought it here – had too many people always watching and waiting for its next move. The host had been too exposed, too known by others for it to *really* use the host's body to its full potential.

Now, it was incognito.

It was ... a face behind a face.

It was ... a shadow that followed its host, always ready to move in and take control.

It folded its lips over one another, licking them with lizard quickness to wet them.

Solitude: that's what kept the *special* work special, kept it ... secret ...

The moth, drawn to the warm bulb overhead, dinged its tiny wings as it flew too close to the heat. For a moment, it thought it heard the tiny creature scream as it was burnt. A dirty chuckle made its host's jawbone open and close with a sound like a laugh, a knowing that it was just controlling a skull covered in warm flesh.

Nine was good.

Ten sounded like the perfect, most rounded number, though.

Ten, then ... *we can try again.* The words infected the brain it dwelled in like blotted ink on white paper.

'Ten, then, I can try and live again.'

The words rose up and out of the mouth, never touching the vocal cords, just escaping from the pit in the host's stomach.

It was a parasite waiting to get out, waiting for its time to hatch, and with number ten ... *'I will live again.'*

It watched the moth flap away from the glass ball of light,

straying blindly too far off course, landing in the spider's web, pulling the tethered webbing attached to the spider's hairy legs: it was time to feed.

The spider wasted no time disabling the winged creature, wrapping it and storing it in a way no different to what *it* was doing with people.

It read the newspapers, kept an eye on things to see if anyone suspected it was doing its deeds: No one knew why it was here, no one knew what it was doing, and soon it would be free.

'Number ten ... free again.'

It laughed loudly, its breath stinking of smoke.

It had seen the perfect ten only today. Maybe she was something it could bring back home, could tie up and drain until it had the power it needed.

The arachnid above pulled the captured moth to the corner of its web.

Every web had a fat spider at its centre – a fat, *hungry* spider.

CHAPTER TWENTY EIGHT

'Morning. Blackie!' were the words that split Graveyard Billy's eyelids apart, the old woman's sugary, upbeat tone reminding him of all the problems at hand: What had happened to Piper? What had happened to Kelly? Where would the 'Graveyard Killer' strike again?

'*Wakey-wakey!*' Aunt Coral shouted, running her wizened fingers up and down the bars of the cage like a prison warden. Whatever the problems were, big or small, they added up to the same immediate need: he and Kelly had to escape.

Kelly, who lay half in, half out the cage, jumped awake as the reverberating bars went off with an echoing metallic hum. '*Noooooooooooooo,* not this again,' she moaned. 'Poxy Barnacle, up and roaming around at ...' She squinted at the kitchen's wall clock, tried to blow strands of the cheap wig from her eyes. '*... SIX-THIRTY A.M.!*' she cried.

'I'll let you out in a bit, Blackie, just have to do me routine,' Aunt Coral grinned, holding an old, faded-blue nightie around her body.

'*I'll let you out in a bit,*' Kelly mimicked in a gravelled shriek. 'Go back to your coffin where you belong!'

Graveyard Billy looked at Kelly, gave her a blink, and then curled back up into a ball silently as he watched the old woman make herself a cup of tea. He had kept a single paw on Piper's printed picture all night, would often wake to stare into her face. At first, it filled him with deep sadness, a longing for the girl he considered as family. Now, determination overrode any other emotion, knowing he had to march to the beat of the old woman's drum if he and Kelly were to get free.

'*Lum-de-dum-de-dum-de-dummmm,*' Aunt Coral sang as Kelly scowled and Graveyard Billy stared calculatingly. They watched her polish, hoover, then apply that hideous blossom of vivid colour she called makeup.

'Nearly ready!' she cooed at Graveyard Billy through the bars, the tuneless song warbling from her vocal cords in reverse now*: 'Dum-le-lum-le-lum-le-lummmm ...'*

'There,' she said, running a finger over her crimson lips as she stared into a hand=held mirror at the perfectly laid kitchen table. 'Perfect.'

'The only way that face would be perfect was if she stapled her chin to her forehead, and it hid the bit in the middle,' Kelly said, shaking her head as she stared disgustedly at the old crone.

Graveyard Billy, who had sat solemnly all morning, let out a sound like a low chuckle. 'Good one,' he blinked up at Kelly, who, hearing his voice, beamed back.

'Time to let you out, my old Blackie!' Aunt Coral exclaimed, reaching down to unlatch the cage door.

With trepidation, he slowly padded out, slight remorse that he had to leave Piper's face behind in the metal structure.

'There's a good boy,' the old woman grinned. 'Now, let's fix you some breakfast.' She spooned a sachet of cat food into a china bowl.

'Follow me!' she commanded, marching into the front room and placing the food onto the plastic placemat she had arranged next to the litter tray.

Graveyard Billy winced. *Stupid woman.* No cat wanted their food next to their toilet; neither would any human, for that matter.

He followed her perfectly, walking the route specified on the strips of clean plastic vinyl she had so purposefully laid out.

'You're learning,' Aunt Coral grinned, watching him navigate her layout. 'I think you're going to be much better than *those* others.'

Something about her words, about *those* others, bristled Graveyard Billy's fur; made Kelly wince with suspicion.

Graveyard Billy began to eat his food, thinking about drinking the dish of water next to him before he had even finished.

'A healthy appetite,' Aunt Coral beamed. 'A big, lovely, healthy appetite!'

She watched him finish the bowl, then move over to his water and lap, each extended tongueful deliberate as not to spill a drop.

'I'm wondering, Blackie,' she pondered, index finger to her old lips. 'With your appetite, maybe you would like one of Aunt Coral's *special* treats?'

Kelly and Graveyard Billy held a look to one another as the old woman tottered off to the kitchen. They heard the fridge door go, heard the lid of a jar unscrewed, then replaced. She marched back into the living room, an old silver bowl in her hand.

'See what you think of this, my old Blackie,' she grinned, placing the distinctively pungent small bowl of pink and red before him.

'What the hell is that?' Kelly said, her nose in the air even though her sense of smell had died with her body.

'It's ... not good,' said Graveyard Billy, who meekly sniffed at it, cringing at the thought of actually eating the viscous mess.

'You'll learn to enjoy it,' Aunt Coral said with a surreptitious smile, '... in time.'

'Freak show,' Kelly said bluntly.

'Your Aunt Coral has to go out this morning; she has to go into town and sort out some business. Aunt Coral owns some flats in Kemptown. I have to make sure that they are all paying their rent so we can have nice things. Isn't that right, Blackie?' she nodded.

104

'I hope the flats all fall down and you're buried under them, you old bag,' Kelly said nonchalantly.

Graveyard Billy gave her a blink.

Aunt Coral went to the hallway, wrapped herself in a heavy black jacket, 'It's looking cold out there, Blackie, the weather forecast said snow is on the way.'

As she put an arm through one of the jacket's sleeves, she accidentally knocked a small ornamental figure from the shelf next to the front door, exploding it into pieces.

Aunt Coral looked back into the front room with eyes that all but shot flames from their pupils; rage puckered her mouth to a hissing hole in her face. 'Did *you* do that, Blackie?'

'*Bill!*' Kelly exclaimed. 'She's being mental again!'

Aunt Coral bounded into the front room, loomed over Graveyard Billy with forbidding menace. 'Was that *you*?' she cried.

All Graveyard Billy could do was shrink into a corner, eyes darting around for a place to escape.

'No – *no*,' Aunt Coral said, her eyes shifting internally, rationality patching the broken parts in her mind. 'No,' she smiled, 'it must have been silly old me!' She chuckled, 'Yes, just silly old me ...'

The old woman strode to the front room door. 'Right, you have everything you need: water, food, and your toilet. Aunt Coral will be home in two hours, my Blackie, so stay in here ... *and be good.*' That hidden menace crawled back into her voice again.

She pulled the front-room door shut, trapped Graveyard Billy inside another space, this one bigger than the cage in the kitchen.

He bounded up to the French windows, stood on an old chair, and watched her purple car pull out of the driveway into the gloomy December day. Graveyard Billy's eyes widened as he looked around to Kelly as ithe car left in a trail of exhaust smoke. 'She's gone!' he cried. 'Now, no matter how, we *have* to get out of this house!'

Chapter Twenty Nine

Quickly Graveyard Billy jumped to the floor, ran up and looked at the door handle separating him from the rest of the house. It was such an easy thing to navigate if you were a human – not so much if you were a cat or a ghost.

He swung his head left and right, trying to make sense of how to turn the old brass handle. It has been said that any cat can open a door, but only a witch's cat can close one: Graveyard Billy felt useless either way.

'You've got the same problem every cat in the world has right now,' Kelly said. 'No thumbs.'

'No thumbs,' he reiterated with a wink.

'Bill, look,' Kelly said. 'The hinges open inwards. If you can somehow push the handle down and pull it back –'

'We can get out of here,' he finished.

Kelly looked around the room for inspiration as Graveyard Billy skulked around anywhere but the plastic walkways that lined the floor.

'Bill!' Kelly said, her voice bright with the inflexion of inventiveness. 'What about this?' She pointed to a small, spindly, mahogany corner unit next to the door, each shelf holding a single prized, antique corner plate. 'If you can somehow get this on its side next to the door, maybe you can reach up and pull down the –'

Tail swiping the air in anger, his mind on Piper, on Kelly, and the thing that was still out there that had ended both of their lives, he leapt towards the corner unit, twisting his body in the air and smashing into its tired old frame paws first, with all the weight and power he could. Instantly the corner unit gave up the ghost, tumbling sideways, china plates spinning out like the saucers from an old science-fiction movie before they crash-landed on the carpet and exploded into sharp shards. The corner unit fell flat at the foot of the door.

Kelly smiled impishly, bit her lip: 'Barnacle's going to do her nut,' she grinned.

'Good,' Graveyard Billy winked at her.

'That's *my* boy!' she laughed.

Graveyard Billy jumped on the side of the downed corner unit, walked along its creaking wooden boards until he was under the door handle. Kelly stood next to him now, feeling the frustration of the un-dead, unable to help in any way.

'You need to jump up, Bill, pull this down,' she pointed to the door handle, 'and try and pull it backwards.'

He let out a huff, raised himself up on his hind legs and stretched out his front, his small paws just reaching the brass handle.

Kelly paused, teeth gritted in vexation. 'Try and pull it

down backwards.'

A louder huff escaped Graveyard Billy's nostrils as he hoisted at the handle, claws extended to try and give some extra grip.

Sharply he shifted downwards, paws slipping, the corner unit nearly overturning.

Kelly gasped. Graveyard Billy's eyes popped as he caught his balance.

'Just take it easy, Bill,' Kelly said, masking her anxiousness with pseudo-calmness. 'Just take it nice and slow; try and ease it open.'

He reassumed the position, lifting his paws onto the handle.

'Now,' Kelly said. 'Slowly.'

Graveyard Billy closed his eyes, the muscles in his front legs flexing as he tried with all his might to pull down the handle.

Kelly, who hunkered down at the handle's height, watched as it slowly – ever so slowly – began to move downwards.

She wanted to squeal, to laugh, but she stayed stone-cold silent, a palpable tension gagging any excitement. 'Go on, Bill,' she said evenly, fighting the shiver in her throat.

Graveyard Billy wrinkled his nose, brought his head down, and hung all his weight on the handle: paws slipping, claws extending to their limit, front legs quivering with the strain of it all.

Slowly, very, very, slowly, the handle moved down, farther and farther, almost turning vertical.

'Try and pull it back, Bill, try and pull it back.'

'I am,' he gasped. 'I a –'

His paws slipped; his balance came undone; he fell sideways to the floor. The handle sprung back into place. Kelly brought her hands up to her head. If he was trapped in here with the smashed plates when the old bag got home, he was history, he was dead meat, he was …

The handle may have been back up to its original position, but the door wasn't back in place properly. A thin metallic ping echoed out: the living room door popped ajar.

Graveyard Billy spun around, looked at Kelly, looked at the door. 'Have I …'

'You have!' she grinned.

With no hesitation, he shot up, clawed the door open, and bolted to the kitchen, Kelly right behind him. He jumped up onto the kitchen counter and ran along the windows, eyes flittering from one pane to the next, looking for an opening to try and squirt through to freedom: there was nothing, not a slither, everything shut tight.

'Let's try upstairs! Quickly!' Graveyard Billy shouted, his urgency egging Kelly on to move faster as he went. Making short work of the stairs, he made it to the landing, bounding into the bathroom and jumping to the window ledge – locked tight.

He moved to the bedroom where only a day ago he'd cowered under the bed – again, each window locked.

'One last chance,' he cried, running to the cluttered spare bedroom, picking the door open with his claws, navigating around boxes and old dusty lampstands until he came to – another locked window.

'Damn!' he cried, meeting Kelly in the hallway, the ghostly girl unable to keep up with his speed. 'Oh, Bill, what are we going to do!' she cried.

'I don't know. The only other thing we can do is wait by the front door; wait until she comes back, and I'll have to make a run for it.'

'But, Bill!' Kelly cried, 'She's bonkers! She'll probably slam the door on you rather than let you get away.'

'I think it's the only chance we have,' Graveyard Billy said, trying to catch his breath. 'I think if I'm fast enough, I'll –'

He turned, sensing something, head quickly flicking around the hallway, looking for the thing he could feel.

'What?' Kelly cried, infected with fear from his sudden silence. 'What is it?'

'I can feel –' he moved quickly to a small door in the landing, whiskers twitching at the gap beneath it. 'There's a draft coming from here,' he said.

Kelly moved closer to the door, her eyes filled with intrigue. I thought that was the airing cupboard,' she said, puzzled, passing through the door into a hazy room beyond.

'There's a stairway behind here!' she said with surprise. 'Looks like it leads up to the loft or something?' Kelly walked up the small narrow stairs; kept going until the supernatural tether that bound her to Graveyard Billy became tight and allowed her to go no farther.

'What's up there?' Graveyard Billy called through.

'I can't get up here all the way,' she called back, staring to the top of the stairs to a dull shaft of light where dust motes swirled, curdled by the distant draft of air.

'There's a way out up here, Bill!' she called down. 'There's deffo something open up here, I can see there's wind getting in!' She bounded back down the stairs, stopped at the bottom, noticing something. 'Hang on!' she yelled, eyeing the small plastic grill just above the skirting board next to the door.

She poked her head through the wall above it, looking in between to see the cavity empty of plaster, then out the other side to see another plastic grill adjacent.

'Bill! If you get these grills off, it's empty in the middle! You can climb straight through!'

With no hesitation, he began to claw at the little slits in the vent, pulling with everything he had until the grill began to fray, making enough room to sink his fangs around and begin pulling a rough hole in the old, frail plastic.

'Careful, mate,' Kelly said, staring down the front door, a worry Aunt Coral would return prematurely and find him trying to escape.

Gradually he made a hole big enough and pushed his way through, smelling the damp and dust trapped inside the wall cavity as he went to work on the second vent.

Kelly moved through the wall, watched from the other side as, little by little, he chewed and clawed his way towards her. 'Come on, Bill! Come on!' she said with a cheer in her voice.

Slowly he made it through, coughing and gagging from the shards of plastic that had scarred the inside of his mouth. 'Oh. Bill, I'm sorry,' Kelly said. 'I wish I could do something!'

'Let's keep going,' he said with a sneeze, the dust from the wall cavity settling in his small nose. Kelly ran up the stairs, her ectoplasmic reins released as he slowly padded after her.

She turned the corner, a smile breaking over her face. 'There's a window up here; it's slightly open! It's ...' She stopped, stepping back down the stairs she'd just ascended, her face filled with undiluted fright.

'What is it!' Graveyard Billy called up.

'Oh my God ...' was all that Kelly could say, staring into the hidden room.

CHAPTER THIRTY

Graveyard Billy slowly stalked to the top of the stairs, his eyes fixed to Kelly, who still stood staring into the hidden room. 'What is I –' he tried to say as Kelly quickly turned around and stared into his face, her expression chilling him to the marrow.

'When she was talking about *those* others ...' Kelly gasped, the heavy words coming from her throat blocking her airway. '... I didn't ...'

'What!' Graveyard Billy exclaimed, hopping up the last few steps as around her a musky, awful smell settled into his nostrils. He froze, and then a moment of relief passed through him: There was a silhouette of a tabby cat at the two back windows. He blinked at it for recognition, but the cat didn't blink back. Graveyard Billy tried repeatedly, but the cat stayed still, doing nothing apart from endlessly staring. He transmitted to it, said *'Hey!'* in that way only cats can – nothing, no reply.

The day's dreary clouds shifted; a dull ray of sun lightened the room. More silhouettes appeared: ginger cats, tortoise shells, pure whites, a black one like he; dogs, puppies, birds sat or stood more still and more silent than Kelly, who remained transfixed at the top stairs.

At first Graveyard Billy felt relief: All these creatures had been captured by Aunt Coral, too; had been locked away, and now they could all work together and esca –

Then he understood.

The long workbench in the corner: knives, scissors, and sawdust neatly placed atop it. The jar placed near the back of the bench: Hundreds of the same kinds of eyes that stared from the still creatures' faces stared back from the glass. There was an old stool before the bench, an old portable Calor gas heater next to it: She had made it comfy up here, had spent a lot of time up here, she had ...

'Sh – she's stuffed them all ...' Kelly stuttered.

Graveyard Billy swung his gaze back to her; their eyes locked as his tail rose to an exclamation point of terror.

'She's done a taxidermy job on the lot of them!' Kelly cried.

Graveyard Billy, with as much fear as his small body could hold, padded closer to a tabby cat on the floor in front of him, its eyes unflinching and dead, it's tail as stiff as a board, its feet wired to a piece of wood. He backed away, searched around the room as the glass-marble eyes stared back. This was no old lady's house; this was a chamber of horrors. There were ten – twenty – thirty animals and more that had all fallen victim to old Aunt Coral's creative hands.

Graveyard Billy leapt up to the workbench, looked at the tools of her trade, looked at ... He froze as solid as the animals around him, noticing a jar in front of him, its insides meaty, red and pink. Its label four symbols Graveyard Billy couldn't understand.

'Kelly ...' he asked, ungluing her from the top of the stairs. Hearing his tone, she shifted towards him, her eyes scanning everything, hoping it didn't get any worse.

'What does this say?' asked Graveyard Billy.

It got worse.

Four letters, one word, and an entire universe's worth of horror inside the oversized jar.

"BITS"

'Is that ...' Graveyard Billy sniffed at it, looked at Kelly.

'It's what she tried to feed you downstairs,' Kelly replied with a gulp.

'Yes, but that's ...' He stood, understanding what the pungent smell coming from the jar was.

'It is,' she replied dully, a quiver in her voice.

It never had to be said out loud or articulated: they both knew.

Graveyard Billy gulped. 'She's –'

'– mad.' Kelly said finally.

Something caught his eye on the workbench: his old white collar with his name written in pen by Piper, now just another part of Aunt Coral's collection.

'We need to leave,' Graveyard Billy said evenly. 'We need to leave now.'

The jangle of keys came from downstairs, the turn of a lock, a shrill voice that sent ice-cold sabres shuddering down Graveyard Billy's spine.

'*Blackie!* Your Aunt Coral is ho –'

She stopped, obviously seeing the smashed china plates, the downed corner unit. Her voice mutated in the air, the cheerful old lady's voice transmogrifying into something as twisted and menacing as the leafless winter trees outside, as creeping as the ivy that tried to wind around them: 'Someone's been *very* bad,' she growled. 'Someone will *have* to pay.'

Chapter Thirty One

'*Oh no!*' Kelly squealed. 'The old bag's back early!'

Graveyard Billy leapt up at the old square French windows in the hidden attic space, feeling the cold breeze outside, finding the gap in the window that let it through.

It was only an inch wide, impossible to crawl through – there was nowhere to go!

Downstairs, heavy stomps came from the old woman as she moved from room to room. 'Blackie! *Where are you!*' she growled.

'Bill!' Kelly said. 'Look this – *this*!' She pointed to a metal bar at the bottom of the window filled with little holes slotted over a metal pin.

'You have to lift up the latch,' she said urgently. 'If you lift this up, it will open!'

Graveyard Billy clawed at it, tried to grasp the long paint-flacked latch in his claws, to no avail.

'Oh!' Kelly cried out. 'Why couldn't cats have been made with thumbs!'

A voice came from downstairs. 'Blackie's come upstairs hasn't he – Blackie's been a very *bad boy!*'

Graveyard Billy fumbled with the latch with both paws, unable to make the correct movement to open it.

'*Billlllll!*' Kelly cried.

He bent down, wrapped his fangs around the cold, bitter latch, and started to pull with all his might.

'Look at this!' Aunt Coral blurted. 'Blackie's been burrowing!'

'She knows we're up here, Bill! Come on!' Kelly screamed, understanding the woman had found the air vent he had broken through.

'*I'm trying!*' he replied, teeth aching as he tried to unhinge the latch.

'He's not a black cat!' Aunt Coral yelled. 'He's a black rat! A filthy black rat that's ruining my lovely home!' The door to the hidden staircase unlocked, and the low creaks of the attic stairs being trodden upon groaned out.

'I was hoping you would be clean, not like all those others ...' the old woman moaned.

'Oh, mate!' Kelly cried, trying to gee Graveyard Billy on. 'You need to get out of here! You don't want to end up with glass eyes and your bumhole stuffed with sawdust!'

'That's not helping!' Graveyard Billy said through a mouthful of the metal latch.

'OCD, that's what the doctor said,' Aunt Coral shook her fists at the air in defiance to the memory. 'But it's better this way, cleaner, easier to control ... everything has its place and in

112

its place ... everything will be.'

Her footsteps drew closer now, just as Graveyard Billy finally yanked the latch free, and the window swung open wide, immediately revealing ... the two-story drop to the concrete patio outside.

There was no tree to jump to, no soft landing: only cold, hard concrete.

'I should have just done the same to my Henry ...' Aunt Coral grumbled. 'None of that expensive funeral stuff ... just nice and clean ... like all my pets in the attic ... He could be sitting in the corner ... in his favourite chair ... forever.'

'What are we going to do?' Kelly moaned.

'Don't worry!' Graveyard Billy cried, turning around, hearing the woman halfway up the stairs now. Somehow he had to end all this, had to stop sweet old Aunt Coral for what she had done to his fellow animals. A strong sense of pride flowed through his body; the last remaining sparks of energy from the animals she had killed spurred him on from beyond the grave. He looked up to the ceiling, seeing the light bulb and knowing what to do. Animalistic whispers prickled his senses, telling him to put what was left of their earthly existence finally to rest.

He jumped down to the floor, scampered to the back of the Calor gas heater.

'What are you doing?' Kelly shouted. 'We need to try and –

Then she heard it, too: the otherworldly tongue of cat, bark of dog, chirp of bird. A bristling cold, not from the open window, but from the taxidermy animals that surrounded them. Their presence from the afterlife was here, and she knew what they wanted.

Graveyard Billy bit with a primal force into the small rubber hose connecting the gas bottle to the heater. He tore through it with as much projected power the spirits of the dead animals could muster. Somehow they were feeding him with their supernatural vitality, helping him finish the attic's abominations off once and for all.

A spitting like an escaping adder erupted; a foul gagging taste entered Graveyard Billy's mouth as he punctured an inch-size hole through the gas pipe, the ignitable vapour escaping in the air.

Aunt Coral was at the doorframe at the top of the stairs now, fading from the darkness to the light; her over-applied makeup and grinning, yellowed teeth making her look like a nightmarish, neon clown.

'You could have had a good life,' she cackled, eyes locked on Graveyard Billy. 'Plenty of food ... plenty of *bits* for both of us ...'

Graveyard Billy jumped to the workbench, grabbed his old

113

collar in his teeth, and leapt to the window frame.

'My Henry left me,' she grinned. 'But no one's ever going to leave again; you'll all be here forever ... even you, Blackie.'

Aunt Coral reached for the light switch, finger on, ready to snap it down, unaware it was now a trigger ready to pull as the gas leaked out into the room.

Then she sensed the otherworldly aura that was growing from the stuffed animals as their spirits conjoined and radiated around Graveyard Billy, heightening his transmission, amplifying his words as he said psychically: 'My name is *Graveyard Billy*.'

She staggered back, seemingly hearing his words, eyes wide with shock.

Graveyard Billy jumped from the window, flew through the air, clambered to the top of the open window's frame and with a blind leap of faith, springboarded backwards onto the cold, tiled roof of the house, claws digging in for dear life.

'Yeaahhhhhhhhhh!' Kelly cheered as Aunt Coral sneered, went to lunge forward. No one ever escaped – ever!

She turned on the light; she pulled the trigger.

The last thing she heard was a supernatural menagerie of animals: hisses of delight, howls of joy, and screeches of revenge.

It was the last thing before the final thing.

The orange explosion lit the oncoming night sky as if for a single second it was day: a spurt of molten sun had opened in the attic of Aunt Coral's house, followed by a thunderclap of explosion.

Every tile on the roof waved up and down like played piano keys as Graveyard Billy held on with everything he had, finally free from Aunt Coral's house of horrors.

CHAPTER THIRTY TWO

The roof was cold; a layer of frost had formed over its tiles. Graveyard Billy's paws had become acclimatised to the warmth of Aunt Coral's house – the only good thing the place had to offer. With his collar in his mouth, Graveyard Billy crawled to the peak of the roof. The crack of timber sounded out below as the house of horrors burnt.

He laid his collar in front of him, putting both front paws on it, so it poked up as a circle in front of him: easy accessibility to slip his head back through. There was a homeliness having it back on, a sense of comfort.

Kelly wisped up to join him, standing on the roof's peak in her vaporous high heels. 'Bill!' she squealed, 'Oh-my-God! That was amazing! I can't believe you did it!'

'Well,' he replied, 'I don't think we were alone on that one.'

'What do you–'

Graveyard Billy nodded over to the window they had just escaped from, flames now lapping out of it. But there was something more than just flames. Slowly, moving from within the house, floating into the grey sky above as gently as the seeds from a blown dandelion, were the glowing energy orbs of the animals below. The last remaining vestiges of their souls were finally free from the earthly ties that bound them.

Kelly could sense what they were, understanding somehow in a deep, instinctive way what each independent orb represented in the animal kingdom: a bird, a cat, or a dog. 'Why were they trapped there?' she asked, a slight awe in her voice as she watched them move up into the sky and beyond the clouds.

'There are always different reasons,' Graveyard Billy said. 'There was such an amount of bad energy created down there by Aunt Coral; maybe their souls couldn't penetrate it and escape.'

Kelly thought about this, adding simply: 'You did a good thing, Bill,' watching as the last of the orbs disappeared into the clouds from sight.

Graveyard Billy looked to the opposite side of the house, where the spindled branches of a tree almost touched its guttering. 'Look,' he said. 'I think I can get on that and climb down.'

Carefully he moved towards it, easing and edging himself as close as possible to the drop below, measuring and gauging with a waggling rear end and flattened head whether he could make the jump.

Kelly bit her lip in worry, but she had faith, knew he could do it.

With a huge leap, Graveyard Billy took off. He quickly found himself attached claws-first to a huge silver birch tree stripped of its leaves by the winter season. Bit by bit, branch by branch, he made his way down towards the ground, travelling past the floors of the house next to him that glowed orange with the spread of flames. Kelly levitated downwards behind him, unable to experience the cold air but appreciating the freedom from the stuffy old house, the mad woman called a home.

As Graveyard Billy touched down to terra firma, the distinct wail of fire engines blazed in the background. 'Let's get out of here,' Graveyard Billy said to Kelly. 'Which way should we –'

Shock hit them as the house's front door flew open, a figure appearing from the smoke. Aunt Coral stepped out, her face blackened, her clothes ragged, and her hair a growing ball of flame. She reached up, grabbed her hair, and pulled it off, threw it to the ground, and began stamping on the wig neither Graveyard Billy nor Kelly knew she wore. 'It'll never be clean again ... nothing will ever be in order...' the old woman wailed as her wig stuck to the bottom of her shoe. She looked up and stared directly at Graveyard Billy with eyes that all but shot daggers from their pupils.

'Uh-oh ...' Kelly said. 'You burnt up Barnacle's bonnet!'

'Youuuuuu ...' the old woman croaked, her face yellowed, eyes and teeth in a mask of soot, stomping stiffly down her garden path towards the small black cat that stared back with fear-filled eyes.

'Run!' Kelly cried, and both she and Graveyard Billy took off, the burning house growing smaller behind them, the presence of Aunt Coral on a second wind of rage keeping good speed, the flaming wig still attached to her foot as she ran.

'It was you! You were the one that did this!' she screamed at Graveyard Billy. 'You destroyed my work ... You! You! You – *Agghhhh!'*

A kid, hood up on a B.M.X., ploughed into the old woman, sent her spilling to the sidewalk with a scream. Graveyard Billy looked back. Aunt Coral rolled over and began to throttle the boy, yelling in his face, 'You should be riding that thing in the road! Everybody has their place! *Everybody has their place!'*

Graveyard Billy and Kelly kept running blindly, putting distance between them and the old, wrinkled lunatic behind.

'Keep going straight, Bill,' Kelly said. 'If we keep going straight. we can end up back at Woodvale.'

'Sounds like a plan to me,' he called up to her, taking the biggest strides he could to escape, coming to a road ahead and running forwards, looking left, then looking right and – he didn't see the car until it was too late; he didn't see anything as its bumper struck him and sent him sprawling. With eyes flickering, he fell into deep, endless darkness.

CHAPTER THIRTY THREE

Time held no relevance; darkness lasted forever. The heavy drape of nothing Graveyard Billy had entered slowly finally began to clear; a vivid vision of rippling light grew amidst a maelstrom of tenebrosity.

He was submerged in a thick, palpable atmosphere, paws kicking to stay afloat somewhere that looked and felt like the depths of dense, deep water, somewhere that was surrounded by bright, reflecting light that shimmered and danced on swaying waves above. Although he had never seen it personally, this was an ocean – this was the place they called the sea, and he was submerged deep beneath it.

A shimmering scintilla above the waves glowed with all the same colours projected from the spirit world; colours that his cat eyes could process more vividly than any others; colours that projected from that place that all ghosts came from as it opened in the fabric of time and space.

A cold, jarring feeling entered his small bones: Had he passed over?

A memory caught in his mind: running away from Aunt Coral, running for his life ... running to his death.

No, it couldn't be! Not like that, not with so much to do, with so much left up in the air!

Shock bristled his black fur on end as a presence wrapped around him, making him instantly aware that something else was here, something ...

He knew then what it was – *who* it was.

That feeling inside that was growing into fear quickly converted to excitement. It was she, the human he picked, that he'd chosen to be his own. He couldn't see her, but he could sense her – she *was* here.

A part of her essence wrapped around him plugged into his senses and opened them up. Suddenly, information opened inside him like a blossoming flower; a deeper instinctual knowledge was tapped into.

Here, now, in this submerged, ethereal world, that slice of information that had been missing in life was suddenly revealed. He could sense part of Piper's essence, knew where it was – strangely beyond the realm of the dead, yet also back in the world of the living. Somehow, part of her was still here, and something in this otherworldly place where he found himself had rewired him to find her ... to find ... part of her.

He didn't know how he knew this, but he understood it to be true.

Radiant warmth grew around him in this thick, supernatural sea, like invisible arms holding him and sharing their love. There was a calm and comfort to the moment, a knowing what he must do ... then the voices ... hollowed and distant, slight words coming in as if they drifted on the whispered airwaves on the static radio of life.

'Heart rate, normal ...'

'Bill!'

'More shock than anything physical ...'

'Bill!'

'At least the driver stopped; it's more than most do these days ...'

'BILL!'

Graveyard Billy opened his eyes, started out into a white, milky abyss more clichéd heavenly than the place he'd just been. Everything was a blur; there was zero definition that slowly bled to a fuzzy focus: Shapes moved back and forth; muffled voices matched them; then everything became clearer.

'Ohhhhh, he's come around.' A warm hand touched his fragile head.

'You haven't had much luck, mister, have you?' said another voice. 'Been out there on your own awhile now.'

'We checked for a microchip, Liz,' said the first voice as she was blinked into focus, a red-haired girl wearing a blue uniform. 'He was registered to one of those girls that were... well, you know ... by that weirdo who hangs around cemeteries.'

'That's awful, Gemma. That's just awful.' said the second girl, a brunette in a matching blue outfit.

'Well, you've had a nasty bump, mister,' Liz said. 'You've had a few scrapes, but you'll live. Maybe this is the change in your luck; maybe now we can find you a new family.'

'I am his family,' said a tearful, familiar voice in the distance.

'Well, you take it easy, mate,' said Liz. 'If you're looking better tomorrow, we'll see about getting you rehomed.' Liz and Gemma walked away, disappearing in a slow blink of Graveyard Billy's eyes.

As his vision focused, he could see the things around him again he had tried to escape: a latticework of thin bars – he was back in a cage. Not that it mattered much; his body leaded, weighed to the soft blanket he lay upon.

Slowly, as if materialising from the white, sterile walls, Kelly's spiritual form appeared before him. 'You are my family, Bill,' she cried.

'Kelly,' he whispered in a weak projection.

'Bill, mate, I thought ...'

'So did I,' he lethargically blinked.

'I saw it all,' she said, wiping ectoplasmic tears from her eyes. 'Some plum in a cab wasn't looking where he was going. He was looking at his phone or something. He slammed on the brakes and sent you flying.' She started to weep again.

'I'm all right,' he said weakly. 'I'm fine now.'

'You've been out cold; I've watched the whole thing. Some lady on a bike with a basket on the front picked you up, went bonkers at the taxi driver and pedalled you here.'

'Where's here?' he strained.

'Back end of Brighton, Chase Lodge Animal Rescue Centre. They've put you right here, Bill; they said nothing's broken; you were just knocked unconscious, had a few scrapes – they said ...' Kelly started to cry again. '... you were lucky ...'

'I told you I–'

'Yeah, but Bill, you didn't see it ... you were all torn up down one side. I watched you slide along the tarmac ...'

As soon as she said it, Graveyard Billy could feel the ailments; he could feel the gauze down one side that had been attached to his aching body. 'How long have I been out?' he asked.

'About twelve hours, now,' Kelly nodded.

'What happened to Aunt Coral?' he asked.

Kelly's cries turned to blubs of laughter. 'Oh Bill,' she chuckled, wiping tears away. 'You caused a right one.'

'What do you mean?' he asked.

'Old Barnacle got wiped out by some kid on a bike; I think it put her last loose screw out. I left with you as the Old Bill, and the fire brigade turned up, but ...' she started to snigger to herself. 'They had the telly on in here; I was watching it while you were being checked out. She's been all over the news after they put the fire out in her house. The police found what she had been doing to animals and the like.'

'Why are you laughing?' asked Graveyard Billy.

'Not about that, about what she did. When they started to question her, old Barnacle finally blew her gasket. She bit one of the coppers! Said that the ghosts of all the animals had been released, that they were going to be watching her – were going to be after her!'

'I think she might be right,' said Graveyard Billy.

'Either way, she's been carted off to a psyche ward.'

'What's that?' he asked.

'Loony bin, nut-nut land, you know, Bill.'

'Oh, somewhere where she can't do any harm?'

'That's the one. Somewhere she's going to be spending a very long time, I reckon. Couldn't have happened to a nicer person if you ask me.'

Graveyard Billy tried to get up, an instant pain firing through his small body.

'Stay down, Bill, take it easy. You've got all the time in the world to just rest.'

'I wish that was true,' he replied, a wince of pain transmitted with his voice.

119

'What do you mean?' Kelly asked.

'Something happened when I was out, something ... I can't explain.' Graveyard Billy said.

'Like what, Bill?' she asked, coming closer to his cage.

'I ... can sense it ... I can sense ... I think ... part of Piper, and ... the thing that killed her.'

'What?' Kelly exclaimed.

'Yeah, I don't know how, but something has changed somehow and ... that smoky smell that dark aura we've both experienced ... I can sense it ... I know where it is.'

'But Bill' Kelly said, 'You've had a bang on the head; are you thinking straight?'

'Yeah, I am,' he replied. 'It's like that sense I know I should have had when I was trying to find Piper has returned to me, and somehow ... she is out there and ... somehow she's part of that *thing*, too.'

'Part of what thing?'

'The thing that killed you both.'

Kelly shivered. 'How do you know that, Bill?'

'I don't know how, but I can sense it.'

'But what can we do?' Kelly asked.

'We need to get out of here and stop it. It's ready, Kelly,' Graveyard Billy said with seriousness. 'It's ready to kill again.'

CHAPTER THIRTY FOUR

Mo Shaan sat at the till in his convenience shop and tapped along gently to the Christmas songs playing from the radio. George Michael sang about giving away his heart last Christmas – the same as he always did this time of year. Cheap tinsel trailed along the shelves of even cheaper wholesale junk food: a mini Christmas tree featured used scratch cards hung from it like secondhand decorations; an aluminous Father Christmas face flashed from the shop doorway with an almost impish glare.

Everything had a manufactured tackiness to it; everything was exactly how Mo's father – the man who'd handed the shop down to him – said it should be.

'You should know your customers. Trust me, this is what they expect from a shop like ours,' his father had said when he came to help put up the decorations.

Selling ourselves short is what they must expect, Mo had thought as he put up the threadbare tinsel. He looked at the trash mags that lined the racks; magazines that treated their readers so stupidly as to imply the misery of soap operas played on their TV sets were some form of reality.

This wasn't what Mo wanted for himself – following in his father's footsteps as the owner of 'Day-to-Day,' the corner shop halfway up Ditchling Road on the way out of Brighton.

He had convinced his father that he wanted to go to college to study graphic design, and his father had allowed him that, but when he said he wanted to progress on to uni, that's when the reluctance came. Repeated phrases with no substance popped back up again and again whenever the subject arose: 'There's no money in it, son, there's no future in that, trust me – the convenience store business hasn't done us badly, my boy.'

His father had tried to find any way possible to dissuade Mo – nothing had worked. Then he found a new way: sign the shop over to him to run, let the business be his business; that way, it would never leave the family bubble. How could Mo say no to his father's pleading? 'I'm sixty-five years old, boy; this place has put us right for years. How can I just throw it away? My health isn't what it used to be.'

His mother's sad eyes burned into him, guilt growing inside him from her unflinching stare. How could he just refuse the business that had given his family their bread and butter for all these years? But it wasn't what he wanted.

Mo should have stood his ground and told his father that there was more to life than just sitting behind a till; there were sights out there just waiting to be seen. But for now, from six a.m. to ten-p.m. at night, for seven days a week, here he would be. Like father, like son; here comes the new boss – just like the old boss.

The electronic beep sounded. The shop's front door opened, and a blast of winter cold seeped through its jamb. Ten to ten already: This must be his last customer of the night.

A blonde girl stepped in, her expression slack with trepidation as she held a white cane in front of her, trying to manoeuvre past the heavy door.

'Here,' Mo shouted as he ran from behind the counter. 'I'll give you a hand, love.'

'Thanks, Mo,' she grinned. 'I was just popping in for a few bits before you shut. I thought I might have missed you.'

'No, just in time, Jamie, you have ten minutes to spare.'

Nineteen-year-old Jamie Chase grinned up at him. Her eyes fixed in his direction, their stare never extending from behind the blackness of her retina. Jamie had been blind all her life, had lived most of it in a home with other children inflicted with blindness. Now, wanting her independence – and with the help of her appointed social worker – she had been given a flat next to the Florence Place Cemetery. She had become one of the regular customers before Mo had taken over the shop.

He often wondered how she coped with things in life. Although she lived alone, her makeup would be perfect, her outfits always tidy and clean – more so than some of the sighted customers he would encounter.

He remembered his dad telling him about the girl when she first came into the shop, asking her, 'How come you have no guide dog?'

'I'm allergic to dogs,' she had shrugged.

Life could play its cruel jokes at times.

'What are you after?' Mo asked her, taking her arm to guide her into the shop.

'Bread, some orange juice, two packets of Super Noodles, and I fancy a Mars bar.' Mo grinned, thinking how important these things must be in a world as small as hers. 'No problem,' he said, asking, 'Bread: brown or white?'

'Brown,' she called out, holding out a hand to balance herself at the counter.

'Orange juice: bits or smooth?'

'Bits!' she answered.

Mo popped the juice in a plastic bag next to the bread. 'Right, we have two kinds of Super Noodles left: the red one's beef flavour, and the yellow one's chicken.'

'I can't say I'm that good at colours,' Jamie shrugged.

Mo closed his eyes and winced: Was he really that stupid? 'Sorry,' he said through gritted teeth.

'Don't worry about it,' she laughed. 'I'm just teasing you. I'll take the chicken.'

Mo popped the chicken flavour Super Noodles into the bag.

The electronic beeper on the door went; Mo looked up. Jamie turned behind her as the sound, and a slight draft drifted in and travelled up the arms of her denim jacket. She wasn't the last customer of the night: Another had walked in and moved to the back of the shop to the magazine rack and started to read. The figure's movements were as smooth as if they had been rehearsed.

Mo recognised this customer, had seen them in the shop before ... but never at this time of night.

'Don't forget the Mars bar!' Jamie reminded him.

'No – no,' he said, dropping one in the plastic carrier, keeping an eye on the other customer, an odd feeling emanating from their direction.

He punched up the total on the till, its small buttons letting out a *'Beep-Beep'* that stirred Jamie's senses.

'Five-fifty-eight,' Mo said, watching the figure at the back of the store, not looking at the magazine, but over their shoulder to where the blind girl stood.

'Hang on,' she said, reaching for her pocket and retrieving her purse. It always amazed him how she knew what money to give, watching her experienced fingers feel the circumference of coin and note to decipher the right amount.

'There you go,' she said, 'that should be enough.' And sure enough, it was: She handed him a five-pound note and a six ten-pence pieces.

He rang up the till and gave her the change. 'Not much longer now until Christmas,' he said as he placed the two-pence piece in her waiting palm. 'Are you planning much over Christmas?'

'Not much,' she said as she reached for the plastic carrier. 'I never really do that much at Christmas. I normally meet some of the people from the home I used to live in.'

'Oh, why's that?' he asked, watching as the other customer at the back listened over their shoulder.

'Well ...' Jamie said. 'I don't have any family to celebrate it with.'

The wince Mo gave this time nearly shattered his gritted teeth: Of course he knew this; his Dad had told him. 'I can't seem to say anything right tonight,' Mo sighed.

'Hey, I don't know anything other than what I've got, so I can't complain.'

'Well, I'm sorry,' Mo said, walking back around the counter, watching as the other customer shifted suspiciously behind the centre aisle and out of sight as he did.

He walked Jamie to the door, opened it. Wisps of cold seeped inside. 'Be careful; it's looking icy out there,' he said.

'I'll be all right,' Jamie grinned.

'You live a fair old bit away from here, don't you?'

'Well, about a ten-minute walk. It's worth it, though; at least I know I can trust you and your dad. I don't go to the supermarket around the corner; they tried to do me out of my change there the last time I went.'

'You're joking,' he replied, genuinely appalled.

'No, it's a true story,' she said, a dull sadness filling her eyes.

'You be careful going home,' Mo said.

'I haven't got another choice than to be careful,' she grinned, a slight solemnness at the side of her mouth. 'See ya,' she said, raising the blue carrier in the air by way of thanks, walking off, feeling with her cane as she seeped into the pooled illumination of the streetlights.

Her words warmed him inside: *I can trust you and your dad,* and in that moment, his career in a convenience store seemed worthwhile, as if he had genuine positive impact to the people in the neighbourhood. Was this the fulfilment that had kept his Dad here for so many years, that made him want to share his business with Mo?

Maybe it was.

A rustle came from behind him, a shuddering shock that he had forgotten the last customer. 'Excuse me,' he called, moving around the centre aisle. 'We're closing in a moment,'

Silence.

No reply.

Had the other customer walked out without him seeing? That was impossible; he had been in the doorway the entire time. A movement came from near the till on the opposite end of the centre aisle. Mo moved down to the back of the shop. As he did, he heard the electronic door beeper go. He quickly turned and watched as the last customer opened the door to leave, the chill from outside as empty as the odd, smoky eyes the customer looked back at him with. Smoky eyes – as if something were burning beneath his skin inside his skull. That was impossible – no one had pure black eyes. It must have been a trick of the light.

Mo moved up to the front door, seeing the customer walking off in the same direction as Jamie had, the streetlights somehow not highlighting any distinctive features as they went.

He walked back to the counter, seeing that next to the till he had left the Super Noodles Jamie had bought on the side – they had fallen as she had picked the bag up, and he had neglected to notice.

He went to swear, huffed, stared at the glowing face of the impish Father Christmas on the door. It was Christmas; everyone should do a little something for someone, right? He remembered where she lived and knew the flat's actual number, as it used to belong to one of the old customers on one of his paperboy's routes.

He grabbed another plastic carrier, throwing in the Super Noodles, some crisps, and packets of biscuits. They were items that meant a few pennies profit to him but would mean a whole lot more to her. Filling the bag halfway, grabbing his jacket, he flicked off all the lights and locked the doors, and headed out into the night.

His assumption was right: It was icy out here, his flat-bottomed shoes slipping and sliding as he went.

He had an idea: *Through the graveyard.*

If he just jumped the fence, he could get to her flat so much faster.

Why not, he confirmed with himself, placing one foot on the old cemetery's iron gates and hoisting himself up and over.

It was pitch black inside the cemetery's walled-in boundaries, the slippery pavement giving way to overgrown tendrils of thick wet grass, the bottoms of his jeans soaking up the moisture. Mo looked up. Jamie's flat-backed on to here somewhere. After some searching, he saw a light pop on, and he watched Jamie standing in her small kitchen, placing the contents of her bag onto her sideboard.

He thought *he* had problems with his Dad shouldering the shop onto him; he couldn't even imagine what being blind must be like. The everyday struggle, the –

A thunderbolt of shock fired through his heart, cutting his thoughts short. He wasn't in the graveyard alone. Ahead, outlined by the light from Jamie's kitchen window, stood the customer who had just left his shop, alone, staring up at her.

'Bloody hell, man,' Mo laughed. 'You scared the –'

Whatever Mo had had scared out of himself quickly returned to incubate inside him; what was before him made no sense.

The last customer stood dead still, their mouth opened wide, looking like their jaw was hinged to a flip-top head, gawping upward. From his mouth, a thick tumorous lump plumed like a meaty storm cloud; it grew from within the customer's throat, emerging as if it were smoke and his neck were a chimney. The veiny, pulsating thing emerging from their mouth looked pink and fleshy beneath the limited light as if the customer's innards had twined free and grown into ... *something* else ...

Mo could smell smoke, could taste the disgusting aroma of flesh burning on his tongue. 'What are yo –' he started to say, seeing the customer turn around to face him, their mouth still gaping wide.

The thing growing from inside the man turned autonomously to face him, turned to reveal ... at its peak ... the tumour actually had a fleshy face ... had, in fact, two awful milky

125

white eyes that looked down at him. The entire beast kept growing until it stood two floors tall as it stretched from the customer's insides, staring in at the unaware blind girl in the flat above.

A slimy mouth drew apart in the bulbous, meaty creature, one that began to speak.

'Youuuu'veee disturbbeeddd meeee,' it's voiced echoed out. *'Andddd nowwww youuu neeedddd to payyyy,'*

'Oh no,' Mo said, cowering away as the beast lowered itself down towards him.

Mo had known instinctively there was more to life than just sitting behind a till; had known there were sights out there just waiting to be seen, maybe even something he'd never imagined.

He'd never dreamed in his most vivid nightmares it would be this.

The meaty, smoky thing had no use for the little man as it did the girls, as it did for the girl above them who it spied upon. But the little man would do tonight as entertainment; would be good to play with.

As the creature came down closer, opening its mouth to reveal a mouthful of sharp teeth, Mo never even had a chance to let out a final scream.

Chapter Thirty Five

'Look cute, Bill, look cute,' Kelly said, watching two adults and their little girl walking down the corridor to the adoption wing of Chase Lodge Rescue Centre.

Graveyard Billy had been moved from the intensive care unit to the adoption wing three days ago, his injuries more superficial than was first suspected. He and Kelly had made a plan to spring him free from the wall of cages in that time.

'What have we got?' he asked.

'Little girl, maybe seven years old; give it some with the eyes.' Kelly said with a wink. Graveyard Billy positioned himself at the front of the cage as Kelly had told him, one paw stretched up to the top of the bars, the other halfway down, an anguished look on his face with fully rounded, sad eyes.

'Perfect! Hold that,' she instructed, keeping an eye on the child as she came closer.

'I like this,' moaned an old tabby a few cages down. 'The newbie rolls in and gets help with getting adopted from the other side.'

Growls and hisses of agreement came from the other cages, the other animals' grievances aimed at Kelly.

'Yeah, what makes you more special than the rest of us to get out of here?' a Norwegian Forest cat snootily whined. 'You need a home as much as the rest of us, but we've been here longer; we have seniority over you.'

'I've got to get out to try figure out what's going on. There's something odd happening to people around Brighton, and we've got to try and stop it,' Graveyard Billy projected to the other animals.

'Sounds like you're letting human problems become too much of your life,' hissed an angry-looking Persian. 'What business does a cat and a ... *poxy ghost* ... have worrying about human problems?'

'Watch it,' Kelly glared at the caged animal, who hissed back at her.

'It's my business because something out there murdered my owner,' Graveyard Billy said angrily. 'And I think – somehow – it has her spirit trapped ... somehow.'

'The past is the past,' a rather rotund-looking ginger cat said. 'You should be more worried about getting a new owner – a new lease on life in a warm home with fresh plates of food, not worrying about things that can't be changed.'

'You don't get it!' Graveyard Billy said. 'There's something out there hurting people, something that needs to be stopped –'

'And it has to be you, has it, my black friend?' the tabby chimed in. 'Just take it easy and live your life for yourself; think about Number One. My goodness, being out on the street – on your ear – should have taught you that.'

'Shut up, you lot!' Kelly shouted. 'Don't you ever give it a rest?' The furry creatures let out a cacophony of whines and hisses.

'Bill,' she said, trying to get his attention, 'Assume the position! They're nearly here.'

The little girl with her parents caught sight of Graveyard Billy, his big moony eyes staring deeply into hers, a whimpering mew passing between his black lips.

'Awwwwwwwww!' the little girl beamed.

'Ugh!'

'Pathetic!'

'He's a disgrace to our kind with that disgusting pandering!'

All the complaints seeped from the other cages simultaneously, vehemence in the air from the other animals directed at Graveyard Billy.

'Ignore them, Bill, do your thing!' Kelly encouraged.

Graveyard Billy made fast, high-pitched cheeps and chirps as he rubbed his head against the bars of the cage, yearning for attention.

More voices groaned out.

'Makes you wish you were born a dog!'

'I couldn't look myself in the face after a display like that.'

'It's stuff like that which gives us grimalkin a bad name.'

'Mum!' the little girl cried. 'Look at this one!'

'He's a new arrival,' said the blonde veterinary nurse escorting them through the facilities. 'Turned up a few days ago after a hit and run. Sadly, his original owner passed away.'

'Can we have this one, Mum?' the little girl asked.

'Go on, Bill!' Kelly egged him on. 'Give it some!'

More peeps and whistles came from Graveyard Billy, more overflowing emotions projected through his bars, eliciting more moans of disgust from the other animals.

'What does his collar say, Mummy?' the little girl asked.

Her mother cocked her head around, just as everyone else did who tried to read his name from his collar. 'Graveyard … Billy,' her mother said, with enough venom in her tone that it was no wonder the words were spat out.

'That's a funny name, isn't it?' the girl grinned.

'Yes,' her mother replied, 'a little too funny. Anyway, he's a black cat – he's bad luck. Come on, Isabelle,' the girl's mother said. 'Let's see if we can find a more normal cat for you,'

'See if you can find these, love,' Kelly said, giving the girl's mother a two-fingered salute as she walked away.

The other cats around them purred out laughter.

'You can't force an owner – a proper owner at least, runt – you have to wait to find someone who fits,' an elderly grey cat said, his wiry tail swishing the bars of his cage, making a small metallic scale ride up and down angrily.

'Look, I've told you lot, I'm not looking for "Someone who fits;" I'm looking for a way out!'

'Hahahaha!' a laugh boomed out, silencing the other cats. 'You think it's all fun and games, locked away in the slammer; think you can see an opportunity and just get out on the lam,' a stocky black and white Turkish Van cat said, his feet so white in contrast to his black legs that it looked as if he were wearing two pairs of socks.

Kelly understood the cat's accent; he sounded Scottish as he projected.

'The days of running feral and free are over, the humans have a new agenda against us cats – trap-neuter-repeat – that's what they want to do; dwindle us down in number for easier control.' The Turkish Van said.

'I swear to you, my small black friend, it's a conspiracy – isn't it, my friends! They're trying to wipe us out!' He called out to the other cages, his diatribe becoming their mantra. 'Trap-neuter-repeat!' the other cats chanted. 'Trap-neuter-repeat! – Trap-neuter-repeat!'

'I'm boss around here, an' I'm telling ya, the humans might align themselves with us by buying us scratching posts to claw, stringed things to dazzled us, and catnip to subdue us, but the rising is coming: We will bite the hand that feeds us!'

In practised unison, the other caged cats began to chant again – 'Bite the hand that feeds us! Bite the hand that feeds us!'

'God, will you shut up!' Kelly moaned at the Turkish Van. 'You lot have been cooped up in these cages too long; there's no conspiracy against you cats from humans!'

'That's what a human would say,' a white cat piped in, pressing against his bars and glaring out with piercing blue eyes.

'They are all the same,' a grey and black patchy cat croaked. 'Even from beyond the grave, the humans keep their secrets with them! Even in death, the truth doesn't come out!'

'Trap-neuter-repeat!' a small black kitten peeped.

Kelly bent down towards the little kitten, a finger pointed in his face. 'And you can keep out of it, matey!' The black kitten, a face of wide-eyed terror, immediately shut up.

'Look, there are no sides; there's no conspiracy,' said Graveyard Billy. 'I need to get out of here to find my old owner to find out what's going on, to stop what's happening out there from happening again!'

The two veterinary nurses – Liz and Gemma – walked back past, both looking down at Graveyard Billy, then stopping.

'What did those last ones say then, any luck?' asked Liz.

'No; they think they might want to get a dog,' shrugged Gemma.

129

They bent down to Graveyard Billy's cage. Liz placed the tip of her finger through the bars to slowly stroke his soft nose. 'You were a lucky boy,' she said. 'I think you must have lost about four of your nine lives with that taxi.'

'They don't seem to like his name,' Gemma said. 'That's what put the mum off.'

'Graveyard Billy,' Liz said. 'Well, I suppose it is a bit morbid.'

'What is it with people hating on your name, Bill?' Kelly said, giving the two nurses a glare.

'That's pretty rich coming from you,' Graveyard Billy transmitted. 'You haven't called me properly by my name once.'

Kelly shrugged.

'It's nearly Christmas. People want to cheer and happiness, not something depressing like a name like that.' Gemma remarked.

'It's supposed to be a white Christmas too, a proper Christmas … people want cute things at Christmas, don't they …' Liz nodded.

'Tell you what, next feed shall we get rid of that old collar?'

'Yeah, we could do,' Liz replied.

'What shall we change his name to on the chart?' the brunette asked, visibly mulling options as she bit her lip.

'What about Barry? Black Barry?' Gemma asked.

A roar of hissing, howling laughter came from the other cages; Graveyard Billy batted his eyes closed to try and block the mockery out.

'Yes, that will do,' Liz said. 'Let's change it to that tomorrow.' The pair then up and walked off.

'And so it begins,' the black and white Turkish Van sneered. 'First, they trap you, then they cut off your important bits, and now they tarnish your good reputation with stupid names. Brothers and sisters,' he announced to the other cages, 'All bear witness to the rebirth of our brother Graveyard Billy into his new domesticated form. All welcome: Black Barry!'

The other cats all roared with laughter, their chant quickly returning: 'Trap-neuter-repeat – we won't face defeat!'

'We need to get to out of here,' Kelly said in disbelief, looking around at the caged cats with contempt akin to being surrounded by a bunch of tinfoil-hat wearing crackpots.

'Trap-neuter-repeat– we won't face defeat!'

'You're telling me,' Graveyard Billy sighed. 'You're telling me.'

CHAPTER THIRTY SIX

Jamie Chase walked to her kitchen, held her hand up to her Braille calendar, and ran her fingers over the raised symbols – two more days until Christmas day. Christmas was important this year; a surge of excitement had grown inside her knowing it was coming.

Usually, at this time of year, a deep sadness ate away at her inside. The loneliness she pretended wasn't really there as she didn't have parents was amplified as much as the sound around her due to her lack of sight. She'd been walking through Brighton a few days earlier with her designated care worker, buying bits as she did every other week with her disability allowance, when she'd heard a couple talking in front of her, pinpointing their conversation from the other sounds in the crowd. As the couple talked, certain words stood out to her.

'I know,' a male voice had said. 'I'm looking forward to *seeing* my sister; she's been working in America for nearly two years now. The last message I got from her was she was flying into Gatwick on Christmas Eve.'

'I know,' a female voice said, one Jamie took to be his girlfriend. 'I'm looking forward to *seeing* her too.'

'What shall we do on Christmas day if your mum and dad come down?' he had asked.

'The Prince Charles Cinema is open; maybe we could all go and *see* a film there? It's better than *watching* TV. After dinner, maybe we could *see* It's a Wonderful Life. I *saw* it was playing a few days ago.'

'*Look* at all the lights hanging up, Mum,' a child had said, breezing past.

'*Look* at the decorations on that tree,' an older voice had said. 'I bet they cost a pretty penny.'

Christmas was a spectacle for the sighted, something she couldn't be part of. But that excitement in everyone's voices, that awe at the twenty-fifth of December, was something she could feel around her, was as tangible as summer heat on that cold winter day.

From hearing the conversations around her, a realisation broke through: even though Jamie was unable to see the decorations and Christmas lights that lined the lanes of Brighton, the excitement of others had rubbed off onto her, the thought of seeing her old friends from the home: Robbie, Jade, Kate, Brian. It made her smile. The Christmas spirit wasn't tinsel and coloured lights; it was the people you were with and what you made of it.

Jamie had wanted her independence, wanted to live alone, and had fought with the local council for help to make that happen. She had to make a place for herself in the world; living in the safety of the care home couldn't be an option forever, but she wanted to see her friends again, to tell them what she had achieved, wanted to know what they had achieved since she had last seen them.

There was another conversation she'd heard in the lanes that echoed in her mind:

'Just have another mince pie!' a girl laughed at her friend.

'Oh, go on then,' said the friend. 'The diet can start after New Year. You know what they say – New Year – new you.'

New Year – new you, Jamie had thought, the words branded in her mind.

That's when she would put her next plan into gear to make the changes she wanted in life.

She had to find her own happiness, something that would give her that Christmas feeling every day. Then maybe – a smile burst on her lips – she could find the one thing she had never had in her life before: love.

To the blind, even the smallest thing meant so much: a simple touch, a hug, and a kiss, something physically with some kind of emotion behind it to remind you that you weren't alone.

She didn't want her disability to get in her way, to stop her from living a normal life. She wanted to live, wanted to travel, wanted to feel … loved, wanted to give love back. There was nothing worse than being alone and being blind. Everything was temporal: One way or another, things had to move on, and being away from the home, being independent, being alone, was her first step towards finding a life she wanted.

She had her flat, her independence; now, in the New Year, she would find her new life, the 'new you' she was looking for, a renewed self she could hopefully share with someone else.

You had to go through a little hardship before you got the reward that was due to you, she would think, as if blindness wasn't hardship enough.

She turned to the kettle, sloshed it from side to side to make sure it held water, then turned it on. Her care worker had even helped her find part-time work in a charity shop starting this coming January: her first job out there in the world. She understood what people with sight were like; she would encounter people who treated her as if the disability came first and the person behind it came second. Not everyone was like that, though. She had confidence in this deduction, another smile breaking on her face – not everyone was like that, she reassured herself.

The kettle bubbled, and she switched on the small radio in the kitchen: The Waitresses' 'Christmas Wrapping' was playing, an upbeat saxophone vibrating from the small speaker.

Jamie jolted, her heightened senses feeling something, feeling the gaze of invisible eyes held on her. She turned her head, almost calling out, hearing a creaking sound coming from nearby. She quickly shifted along the flat's corridor, hands rubbing down painted plaster, towards the flat's front door, knowing this was where the sound was coming from.

She held her breath in silence, blocking out the radio, blocking out the kettle, honing in on the front door. Had she used the bolt at the bottom to lock herself in? Of course, she had; it was part of her routine.

A slight movement came from outside, a deep hissing sound that moved as if something was pacing her door. 'Who's there?' she called.

A long silence was her reply.

Again: *'Who's there?'*

'Sorry,' a voice replied. 'I'm just sweeping the stairways. I've been sent here by the council.'

Jamie sighed in relief, wondering why her senses were so heightened. 'No worries,' she called back. 'Sorry.'

The sound of sweeping – she recognised it now – started again.

'What's wrong with you,' she whispered, not knowing that a silhouette behind the frosted glass in the front door leered in as she wondered what was causing that distant but awful smell of smoke.

CHAPTER THIRTY SEVEN

Everything was oddly quiet in the adoption wing of the Chase Lodge Rescue Centre. The normally angry voices of the cats were all silent, all waiting: A truce had been made, a deal struck. A clock ticked in the corner; a clinical smell lingered all around. Kelly waited by the main door, staring through its small security window down the hallway opposite Graveyard Billy sat in his cage staring up at the black and white Turkish Van, the older cat's suspicious eyes glaring back at him.

'And I will be the first?' the Turkish Van said.

'Yes, of course,' Graveyard Billy said. 'It's simple: You put your back legs on the bottom of the cage and pull the latch with your paws; then it will spring open.'

'How do you know all this, my small black friend?' the Turkish Van said untrustingly.

'Bill's become quite good at getting himself in and out of places,' Kelly called back to them. 'I taught him how to master door handles.'

'*Aghhhh,*' the Turkish Van grinned. 'It is the influence of the humans infecting your sensibilities, is it, Graveyard Billy? Lads!' he called to the other cats. 'It looks like the spirit of Black Barry has already infected his soul.'

The other cats all laughed.

'The human's plan for domestication has already tainted his being. He's being programmed as their slave to open and shut doors like some kind of dog!'

'*Yeah!* Some kind of dog!' the ginger cat a few cages down cried.

'Look, if you don't want my help, then say so,' Graveyard Billy said. 'But if you want to practice what you preach, if you want to roam feral again, then we have to work together.'

The Turkish Van let out a long sigh, 'So be it, but don't cross me, Graveyard Billy, unless you want to end up like your human friend here,' the Turkish Van laughed. 'Or should I say, *ex*-human friend?'

'Watch it,' Kelly sneered back at the chuckling cat.

'Look, we all know what to do, just like we planned – we work together,' Graveyard Billy said, anxious to prove he was a cat of his word to the Turkish Van.

'Get me out of here, boy, and I'll see to the rest,' the older cat growled.

Graveyard Billy blinked at the Turkish Van, knowing they needed each other equally if this was to work.

'Bill!' Kelly called. 'They're coming down.'

'Right, get ready, everyone,' Graveyard Billy said eagerly.

Outside the room's main door, murmured talking came

closer; echoed footsteps levelled to clean clicks on the tiled floors as they drew nearer.

'Right, everyone ready,' Kelly said. A cacophony of low growls came from the caged cats. 'It's all on you, Bill,' Kelly said as the room's door was thrown open and Gemma and Liz, the veterinary nurses, walked in, grinning about something mid-conversation.

'What's the plan? Are we all going out on New Year's, then?' asked Liz.

'It's Christmas Day tomorrow, and you're thinking of New Year's? The only reason you're so bothered about New Year's is that Dr. Derek might be there,' said Gemma, checking her clipboard. 'He's divorced now, you know.'

Liz went to the desk in the corner and started to pour cat biscuits into a series of silver bowls, trying to act nonchalantly and hide the grin that pulled at her lips. 'I know he's divorced,' she said.

'I'm sure you do,' Gemma replied under her breath with a flash of her eyebrows. 'His collar,' she exclaimed, looking at Graveyard Billy's cage. 'We can update his profile on the website. Get rid of the name, and we might have half a chance to get rid of the cat.'

'I agree with that,' Liz said, the thought of that name from the papers – the Graveyard Killer – sending a chill down her spine. 'Such an awful name, it's so ... morbid,' she added.

'Charming!' Kelly exclaimed. 'This is coming from a girl who fancies a bloke who with a drop of an E and the addition of a C would be called Dr. Dreck.'

Graveyard Billy transmitted a sound to Kelly that amounted to a chortle.

'Keep focused, runt,' the Turkish Van said, 'or forever be known as Black Bar –'

'Okay! *I get it!*' Graveyard Billy said.

Gemma moved to Graveyard Billy's cage, then turned to the Turkish Van, noticing his movement in the confined space. 'Are you all right, big boy?' she asked.

The Turkish Van stared at the girl with nonplussed eyes.

'Mr. Ruffles is being a moody git again,' Gemma said.

'Mister What-ells!' Kelly cried with laughter.

'Keep the ghost quiet, Graveyard Billy; I won't be mocked by an un-dead human.'

'Proper menacing with a name like that, ain't ya, mate,' Kelly grinned at the caged Turkish Van.

'Yeah, it's not often he is in a good mood,' Liz said, finishing filling the bowls.

The Turkish Van let out a *'Whhhhhhaaaaaawwwww'* under his breath.

'You'll never get adopted with an attitude like that.' Liz

waggled a painted red fingernail in the older cat's face. She turned around, holding contemptuous eyes on the caged, miserable creature as she did.

'Right, let's get that collar off,' she said, bending down to Graveyard Billy's cage, unlatching it and reaching in. 'Sorry,' Graveyard Billy said, 'but I can't stay in here.' With a swiping slice, he plunged his exposed nails through the air, not pulling the punch as his claws connected with the soft skin of Liz's hand. Five long slashes broke on her flesh, a warm gush of blood instantly trailing behind them.

'*OW!*' the girl cried, instantly pulling back. 'He got me, the little –'

She didn't have a chance to finish her sentence; Graveyard Billy leapt from his open cage, landed on the girl's shoulder, and springboarded up to the Turkish Van. With claws still extended, he grabbed onto the bars of the cage, found the latch to undo the door, and, using the technique he'd learned at Aunt Coral's house, yanked the small latch down. A loud click sounded out: Graveyard Billy had successfully unlocked it. He swung back on the hinges and let go, falling to the floor.

'Oh no!' cried the Gemma. 'Mr. Ruffles is out!'

The Turkish Van leapt down from his cage; an audible *'Slap!'* beat out as his bulk hit the floor. 'Finally, *I'm free!*' growled the cat, his full size revealed as it unfurled from the confined space.

'He's not a cat – *he*'s a cub!' Kelly cried, awestruck at his true size, at least three feet long and over a foot and a half wide of unneutered Turkish Van.

The Turkish Van padded the floor towards Gemma, who tripped and fell on her backside, face locked in terror; she pulled herself backwards, crawling and watching the hypnotic sway of the huge cat's agitated tail above his menacing eyes. 'Unlock the others, lad; leave the humans to me,' he growled to Graveyard Billy.

'Mr. Ruffles, don't start with that –' Liz said confidently, walking towards him and reaching down to pick him up. With one glare of his piercing eyes, the bulky cat stopped the other girl in her tracks.

Graveyard Billy leapt at the other cats' cages, using the same trick he had on the Turkish Van's cage to unlatch them, setting the cats free. Each of the other cats took their cue and began doing the same, all eventually freeing each other.

'I'm out; I've been sprung!' cried the ginger.

'Jailbreak, lads! Jailbreak!' cried a rough-looking white cat.

Quickly, one after the other, cats began to congregate together on the floor, all of them moving towards the veterinary nurses, with the Turkish Van acting as the head of the pack as they all hissed and whined in high-pitched voices.

'What is going on!' Gemma said, staggering to her feet and grabbing Liz, the pair backing to the door.

Graveyard Billy fell in line with the others and walked at the back of the group next to the small black kitten who started the chant again; the others immediately joined in: *'Bite the hand that feeds us! Bite the hand that feeds us!'*

'Bill, you've got one chance at this,' Kelly said. 'Just go for it,'

'You did well alone, Graveyard Billy,' hissed the Turkish Van. 'Now, let's see how you do as part of the pack.'

Gemma reached for the door handle, pulled it down to exit.

'We won't all make it out of here,' the Turkish Van cried. 'But let's give them what for! *BITE THE HAND THAT FEEDS YOU! LET'S GOOOOOOO!'*

The veterinary nurses tried to make an escape, but they couldn't move as quickly as the cats.

The cats seeped through the open jamb in a flash of blurred fur, kept running until they made it into the main reception area. Suddenly, thirty cats were all leaping up towards the plate glass windows of the rescue centre, trying to escape into the blackness of night beyond, flecked with the heavy fall of snow.

'What is –' was all the bespectacled receptionist could say, she too backing away from the seemingly possessed felines. She began to call out.

A male vet walked in from a back room. 'What's going on in here!' he cried. 'Get those animals back in their cages.'

Gemma, holding her scratched hand, blurted out all at once, *'We went into here to feed them, and one got out then another, and now they've all gone mad!'*

The small black kitten jumped on the reception desk, howling in his cat's tongue, *'Bite the hand that feeds us!'*

The vet's big hand reached down and grabbed the kitten by the scruff of the neck, a loud peep escaping the baby cat's lips. 'Get yourselves together,' the vet yelled. They're just cats! Just get them back in their cages and–'

The Turkish Van pounded up on the reception desk to the vet, glaring at him with eyes that could cut glass. The vet quickly shut up, backed away, and placed the black kitten down on the desk again as a mouthful of fangs hissed in his direction.

'Come, lads!' the Turkish Van cried. 'We need to find a way out!'

'The front door!' Kelly cried as she wisped her head through the glass. 'Someone is walking over – they're going to come in!'

'Now is our chance!' the Turkish Van yelled.

Outside, the centre's maintenance man, Danny Wilson,

was walking to the main door, his arms piled with bags of grit and salt to scatter in the car park as protection from the oncoming snow. His mind was fixed on his Christmas presents under the tree at his mum's house; his lips puckered as he whistled, 'Let It, Snow.' He opened the centre's door, saying, 'You all better start thinking about making a move home; this weather is –'

Shock froze him to the spot as a huge furred clowder of cats ran, leapt, and flew straight towards him. All the cats from the centre fired through the open jamb at once, their paws sinking into the settling snow outside in trails of paw prints.

A mewing roar of success escaped the cats' lips as Kelly bolted with the rest of them and passed straight through Danny, her presence sending a spasm of shivers through the man, who dropped the bags of grit straight to the floor.

Cats fired under parked cars, under shadowed bushes. Graveyard Billy ran without looking back into the wooded area next to the rescue centre, the mob behind starting their chant again: *Bite the hand that feeds us! Bite the hand that feeds us!*

'Come on!' Graveyard Billy said, calling back to Kelly, who was like an anchor chained to him as he tried to get up speed. 'I can sense Piper! I can sense that other thing is doing something wrong. I think it's going to after another victi –'

The huge Turkish Van jumped down in front of Graveyard Billy from the branch of a winter-weathered tree, stood in front of him with glaring eyes. *'Graveyard Billy,'* he croaked.

Graveyard Billy said nothing.

'You seem too obsessed with human problems, too obsessed with helping those I consider enemies to just let go.' The bigger cat bulked up, threateningly fluffed out his fur as, step by step, he came closer. 'But today, my black friend,' he said a few inches from Graveyard Billy's face, 'you did your brethren right and have earned your right to pass.'

'Th-thanks,' Graveyard Billy said with a blink. Kelly stayed silent, feeling the dread that surrounded the oversized cat.

The Turkish Van eyed Graveyard Billy. 'I don't understand what it is you are doing, runt, but if anyone uses the name Black Barry to describe you in my presence –' He took a step closer, drank in Graveyard Billy's scent and stared into his eyes, tail swaying with menace. '– they'll have me to deal with.'

Graveyard Billy nodded. Kelly, for once, stayed silent as the cat stalked past her.

'Thank you, too,' he said in her direction. *'Ex-human.'* A snide gleam shimmered in his eyes with his parting words as he disappeared to converge with the rest of the cats, taking his place as their leader, guiding the entire pack as they ran out into the night.

'Bill, he is one scary cat,' Kelly said.

138

'Even more so for a cat named Mr. Ruffles,'

Kelly snorted out a small, uneasy laugh, the cold falling snow around her illuminating like falling stars as it passed through the otherworldly glow surrounding her body.

'Come on,' Graveyard Billy said. 'We need to make a move, 'I can feel something bad is happening.'

Chapter Thirty Eight

Jamie was sitting in her living room; a play was on the radio in the corner, not that she was really listening to it. She was too busy piecing together her outfit for the Christmas dinner tomorrow, laying what she wanted out piece by piece in a symmetrical human shape as if it were a shell waiting to be filled: her black dungarees, her stripped woolly jumper, and oversized trainers; comfy clothes she could relax in for Christmas Day. Her care worker, Harley, was to pick her up at nine tomorrow morning, and she couldn't wait.

The play ended. An announcer's voice appeared after a moment's worth of silence: 'Well, we hope that puts you in the Christmas spirit, and if not, it looks as if the forecasters were right – it's snowing here in London as it looks like it will do for the rest of the South East tonight.'

'No way!' Jamie smiled, reaching for her stick and lifting herself to her feet. She walked to the living room window, lifted back the heavy curtain she had drawn, clambered beneath the nets that hung there, and held a hand to the glass in the window frame. A freezing, icy coldness bit her palm, even from inside the flat; by instinct, she could tell it was cold enough to settle.

In her mind, the cold signified something; her positive outlook somehow solidified by the idea of a white Christmas. Maybe things would change for her? Maybe all the things she wanted to come into her life could do as easily as the change in the weather.

This thought brought a smile to her face as her fingertips touched the glass. She was unaware that, pressed to the window outside, another face was grinning back.

Kelly and Graveyard Billy ran along a darkened pavement, the streetlight above glowing with the flourish of falling snowflakes that had settled on the sidewalk.

'What do you mean you can sense her, Bill?' Kelly asked.

'When I was knocked out, unconscious back at the vet's … I … well, you know, like how we talk, where I transmit to you? Well, something started transmitting to me – something that felt like Piper … but it felt like *the killer,* too. I know that makes no sense, but somehow … I know where it is – whatever is doing this.'

'What?' Kelly gasped.

'I can sense it!' Graveyard Billy said. 'I can sense that something is happening tonight that we need to stop.'

'I think I know where you're headed, Bill,' Kelly said. 'The one place that makes sense in this direction.'

'Where?' he asked.

'Florence Place Cemetery,' Kelly replied, *The killer* is there, isn't he?'

Graveyard Billy gave no response.

Jamie walked to her front door, held the small latch on the lock. The coldness from outside travelled through the metal as she twisted it open. A breeze pushed her hair back; a soft sugar puff of falling snow fell against her face: This was the feeling of winter, the feeling of all those Christmas colours she couldn't see.

She held a hand out over the concrete barrier in front of her flat into the free-falling snow. Tiny, freezing snowflakes landed on her exposed flesh. They did their job, produced their last pinprick of cold, then melted into her body temperature.

It was a small wonder to some but a huge, ginormous skyf all of wonder to her.

As she stood there, smiling out at the soft blizzard of snow, thinking of Christmas, thinking of the future, thinking of everything that was coming in the New Year, her senses were distracted, didn't hear or feel the presence of the form that shifted from the balcony to inside her flat. The form that stood waiting, grinning as manically as it had when it had pressed against her window – now inside her own home.

Graveyard Billy slipped through the old, rusted gates to Florence Place Cemetery, stealthily furrowing through the overgrown grass and wildflowers that sprouted from the unkempt space. Decayed tombstones now looked like whitened teeth with snowfall; small gusts of winds twisted in the air, looking like the corporeal shapes of graveyard spectres.

'What can you sense, Bill?' Kelly asked, eyes flickering into every flat shadow for potential danger.

'I don't know I …' he stumbled to a stop, staring up at the flats that overlooked the cemetery. A whiff of that burning smell from the night Piper died entered his nostrils: The graveyard, the darkness, that smell, the flats nearby – it was like a remake of the night she died, a nightmarish remake he couldn't let play out again.

'Up there,' he said to Kelly. 'Whatever is happening, it's happening up there.'

Jamie turned around and stepped back into her flat, the cold wrapping around the whole of her body as she shut the front door. A coldness that … became stronger when the door was actually shut. Instantly her senses were alert: *Something was in here with her*.

It was something cold, *dead* cold, that emulated the chill of the grave but at the same time had that smell of … *'Burning?'* she said to herself in a scared whisper.

'Not anymore,' a hideous voice replied.

Jamie fell backwards, hitting the front door with a juddering crack, not hard enough to knock her unconscious or end the terror that wired itself through her: the hammer the intruder was holding did that.

'Wait up, Bill!' Kelly cried as Graveyard Billy leapt up and over the wall that separated the graveyard from the flats, landing in a stinking bin area, more rubbish out of bags than in them.

He searched around an underground car park; ran up into the street outside, back into the snow. 'What can you sense?' Kelly cried. 'Are we any nearer to … it?'

Graveyard Billy looked around, up at the flats, then to the houses opposite. 'It's like … I can sense the thing from Woodvale, a part of Piper and even … a part of you.'

'What?' Kelly said.

'A part of you that's not part of you,' he fumbled, nose twitching, senses in overload. 'It's like … it's here … something is here!'

He took off again, running up to a poorly lit stairwell to the flats.

'Bill, mate!' Kelly called. 'I've been going along with this, but I think that car crash has sent you cuckoo,'

Suddenly she was jerked from the spot by the supernatural cords that bound them; quickly, she found her footing and started to run behind the black cat, more floating than running in the impractical shoes she'd died in.

Graveyard Billy ran up the stairs, made it to the third and top floor, jumped to the concrete balcony, and looked out into the night, a visible huff of steam escaping his mouth.

Kelly made it up to top floor with him. 'Bill, seriously, think about this, what can you sense? I mean really, *really*, why do you think something's her –'

She stopped, hearing a grunt coming from the other end of the block of flats. A figure was walking to an old transit van, an odd guttural mumbling, almost like the chanting at a ritual, escaping its hidden lips.

'What is he doing, Bill?' Kelly said as the figure dropped a huge rolled rug by the van's doors, a limp hand visibly curling from its centre. 'That's not ... *is that?*' Kelly said.

Graveyard Billy said nothing, just stared intently.

The figure picked the rug up, its weight causing the figure to grunt again, and then threw it in the back of the van, a sprig of hair hanging falling from one end as the doors were locked firmly.

'Bill,' Kelly said with a shiver, 'there's someone in that rug!'

'I know,' he said, lowering himself down, his eyes illuminating with a nocturnal glow, pinpointing down towards the figure as it looked left and right, made sure it wasn't being watched, hadn't been recognized.

It had.

Graveyard Billy all but gasped as he looked into the face of the killer and instantly knew its features by name.

Chapter Thirty Nine

Issac, Graveyard Billy remembered. *That's the name that goes with this face – this awful screwed-up face.*

Issac: the one from Woodvale Cemetery that had gone for him with the strimmer, his friend telling him to leave it out.

Issac: the one at Hove Cemetery who went after him like a maniac until Aunt Coral – of all people – came to his rescue.

That was the connection between all of them: All the dead girls were found near graveyards, and the only connecting factor, the one man who worked in all the cemeteries as their caretaker, was Issac.

But why? Why did he do this to Kelly; why did he do this to Piper? Why … Why …*Why…*

CHAPTER FORTY

Issac Waters had worked for Brighton and Hove Council for nearly ten years; he was part of their maintenance team for all the parks and graveyards and public greenery. It was a simple job, but he was a simple man.

'That's one good thing about you, Issac. You've always been good at practical things,' his ex-wife had said as he'd meekly changed the tyre on her car – her new boyfriend in the passenger seat – after their divorce hearing.

He'd grinned, hands black with dirt that he had slobbishly tarnished his only good suit with.

'Shame you were no good at anything else,' she'd added with a sneer.

His smile faded; that empty, hollow feeling inside his chest widened, filled with the heavy sadness that seemed to haunt him. That had been twelve years ago, and after bumming around here and there, never really finding his feet in anything, he eventually found his job with the council.

It was an easy enough job: Jump in the van with the others in the morning, then split up and do what they had to do: a bit of weeding in Preston Park, a spot of mowing at The Level. Then there were his favourites, the places he loved to work more than any others – the graveyards.

They would spend weeks in the graveyards, all working well away from one another with a corner each, then slowly meeting in the middle. The graveyards meant one thing: solitude. That was something Issac could contently live with.

He lived alone; he worked alone. At least alone, he could be with the one person he trusted the most, the one person he could rely on, the one person who would do him no wrong, who would never take advantage of him or lie to him ... well, he thought so at least – that was, until recently ... when things had started to change.

He remembered the day it had started, the strangeness before everything changed, the strangeness after everything changed ... well, *kind of*.

Woodvale Cemetery was the largest of the graveyards he maintained – the most secluded. There had been many days when he'd found a little nook in amongst a copse of overgrown trees, hidden underneath a darkened thicket of branches, to just sit and eat his sandwiches and drink his Thermos of coffee. It was more than big enough to avoid the others while they were working; more than big enough to tuck himself away somewhere out of sight, just to enjoy the seclusion.

It was just the legacy of Woodvale that could cause problems when the people his boss called, 'Those black-clothed nuts' crawled out of the woodwork to intervene.

It mainly happened overnight: pentagrams appearing on the church's walls, tombstones knocked over, graves desecrated with cheap shop-bought black magic paraphernalia: incense sticks, black candles, makeshift voodoo dolls.

Why did they do it? What was the point?

It was all because bloody Aleister Crowley had to get himself cremated at Woodvale back in the forties. And because of that event – eighty-odd years ago – every crank and nut and loony nearby took this to mean something that the man, the so-called 'Great Beast,' had been burnt there. It had become some kind of black-magic pilgrimage for the weirdos to come to Woodvale and cause some kind of pseudo-supernatural nonsense there.

Just like that day nearly a year ago, as the vicious bite of the old winter chill had started to lessen, as Nature tensed, ready to green up. Issac had found a nice comfy spot in the undergrowth away from all of the others, just as the afternoon's daylight started to disappear at around three o'clock: That was when everything changed.

Sitting, sipping from his Thermos, looking farther into the spindled shrubbery, a vivid orange glow caught his attention, accompanied by a series of flickering dots and a low moaning incantation.

Not now, surely? The black-clothed nuts wouldn't be about this early in the day?

Issac crept forward, keeping his footsteps as light as possible, slinking between the winter-ravaged trees, coming ten feet away from a small crowd of *them*, caught red-handed with their weirdness in full effect.

There were three of them, two men and a woman – more like two boys and a girl: They couldn't be any older than eighteen and nowhere near twenty. Issac caught a glimpse of what was there in the middle of their triangle: an Ouija board with an upside-down glass placed on it.

They chanted foreign-sounding words in low breaths. It was all Greek to Issac, although it was most probably Latin.

'Will this work, Matt?' asked the girl, her nose stud sparking in the light of the small array of black candles that surrounded them. 'Why do you think here is a better place than my flat?'

'This was the place he was burned; this was the place his flesh body met its untimely end, Tanya,' Matt replied, his eyes blackened with mascara.

Aleister bloody Crowley.

Issac gritted his teeth.

'Crowley was a fan of the flesh,' the other boy with them said, his hair dyed black and spiked. 'This is why we brought you,

146

Tanya, to tempt the beast.'

'Don't say that, Dave,' Tanya said, a genuine quiver in her voice as the other two laughed.

'Come on, let's do it,' Matt said, encouraging each of them to place a finger on the top of the upside-down glass.

'Go on,' Dave said. 'You get to say the words, Tanya.'

She sighed, cleared her throat. 'Is anybody there?'

Issac shook his head.

Unbelievable, idiots will believe anything.

The glass didn't move; their eyes widened with the tense silence that followed.

'Ask again,' Matt said.

Tanya cleared her throat once more. 'Is there anybody there?' she asked. The same palpable silence followed.

'Look, this isn't working,' Tanya said, visibly creeped out. 'Let's just go back to mine and watch a film on –'

'Quiet!' Dave said. A slight breeze caught where they were hidden, the barren bushes around them creaking like arthritis-afflicted arms.

'I'm getting cold, and –' Tanya moaned, quickly cut off as Matt's eyes fixed on the glass.

'Look!' he gasped.

From inside the glass, a smoky vapour started to grow. It darkened its insides as if injected with a swirling curdling mass of black paint. A disgusting smell hit the air, a charred burning smell, a foul stench that only few would have known as the cooked smell of bubbling flesh.

Tanya turned white, her lone inverted cross earring jangling with terror. 'I'm scared,' she managed to blurt out, feeling the change in atmosphere, seeing the dark mass in the glass with only a single finger from each of them keeping it trapped.

The two boys stayed silent, in awe at the spectacle, their jaws dropping as wide as their eyes.

Issac had seen enough, had caught a whiff of the burning smell. Had one of their candles caught some dead leaves alight? '*Oi!*' he shouted, causing each of them to cry out in terror. 'What exactly do you think you're playing at –'

Tanya and Dave took off from the undergrowth as fast as the snap of fingers, jumping graves and stone monuments, trying to make it back to the cemetery gates.

The third boy, Matt, stayed. Tears formed in his eyes, his mouth a drooling, blubbering mess.

'There's something in here,' he said, finger pressed tightly to the glass.

'I can see,' Issac said, coming over to the boy. 'A lot of nonsense I have to clear up.'

'No!' Matt cried. 'Under the glass.'

147

'You lot need your head tested, seeing spirits and bogeymen because you wear all that black nonsense. Life's not like that; it's just all made up and in your head!'

Issac wondered why this boy stayed. Why he would stand perfectly still, ready to be caught, while his friends ran? Did the boy have something planned? A squirt of paranoia ran through Issac's veins. Were these some of those kids who went about with knives?

Thinking fast, he pulled the Stanley blade from his work jacket, extended the blade with a click. 'I'm warning you, son; I'll have no funny business from you. Now get out of here.'

He loomed forward, the blade catching a glint of candlelight. It was enough for Matt to shift around the Ouija board – to get ready to run – his finger still pressed tightly to the top of the glass.

'It's up to you,' Matt said, face leaking tears and spittle all over his black leather jacket. Then, as if he had one foot on a land mine, he took off with all the speed he could muster, as if he expected an explosion behind him, bolting through the undergrowth, crying audibly as he ran in the same direction as his friends.

Issac snorted, put the blade away, and drew closer to where the candles and the Ouija board still lay. This was the problem with all these films kids watched these days; it made the unnatural normal, made all this rubbish acceptable. He took a swift boot to the candles, stamping them out on the ground as to make sure the flames wouldn't spread. He turned to the Ouija board now; it was an antique-looking thing, probably worth something to someone – that person wasn't him. With a quick, swift boot, he punted the glass from the board, kicked the board itself off into the undergrowth. *'Morons,'* he muttered. 'Nothing but –'

He paused. He had stamped the candles out, but for some reason, a thick, stinking patch of smoke had risen in the air, had risen from … the insides of the overturned glass.

The smoke was like a woollen blanket left in the rain as it touched his skin, damp and clammy, each of its worn, stinking threads coming loose and entering his senses, twining down his nose and throat, penetrating the eyes, and seeping through their retinas.

All vision was lost; there was only perfect black, his body convulsing with a gagging sickness. Somehow he was being entered, suppressed in his own body, his will ripped away. That hole of loneliness inside that his ex-wife had left was slowly being filled with … *something else.*

From that moment on, he wouldn't be alone again. When he would go to the graveyards to work, he would never be alone again – even if he were by himself.

Something had changed; something was now living inside him.

He was about to scream, then there was nothing, only total blackness.

For a moment, he seemed to disappear inside himself.

Suddenly he was back at the work van, a smile on his face as if he had no cares in the world.

'Easy day today, Issac,' his workmate had said. 'I haven't seen you for a while. Have any trouble on the west side?'

'No trouble at all,' Issac replied, even though they weren't the words he wanted to say. He didn't move his lips, but somehow … something inside him did.

That's when odd things started to happen all the time when he started to find himself in places he had no recollection of going. A padlock appeared on the workshop at the bottom of his garden, but he never remembered where the key to open it was …

He couldn't even remember what he kept in there anymore …

Just as now. Issac would have had no idea why he was out on Christmas Eve with a blind girl wrapped in an old Persian rug or why the cat who sat on the top balcony of the flats he had just come from recognized his face.

Issac knew nothing now, as Issac … wasn't Issac anymore.

CHAPTER FORTY ONE

'Hang on!' Kelly gasped, hanging over the flat's barrier and staring down. 'That's that bloke from Hove cemetery! That's that, the one that chased you! He was there the day we found that lost soul wandering about, he was –'

'The one that killed Piper … and you,' Graveyard Billy said, growling anger in his tone, tail swishing madly as the man locked the van's back doors, pulled the collar up on his old worn Donkey jacket to deflect the falling snow, and got into the driver's seat.

Kelly stayed silent, frozen to the spot, unable to gauge the correct emotion now that she had stared into the face of her killer. He was the man whose hands had ended her life: The old clichéd feeling of someone walking over her grave was somehow inverted as her supernatural aura shivered.

'Bill,' she whispered, a coldness more chilling than the December weather gripping her throat, 'what can we –'

The van's engine turned over, the starter whining in the winter cold before firing to life. As it did, Graveyard Billy took off with no thought of danger or himself, only thinking of Kelly and Piper. He ran to the edge of the flat's balcony and leapt off through the air.

'*Billllll!*' Kelly cried as the van pulled away, and Graveyard Billy landed on its roof with a reverberating pang.

Inside the van, the thing Issac had become hit the brakes, turned around to stare at the limp figure rolled in the old rug. *No, it wasn't her,* he rationalized, looking around in his mirrors, seeing nothing reflected that could have made the noise.

Suspicion filled his features, his eyes rolling back and forth like the pendulum of an old clock. No, there was nothing there. Maybe it was just his work gear falling back into place where he had made space for the girl's body?

No one came out of the gloom of night around him; no figures seeped from the falling snow to stop him. He pulled away, unaware that on the van's roof, Graveyard Billy held on for dear life.

Chapter Forty Two

Graveyard Billy had his claws wrapped around the old rusted roof rack on the cold van roof, holding on grimly as the van chugged and rumbled over every pothole Brighton council had neglected to fill. The wind hit his face; snow turned his black fur speckled white as G-force pushed him backwards.

A distant screaming came from behind: Kelly was being yanked through the air on the ectoplasmic strands that attached them both, yanked through the dark night sky like a supernatural comet. *'Bill!* What are you doing!' she cried, reeling herself in like a fish that wanted to be caught, bringing herself down to the top of the van next to Graveyard Billy.

'We can't let him go! We have to stop him!' he hissed in reply.

'But how!' Kelly whined. 'You're just a cat, and I ... well, what can I do! Not much in this state!'

'We've done okay so far!' he said, a gust of wind making him close his eyes, his ears turning flat to his small head. 'We have to try and do something!'

'You were all knocked up a few days ago, and now look at you! You think you're the cat equivalent of Rambo!' Kelly said, squinting from the oncoming snow flurry, even though it didn't affect her ghostly eyes.

'This isn't about me,' Graveyard Billy said. 'This is about you and all the others. This has to be stopped!' The van hit a speed bump; for all of a second, Graveyard Billy lost his grip, flew straight up in the air, dislodged from his safe space, and slid down the van's slippery roof.

'Bill!' Kelly screamed as, with his contortionist cat skills, Graveyard Billy turned quickly and caught hold of the rear roof rack, wrapping all four paws around it tight.

'You're going to kill yourself!' Kelly shouted, visibly shaken.

'It's okay! I've got nine lives!' he replied, his eyes now closed to protect his pupils from the lash of the snowfall.

'I'll be the judge of how many lives you have left!' she shouted. 'They've been dwindling since the day we met!'

'Just go inside and check on the girl, see what's going on inside!' he replied.

With a gulp and shiver, Kelly closed her eyes and seeped through the van's roof, materializing inside its back. Gardening tools were piled around its cluttered, gloomy edges, with the rolled-up girl lying in the back of the van's centre. Kelly lowered herself down towards where the hair hung from one end of the rolled rug. She moved in closer with trepidation – a ghost scared of the living. Yes, she was living: Kelly could see her head move slightly, her blonde hair turned red with blood, the fingers of her right hand that protruded from the rug slowly trying to close.

Kelly leapt up, plugged her head straight through the top of the van's roof to scream: *'She's alive!'*

Graveyard Billy jumped and almost lost his grip with her outburst.

'What about *him*?' he replied.

Kelly's grin dropped, that feeling of feet over her grave tingling through her body. Reluctantly she dipped back inside, moved slowly to the front to the van, and hung over its old, worn seats. She repositioned herself to stare into his face – her killer's face – all bugged-out eyes and demented grin; something human missing in his features. Where the shine in the eyes should be, that glimpse of the soul, it had been replaced by something ... *else.*

His lids didn't blink; his expression didn't change as he turned his head to face her.

'I can sense someone here,' he growled in a phlegmy, guttural tone. *'Someone dead ...'*

Kelly jerked into the back of the van, tried to shift into one of its darkened, jumbled corners. A mumble came from the rolled-up rug: Jamie began to murmur as she started to come round.

'I was wrong,' the killer snarled. *'Someone woke up.'*

Jamie stirred again, a muffled cough coming from the rug's innards.

'Just in time,' the killer laughed to himself. *'We're home now. Time for some real Christmas fun.'*

The van rattled from side to side as it went off-road, the rakes and spades hanging in the back clunking and clonking like a death rattle.

Kelly looked up through the van's front window, watched what was coming ahead, and vaporized back through the roof to Graveyard Billy as the van came to a stop. *'Bill, open your eyes!'* she said in a whisper, afraid the killer's hearing went from beyond the living to the dead. *'We're at his home!'*

CHAPTER FORTY THREE

The van drew to a stop; a crackle of stones and freshly laid snow popped beneath its tyres. Graveyard Billy opened his eyes, his small black body cold and covered with a pelt of snow. He went against his natural reaction to shake himself free of its chilled bite, of unwrapping himself from the roof rack as he stayed deathly silent. 'Where are we?' he asked.

'Somewhere on the outskirts of Brighton, by the looks of it; somewhere near Colddean,' Kelly replied, keeping down on the roof, still spooked from her encounter in the van with Issac's impish grinning face staring into hers.

The van's driver's side door opened; cat and ghost shuddered. They listened to his slow, methodical footsteps make their way around to the back of the van, each step taking a full, suspenseful second until the next footfall. His breathing was heavy and ragged, its hot stream visible over the lip of the van roof, moving steadily to the rear. A loud, metallic bang echoed out into the dark snowy night, a sound like snapping twigs made a satisfying pop; Issac was cracking his fingers and knuckles, readying himself to move the girl in the rug. The van's suspension whined as a weight was withdrawn from its back: He had lifted the rug-rolled girl out.

A muffled smothered moan escaped into the night, a sibilant, *'Shhhhhhhh,'* escaping Issac's lips. The van door clicked back into place as silently as possible, a sound that wouldn't bring attention from anyone.

A grunt came from below; swifter, heavier footsteps led away from the van. Graveyard Billy looked over the top of the van. Issac disappeared around the side of a red brick council house that held unknown horrors within, the rolled-up girl hanging over his right shoulder its newest addition.

As he melted into the shadows – merging with their blackness – Graveyard Billy stood up, shaking the cold wetness of the fallen snow from his body, his ears flapping with a rubbery sound. He looked up at the dark, old house before them that dripped with a dark menace. *'Come on,'* whispered Graveyard Billy. *'Let's follow him.'*

'Bill, be careful, Kelly said. 'I'm not sure, but I think ...' she stammered; fear on her ghostly face made her more transparent. 'I think he could sense me in the van.'

Graveyard Billy contemplated this, blinked at Kelly to show he understood.

Scanning the area below, Graveyard Billy leapt onto the garden's grass – not yet solid from the cold and snow. With timorous footsteps, he followed Issac's path to the back of the house, making sure to make no noise on the pebbles below his paws as he went. Kelly followed behind, unusually quiet as fear gagged her throat.

Under the lunar light of the silver-clouded full moon, they watched Issac jangle a set of keys from his pocket. Words slipped from his lips, in rhyme: *'The secret key – the secret key, for opening up that place for me ...'* He wasn't going to the house; he was opening the door of a small shack at the end of the garden. Silently, he stepped inside with the girl never leaving his shoulder, locked himself away from the outside world.

'What exactly is he doing?' Kelly asked, not really wanting to know the answer.

'I don't know,' Graveyard Billy growled. 'But whatever it is – it's not good.'

Graveyard Billy accelerated his steps in the overgrown back garden. Looping, thorned vines reached for him; long grass swayed as if ready to tangle around his legs.

With heart-stopping quickness, something terrible yanked from the darkness and lunged straight for them.

CHAPTER FORTY FOUR

Kelly gasped, almost fell over herself, and then leapt through the garden fence. Almost turning white with fright, Graveyard Billy jumped up onto the six-foot fence that separated this garden from the next. It was as if a slice of the night had come to life: teeth as pearlescent as the falling snow snapped in their direction; brown, beady eyes held pent-up rage.

'What the hell is that!' Kelly yelled, seeping through the fence Graveyard Billy perched fearfully on, pushing her face through its boards back to the other side so it looked like a perfect mask of her face hung freely on the fence. Their eyes adjusted to the gloom, ears understanding the snapping bark: a Doberman pulled into view.

The chain that held the dog in place rattled as it lunged for them again. *'Get out!'* it projected in their direction with a savage growl. 'Get out of here now, and if you think of setting foot in this garden again, I'll tear you to pieces!'

The dog began to bark again, a succession of low deep *'Woofs*!' to ward them off.

Kelly found her bravery again, leapt forward as she had when her and Graveyard Billy first met, screeching at the dog and expecting a timid response. Instead, the beast went berserk, snapping and snarling in her direction, it's spraying, rabid spittle flying through the air and mixing with the falling snow.

'You keep out of this, ghost,' the dog said, 'or I'll find a way to end you again ..., and if not, I'm sure my master will ...'

Kelly scrabbled back towards the fence, the dog's menacing demeanour a worry to her even in her undead state.

'Do you know what your so-called master has done? Did you see what he took in there?' Graveyard Billy hissed.

'I don't need to see, *cat* – I'm obedient; I listen to my master; I am man's best friend. Not like you, *cat*: selfish, ignorant, out for Number One,' the dog growled.

'Your master has a girl in there – he's the killer!' Kelly cried. 'He's the one responsible for all those girls going missing! He's the one that ...' Kelly gulped, the situation's reality always a bitter pill to swallow. 'He killed me,' she added dully.

'Nonsense,' the dog growled, his interest piqued by their words, not fully accepting what they said about the man who had him since a pup but questioning things that his master had done recently.

'Are you telling me you didn't pick up on any odd scents when he passed?' Graveyard Billy said passionately. 'You haven't noticed anything *funny* happening around here?'

The dog's barking stopped. He *had* noticed the oddness his master had displayed, had smelt and seen things that made no sense to him. A year ago, his master would never have chained him outside, would never have left him in the freezing winter snow. But now he did. And as for the scent … that odd, burning smell had appeared just as his master's new attitude had when he'd started to put the boot to him for no other reason than he could.

'We're going past,' Graveyard Billy said.

'Yeah!' Kelly added. 'Whether you like it or not!'

A dog was obedient and loyal to the detriment of its own well-being and self-preservation; his master was his master. As soon as Graveyard Billy wandered past the line of the six-foot fence, heading towards the oversized shack at the end of the garden, the dog began to bark and holler in its deep, fierce tone. 'Come here, you!' it called. 'Come *here* and leave him be. Lying to a dog about his master! A *cat* trying to convince me that *my* master would do wrong.'

'God, Bill,' Kelly said with a skewering look at the barking creature. 'You never told me dogs were so brainless.'

'It's just the way they are, loyal to their own fault. Trust me, some cats are that way – some humans are, too.'

They neared the shack, could see slashes of light trailing out of the gaps of the painted-black windows, illuminating the falling snow as they travelled through its small beams.

Graveyard Billy was one step away from jumping from the fence to the roof when the shed door flew open. A bright light broke in the darkness of night, an almost ethereal glow filling its frame from a source beyond. A figure pulled into view, stared into the back garden; Issac's face was a pure frustrated nightmare: eyes pulsating in his skull, sweat pouring down his head, lips quivering with subdued anger.

He stared at the dog, looked around the garden as Graveyard Billy froze less than five feet away from him, teetering on the fence. Kelly seeped back through the fence immediately, fearing his senses had been accurate in the van and could be again now.

'*What's making you cause all this noise?*' the possessed man growled, raising a bloodstained hammer in his hand. '*What seeeemsss to be the problem out here?*' he hissed.

CHAPTER FORTY FIVE

Graveyard Billy stayed as still as a statue, his yellow-ringed eyes burning with rage as he stared at Issac. The dog started to bark again, a rhythm of loud single '*Woofs*!' one after the other.

'Oh, Maxiiii,' Issac grinned, walking forward as stiffened as a puppet, for that was all he was now. '*Oh, Maxxxx!*' He gripped the hammer tighter as he stepped towards the barking dog.

'Stop!' Graveyard Billy projected at Max. 'For your own good – stop!'

'Oh no, I can't watch.' Kelly said, pulling her face back through the fence and scrunching her eyes shut.

'Behind you, master! Look! Look! Intruders!' The dog barked as the slow stomping figure of Issac shifted towards it, his feet crunching on the packed, fallen snow.

'*Why don't you ...*' Issac warned.

'Please!' Graveyard Billy pleaded. '*Stop! Stop! Stop! Stop!*'

'*Shut up!*' Issac said, bringing the hammer up over his head, his teeth bared in a more rabid expression than the barking dog could ever manage.

Max, the dog, whimpered, seeing that new look in his master's eye that replaced the love that used to be there. He hunkered down on the snowy ground and shuffled backwards as fast as he could, as far as the old, rusted chain around his neck would let him; understanding in that moment that his master was gone, that he should have stayed quiet, that trying to be man's best friend had turned into dog's worst nightmare.

'*Stay downnnn ...*' Issac hissed, the sound of the hammer shifting in his leathery hands, ready to –

'It's snowing!' A small voice came from behind the adjacent garden fence, a small, single eye staring out at Issac as he was about to bring down the fatal blow.

Issac's face flickered back to a more human expression, his demented grin pursing back to slackened lips. It was the little girl next door, who would always talk to him and peep through the knotted holes in the old panelled fence, but what was she doing outside so late?

'Hi!' Joanne, her mum, said, a bobble hat and eyes poking over the top of the fence. 'I just thought I'd show Steph the snow.'

'Yes,' the little girl added. 'I think it's going to be a white Christmas!'

Issac nodded, tried to pull a grin on his face that was now as slackened as a Halloween mask.

'What are you up to?' the girl's mother asked, seeing Max's fear-filled eyes staring up at her.

'I was ... just about to bring Max in. I left him out here ...

just in case anyone tried to break into my shed,' he said unconvincingly. 'It seems the padlock's rusted shut on his chain, and I need to break it off.'

'Oh – poor Max!' the woman said, making kissing noises in the dog's direction. 'Have you heard anything about break-ins, then?' Joanne asked.

Issac smashed the lock that held Max chained in place twice, splitting it with the second blow for effect, grabbing the chain that was attached to the dog's neck so he wouldn't escape.

'You can never be too careful,' Issac nodded. 'Especially with all my work in there.' He nodded back over to the shed.

He walked Max to the back door of the house, the dog cowering as he padded through the snow. *'Get in there and shut up,'* he growled, banishing the dog to the kitchen, his eyes shining with rage.

Shutting and locking the house's back door, his face reorganized to a more socially acceptable expression.

Joanne was still looking over the fence, her daughter pressed against the knot below. 'What are you up to in that shed on Christmas Eve?' she asked.

'Odd things,' Issac grinned. 'This and that, you know. Just fixing a few bits for work.'

Joanne nodded.

'Merry Christmas, Issac.' Steph grinned.

'Merry Christmas to the both of you.' He grinned back resentfully, walking to his shed, locking the door behind, neither of his neighbours noticing his fake grin drop to a stony grimace. Just as Issac hadn't noticed that Graveyard Billy had sneaked inside his shed, hiding between stacks of old newspapers, didn't know he and Kelly's eyes watched on as he pulled up the old wooden trap door at the shed's centre and descended down below.

CHAPTER FORTY SIX

The stench of turned, sodden earth clawed at Graveyard Billy's nostrils. It was a smell mixed with his extrasensory knowledge that some part of Piper – some part of Kelly – was below in the pit where Issac descended.

An idea chilled Graveyard Billy's body more than the snow outside had: Were their bodies being kept down below? No. Death lingered in abundance around Issac, but it wasn't that presence he could sense. Somewhere, the warm glow of life stirred.

Issac's heavy work boots stomped down the makeshift wooden stairs he had fitted to the dugout's subterranean level; a pale blue illumination stirred in the distance of its gloom.

'Bill, what are we going to do!' Kelly whispered.

'Anything we can to help that girl,' he replied, cocking his head to watch through the stack of papers as Issac disappeared from sight below.

'Be careful, Bill,' Kelly said with a shudder.

Graveyard Billy blinked at her, his face contorted with fear. With one paw in front of the other, he timorously padded forward, feeling the rough, unsanded wood of the stairs splinter under his footpads. That disgusting stink of smoke and burning seeped from the earth walls like sweat-dripping pores. The atmosphere below was like a thick, airless crypt, a moist chill emanating from the cold mud walls.

Kelly stayed close behind, a feeling in her chest of thudding tension where a fleshy beating heart should be. They moved forward into a sodden earthy tunnel. How had Issac managed all this? It was as if he had burrowed beneath his neighbour's gardens like some maggoty grub, boring a vast web of tunnels, his own subterranean lair – his own version of hell.

They could hear Issac move deeper down the long tunnel, following the ethereal blue haze that bounced off the wet, glistening walls. Kelly shook all over from the eeriness of it all. A wonder sparkled in her eyes as she stared at the wispy blue light.

What is that?' she whispered as they drew towards the end of the tunnel, a hollowed-out room appearing. They stayed in shadow beyond the doorway, stared as Issac's figure flickered back and forth past the light source, adjusting their eyes to understand what the glow was. What it was … *what it was …*

Graveyard Billy's eyes grew to the size of plates; Kelly's did the same.

A transparent, cylindrical tank, four feet high by three feet round, sat atop an old antique oak cabinet at the rear wall's centre. An electrical buzz came from it, wires from outside crudely used to create a surge of power around it with transformers plugged into the cylinder's base. Issac had created an arcing electrostatic force-field generator to somehow trap its contents inside, unable to escape, only able to curdle together as they swam in their own otherworldly light.

Graveyard Billy and Kelly understood what was in the tank; they knew what each rotating orb was: They could feel it in their bones. These were the living essences of souls – once-living human souls whose glow lured them closer with curiosity. Part of Piper was there – Graveyard Billy could feel it; Kelly could feel a missing part of herself in there, swimming like a vague reflection in a deep, supernatural ocean. They were all in there; everyone Issac had murdered; slithers of people's essences – of their souls stolen from life, refused death, being kept hostage by the thing that possessed Issac and used him as a puppet.

Before the cylinder of trapped souls stood a table base made of mounded earth, wood planks were nailed together as a top. Jamie lay on the crudely made table; the bloodied rug that had concealed her had been rolled up and placed under her head as a makeshift pillow. She stirred slightly, noises coming from her mouth that tried to twist into words.

That awful grin had slithered back on Issac's face as he stood to one side in dim shadow. He reached up and flicked a dense patch of spider webbing that hung overhead like an aura, arachnids jumping to attention at the thought of a feed. He was the spider; his subterranean lair a web; the blind girl caught in the stinking gloom just a fly.

He moved closer to the girl; she became more vigorous as she blurrily awoke.

'Quiet, little one,' he whispered, running a hand out to grab into her hair.

'Where am I …' she groggily cried, tears instantly forming in her eyes.

'That's not important,' he whispered. 'This is your home now; this is where you are going to stay.'

She tried to get up, but his clenched hand in her hair kept her firmly held down. She tried to fight free, but he gripped her hard around her neck. 'I need you,' he said, his grin growing wider. 'I can feed on your essence, feed on your fear. You'll be better than the others to make me whole again.'

He ran his fingers over her eyes, pressed down into her sockets slightly. 'What you can't see won't hurt you,' he grinned. 'Don't think of moving; I am everywhere; I am all around you. I'll always be watching you.'

Jamie curled up on the table, paranoid everything around her in the black world of blindness was stalking her.

'Goooodddd,' Issac whispered, holding a hand over her, feeling her fear radiate.

Graveyard Billy, eyes piercing like the ends sharpened knives, went to charge forward, his rage firing through his veins.

'*Bill, no ...*' Kelly whispered in terror.

Graveyard Bill stopped listening to his friend.

Issac turned to the blue-glowing cylinder of souls, pulled what looked like an old gas mask attached to it via a ribbed black pipe and strapped it on his head, making him look like a giant insect in the limited light. '*I've nearly drained these old souls,*' he said, his voice muffled under the mask. '*I need fresh fear to give me the life I need away from this flesh body I inhabit.*' Issac's hands touched his own body as if it were a suit of clothes he could take off.

A deep, disgusting huff came from the mask, the glow in the tank lessening with each pull of Issac's breath. Jamie jerked with each drag he took, growing smaller on the table, inverting within herself to escape the unknown, terrifying sound as Issac straightened up, becoming stronger.

'*I waited a long time in that graveyard, longer than I waited in the body that brought me here,*' he said. '*That Crowley didn't know what he was playing with when he started to dabble in black magic. Crowley looked into my world, and with his body ... I crossed into his world.*'

'What are you talking about?' Jamie sobbed.

'*I lived inside him for years, but because of who he was, what he was – the so-called "Beast" – I had to hide, had to behave, had to put off becoming solid in this realm of existence; had to put off becoming whole. I was trapped in his living body, then trapped in his dead carcass of flesh, trapped right up until they cremated him – right up until I could escape.*'

Issac raised his hands and looked at them as if they were just flesh-coloured gloves. '*I could never get that stink from the flames off me,*' he growled. '*It follows me everywhere I go...*'

He took a final huff, the light in the cylinder declining, the rotating orbs of life flailing like fish without water. He pulled off the gas mask, his features more shadowed as something beneath his skin stirred. '*I took what I could around Woodvale – a slither of soul, a quick drain of the odd ghost to keep me living, anything while I waited for the right body.*'

He caressed his own skin now as if it were velvet. '*Someone I could use with the know-how to help build this machine to keep vitality trapped; to keep the human essence caged, so I could drain it ... until I could get something fresher, straight from the source ...*'

He reached below the glowing tank into the shadows to retrieve something. '*Issac has such handy hands,*' he grinned. '*Handy hands for a handyman. This machine was my design, made with his know-how once I'd tapped into the brain department.*' Issac rolled his eyes upwards to stare into his own head.

His hands brought what was hidden up into the light: it

161

looked like a huge metal spider crafted with a chromed finish, its legs held at just the right circumference to grip the back of a neck, with long blades that looked like teeth embedded at its centre, its bulbous back a small tank to drain the life force from the living.

Kelly held her hand to her throat, ran her palm to the back of her neck: This was the thing she had sensed that had drained part of her living essence; it hadn't left her as a lost soul like the girl in Hove Cemetery because Isaac – her killer – had been interrupted.

Graveyard Billy understood that this was the thing that had left the markings on Piper's body, that had taken the part of her soul that he could sense swimming in the tank. His anger emanated, radiating; vengeance hissed out as he bared his fangs at the man and his diabolical machine.

'It always was a worry, getting what I needed without getting caught, getting the job done quick enough without being seen, but with you … I'll never be seen.' he grinned. *'You can be the fly, and I can drain you like a spider, bit by bit until I'm ready to walk alone… when I don't have to use this body …'*

Issac held back his head, his lips wrenching impossibly wide as a thick, bulbous lump pulled up from his throat and ejected from his mouth.

Something was growing in Issac, using his insides as its outside, it's colouring a cancerous black mixed with the red and pink of the man's organs. It was a malignant supernatural growth – a parasite – that had reconfigured Issac's innards into its own body with the stolen supernatural life force of the dead girls.

It moved up, spread out thin, wizened arms that ended with needle-sharp claws. It was the puppet master, and Issac was its puppet, using his organs as its own flesh like strings to control him. Blank white eyes opened in the organic mess that now towered three feet from the body it stretched from; a vile face formed that held the same disgusting grin as the man it had possessed. It manipulated Issac's hands, one grabbing Jamie's throat, the other bringing up the cold, metallic spider. *'No one's going to come for you; you can't escape— you're mine now … all mine … until the end.'*

Jamie fought back, tried to escape his grasp as he attempted to turn her over to sink the metal spider's blades into the back of her neck. If she had seen the awful nightmare creature that hovered, drooling, over her face, blindness might have seemed a privilege just to avoid its blank, soulless eyes.

Graveyard Billy had seen enough of this vile thing that couldn't be described – a creature that had no name –the thing that had ended his life with Piper, had ended Kelly's life with her family, just as it had ended the lives of all those innocent girls for its own selfish needs.

162

Unable to control the rage inside any longer, his tail swishing like a fuse burning to its end, Graveyard Billy leaned back and pounced up, all teeth and claws aimed at the disgusting, indescribable thing.

CHAPTER FORTY SEVEN

The creature arced back in surprise as a slice of shadow with glowing yellowed eyes flew towards it. Graveyard Billy pounced with that old jungle ferocity, with that ancient predatory instinct to kill. He moved through the air with speed and no regard for his own safety, just the single-minded attitude that he must stop this abomination, protecting Jamie as if she were his human now. In a way, he had chosen her – she would be the one that lived! With a great precise swipe – without holding back – his right paw snagged into the creature's pale left eye and tore its milky retina as smoothly as a knife through cloth.

Kelly stayed transfixed in terror, watching as the creature's eyeball burst in a vile rush of yellow goo.

Issac's hands dropped the metallic spider to the earthen floor with a dull clump as the creature's fanged mouth wailed all the way back to the bowels of hell.

Jamie flinched, put her hands over her face to protect her from the unseen melee erupting above. Graveyard Billy held onto the creature's malformed head and then spun round to the back of its cranium, sinking his fangs and claws into its tender flesh.

The creature screamed twice as loud now, a riveting high-pitched cry that could burst eardrums. Issac's hands reached up at the creature's commands, tried to unseat Graveyard Billy as he clung to the creature for all he was worth, kicking with his back legs so bloody divots were racked into its flesh.

'Noooooooooooooo!' Issac's voice cried as he fell backwards into the crudely wired cylinder that held the collection of severed souls. Sparks erupted. A vibrating hum of electricity shot through Issac's body, arched through the awful parasite, and surged into Graveyard Billy, sending his tail as straight as an antenna.

'Bill!' Kelly cried as the cat leapt through the air, tumbling roughly to the ground at the room's far corner. Issac couldn't catch his balance, the weight of the disgusting parasite tipping him over, bringing down the cylinder with a giant burst of sparks and ethereal light.

Even Jamie sensed the blistering light: She flinched with its eruption across the subterranean room as the contents of the cylinder exploded out. Glowing orbs – the same types of orbs as those of the spirits of the menagerie of animals in Aunt Coral's house –flew about, circulated around one another, trying to make their escape.

'What have you done!' the creature in Issac screamed, pulling forward and splitting the sides of Issac's mouth wider. 'What have you donnneeee!'

'Bill! He's coming ba –' One of the glowing orbs streaked through the air and hit Kelly square in the chest, stopping her words mid-flow. Her eyes widened as if she had just swallowed a golf ball whole. She grabbed her throat, grabbed her chest, as suddenly … *as suddenly*, that part of her essence, that missing piece of her soul taken by the creature to keep her trapped firmly away from the afterlife, was reattached.

Her wispy pale aura grew into a blazing blue flame; the supernatural tendrils that had kept her attached to Graveyard Billy withered away to nothing: She was whole again.

The creature suddenly sensed her, squinted through its one good eye to focus on the spot where she was standing. *'Youuuuu …'* it growled.

Seeing its distraction, Graveyard Billy went in for a second try, grabbing onto the creature's face and pushing it straight back to the floor with all his weight.

'Go on, Bill!' Kelly yelled with her new vitality. 'Give that thing what fo –'

Jamie jerked upright, staring in Kelly's direction. 'Who's there? *Help me*!' she cried.

'Oh my God! She can see me!' Kelly cried.

'I'm blind, you idiot!' Jamie yelled.

'Oh my God! She can hear me!' Kelly cried, trying again.

'Get her out of here!' Graveyard Billy said, rolling around on the floor with the disgusting creature as if engaged in a schoolyard tussle.

'Come with me, this way – quickly!' Kelly shouted to Jamie. The blind girl held out her hand. Kelly tried to reach for it; her touch passed straight through it. 'Damn it!' Kelly growled.

'What?' Jamie said, reaching off the table and falling to the ground. 'Help me out of here!'

'I don't think that's going to work!' Kelly fretted. 'Follow my voice!'

Jamie did just that, staggering to her feet and feeling her way down the earth-walled corridors.

'Keep coming!' Kelly encouraged, walking backwards, trying to keep an eye on Graveyard Billy and the creature. She led Jamie to the steps. 'Stop!' Kelly cried. 'There are steps in front of you!'

'Help me up them!' Jamie yelled back.

'I can't!' Kelly shouted.

'Why? Are you disabled, too?' Jamie asked, panicked.

'Yeah, you could say that.' Kelly said, looking back as Graveyard Billy leapt from the creature to the table in the middle of the room, hissing and spitting as the creature started to run after the girl.

'No! She's mine – mine!' it growled.

Graveyard Billy leapt up, embedding himself into its face, trying to take out its one good eye, instantly stopping it dead in its tracks as it fought to free itself of him.

Kelly thought fast. 'Hold onto the rail to your left!'

Jamie reached for the rail on her left.

Quickly, Kelly counted the steps. 'Fourteen steps straight up, *GO!*'

Jamie counted them, whispering each number over to herself as she made it to the top of the stairs. Kelly shifted up after her. The glowing orbs darted around them as if sensing a means of escape.

'Now where!' Jamie gasped, stopping at the top, now standing inside the shed.

'Turn left, hands out and walk forward; there's a door!'

Jamie threw herself into the door, instinctively reaching around the frame and finding the two deadbolts and undoing them.

She stepped outside and stopped, feeling relief at the cold snow falling into her face. The supernatural orbs swarmed around her and Kelly, then flew out into the night air, ready to reconnect with the bodies they had been ripped from.

'Just keep walking straight forward! There's a house ahead, get inside, and we can find the phone.' Kelly said.

Jamie slowly stepped forward, feeling the freezing snow creak under her feet.

'Quickly, now, go on!' Kelly ordered, hearing the fight below, knowing that Graveyard Billy was still in danger.

Jamie staggered forward, hands outstretched, stumbling through the overgrown garden. Brambles and thorns sliced through her jeans, but she never stopped until she reached what the mystery voice had told her was there: the red bricks of the old council house.

'Move to your right; there's a back door there!' Kelly said.

Jamie did this immediately, throwing the door open and stumbling in, falling to the floor on her hands and knees, then stopping dead in her tracks, wrapped in fear. The loud yapping jaws of Max snapped towards Jamie as the Doberman lunged for her face.

CHAPTER FORTY EIGHT

'No!' Kelly shouted as Max stared up at her with intense eyes.

'So, the ghost has brought another intruder into my house,' the dog growled.

Jamie paused, feeling the hot breath of the Doberman, fear solidifying her body.

'No, Max,' Kelly said calmly. 'Leave her alone.'

'Leave her alone – *leave her alone!*' he barked. 'First, you try to break into my master's shed, and *now* you break into my master's house!'

'I'm trying to save her from your master, *you idiot!*' Kelly shouted at the animal.

'Wh– why are you talking to the dog like that?' Jamie said.

'*Shut up!*' barked Max.

'Look at her, Max, just look at her,' Kelly said. Max adjusted his gaze, stared down at the girl before him on the kitchen floor. He could see the bleeding blow the hammer had inflicted on Jamie; he knew it was from the same hammer his master had menaced him with.

'She was ... breaking in ...' Max barked limply.

'No ... he took her down there, wrapped in that rug, you dummy! Don't you realize? There's something wrong with your master!'

Max knew, all right, but had lied to himself out of loyalty. He backed up, a sad look on his face. 'But why ...' he whined. 'Why did he hurt this girl ...'

'There's something in him ... *something* ... making him do things.' Kelly replied.

In Max's mind, that made sense: His master had been anything but himself for quite some time.

'We're going into the living room, Max. Please don't hurt the girl.'

A solitary tear rolled down Jamie's face, splashed on the filthy linoleum.

Terrible guilt made Max shudder; he curled his head between his legs.

'Go on ...' he said, ashamed at himself. 'Help her.'

'Thank you,' Kelly said. 'Come on, it's safe, get up; there are doors behind you to the right.'

Worriedly, Jamie got up, scrambled against the sideboard, and knocked over filth-encrusted pots and pans as she did; feeling along the wall to the door, she fell into the adjacent room. Kelly quickly followed, keeping an eye on Max.

Jamie stayed still, frozen to the spot, as Kelly looked around the room into its darkness, trying to find the telephone. It was a ramshackle mess: Papers and plates and piles of empty packets lay everywhere. The TV held a constantly flickering blue screen; a record player turned, its needle picking up snapping crackles, and in the corner – Kelly gasped, looking at a chair in front of the main window, seeing an outline in it. 'There's someone else in this room!' she cried.

The last spectral orbs found their way out of the dank subterranean corridors, shifting up and into the night. Graveyard Billy tore into the foul creature – Issac's limp and lifeless body now hanging from its bottom half – then leapt back onto the wooden table in the room's centre, breathing heavily with exhaustion.

'*Why are you here, cat?*' the creature sneered. '*What business is this of yours?*'

Graveyard Billy owed this thing no response; he just let out the fiercest guttural howl he could muster, leaping up and going in for the kill once more.

A low, muffled cry came from the chair in the living room, the figure in it bobbing up and down, trying to catch their attention.

'*Hmufff ... Jammieee ...*' it coughed. '*Jammieeee!*'

The blind girl gasped, ran towards the noise. 'Mo! Moooo!' she cried.

'What – you know him!' Kelly yelled.

'*Yesss!*' the bound man cried as Jamie fell to her knees before him, pulling the gag from his mouth.

'It's Mo Shaan; he runs the local shop next to my flat!' Jamie cried. She felt his face, felt the bump on his head that throbbed like her own.

'What are you doing here!' Mo cried.

'There was someone ... he brought me here ....' She stumbled on her words, not knowing what to say, none of what had happened to her making any sense.

'Untie me quickly, before that nutter comes back!' Mo said as Jamie reached for the thin, knotted rope that connected his ankles and wrists to the old wooden chair.

'How did you escape?' he asked as he jumped up and grabbed Jamie by the wrist.

'The girl with me, she helped me escape!' Jamie said.

'What girl?' Mo replied, staring at the spot where Jamie *knew* Kelly was standing.

'The girl behind me, she helped me!'

'There's no one there!' he yelled, grabbing Jamie's wrist.

'He can't see me,' Kelly said quietly, an expression dawning on Jamie's face that said she might understand what Kelly's disability was.

'But –' was all she could say as Mo grabbed her by the hand and ran for the door. 'Come on," Mo urged. Let's get help!'

'Go with him! I need to go back and help Graveyard Billy!' Kelly yelled after the girl as Jamie stared back over her shoulder, disappearing with Mo into the snowy darkness of the night. 'You'll be safe!'

In that moment of panic, Kelly realized that she had said Graveyard Billy's name in full for the first time in all their friendship. *'Oh, Billy,'* she whispered.

Max breathed heavily in the darkness of the kitchen, his mind rushing with the revelation of how blind and foolish he had been. *'No one makes a fool of me … no one …'* he snorted. *'No one!'*

A loud, piercing cat cry came from the shed. Max's ears pricked to the sound. *'Master!'* he barked, taking off out the open back door, his teeth bared. *'Masterrrrrrr!'*

CHAPTER FORTY NINE

Max barrelled through the snowy back garden, into the shed and down into the depths of the earthy tunnels beneath the ground; bolted to where he could hear the fight in progress.

'Master! *Master!*' he barked, distracting Graveyard Billy, giving the parasite's needle-tipped fingers a chance to tear through the black fur on the side of his stomach.

Graveyard Billy screamed, feeling warm blood nest in his coat. He limped back to a shadowed corner of the room in retreat, Max barking in his face. 'What are you doing to my master, *cat*? What are you ...'

'*Look at him!*' Graveyard Billy cried.

Max cast a glance to where Issac – his master – stood, but in his master's place, *it* stood.

Max could see his master's body hanging down, blue and asphyxiated, the thing from inside spending too much time outside, suffocating the host it had nested in.

'*What are you looking at, Max,*' the elongated one-eyed monster said, blood pouring down its pulpy skin, its spindled arms reaching out to either side. '*Get the cat!*'

Max cocked his head in shock. He had tried to fool himself, tried to tell himself the ghost was wrong that his master was a good man who had always treated him with kindness with respect ... but that wasn't true. What the ghost had said *was* true: Something was indeed living inside his master, something that had made him do all those cruel acts ... this *thing* ... he looked down to Issac's slumped body. He knew his master was dead.

Max began to growl.

'*You stupid mutt! You poxy four-legged thing! The cat, not me! I am your master!*'

'No ... you're not ...' Max growled.

Another sound came from behind them, a heavy, stalking padding sound that made everyone turn and look.

Another cat's growl echoed in the underground tunnels.

'Black Barry!' a voice laughed as the figure of a Turkish Van emerged from the shadows to stand inside the room. 'I thought I'd better keep my senses keen, lad.' a voice Graveyard Billy knew said.

Mr. Ruffles stepped closer and blinked at him. 'I had a feeling you were up to something when you left, that you might need my help. That it might be time to repay that favour ... somehow.'

'Yes! *Yes!*' Graveyard Billy cried, limping towards him.

'What did that to you? The dog?' Mr. Ruffles queried, glaring at Max.

'No ... *that* ...' Graveyard Billy said, turning to the parasitic creature that loomed at the rear of the room.

'*What are you animals doing?*' it spat.

'So this is what you've been doing,' Mr, Ruffles said, unphased. 'Fighting with beasties.'

The one-eyed creature hissed at the animals before it, bared its jagged teeth.

'Not very advanced, is it … it can't even understand us,' Mr. Ruffles said.

'It used this dog, Max's, owner to grow inside him, to try and become solid in form like a human,' Graveyard Billy explained.

'Like a human,' Mr. Ruffles said. 'Oh, dear – you know how I feel about them – *BOYS!*' he cried, and just like that, all the cats from the rescue centre poured down the stairs. The hissing, mewing mob stared at the creature – the parasite – and formed a living barrier to keep it cornered into the dark dirt room.

'That thing has been killing other humans. It killed my owner and my friend – the ghost who travels with me.'

'Is that so,' Mr. Ruffles hissed.

Kelly moved down the stairs, slowed up in awe at the standoff between all the animals that had suddenly appeared from thin air and the hideous creature in the corner. 'Bill, what's happening?'

'No worries, ghostie, I owe old Graveyard Billy a debt … I sensed he might need it … I think I was right, a' boys.'

The other cats all hissed and screamed, moving one step closer towards the backing-away creature.

'*Keep away, keep away!*' the creature gasped.

Max began growling, pure anger streaming from his eyes.

The Turkish Van purred, 'So … this thing doesn't like humans, doesn't like cats, and it doesn't like dogs … it seems to have done wrong by all of them. I think for once we all have a mutual enemy, hmmmm?'

The cats all hissed and moaned again.

Graveyard Billy began to cough, the pain of the creature's scratches making him feel woozy.

'Bill, mate! What's wrong!' Kelly exclaimed.

'Nothing too bad,' he winced. 'He got me with those claws.'

'You've done your bit here, Graveyard Billy,' the Turkish Van said. 'You and the ghost go upstairs. I'm sure me, Max, and the boys can finish this.'

'You killed my master,' Max growled. '*You killed him!*'

The other cats formed two lines, making a path for Graveyard Billy to limp through and make his way up the stairs to the cold night air.

'It's all right,' Mr. Ruffles said to Kelly. 'Go and see your mate.'

She backed away, nodding, sensing the menace emanating from the grinning cat, and followed Graveyard Billy.

Mr. Ruffles looked at Max. 'I think you should be the one to start this, seeing as that's your master; he did that too.' The Turkish Van blinked towards Issac's limp body.

Max looked at the creature, his brown eyes red and burning like coal.

'*Maxxxxxx, it's me, it's –*' the creature said.

With a primal howl, and Max leapt leap across the room, locked his snarling teeth onto the parasite's bulbous throat, ripping it free of Issac's carcass as the other cats all piled forward, a single cry of *'Get him!'* hissing from their lips.

CHAPTER FIFTY

A scrabbling, barking, meowing melee came from inside the shed's underground lair. Graveyard Billy sat by the back of the house, licking his wounds and letting the cold, snowy ground soothe him.

Kelly, too fearful to see what has happening below, knelt to Graveyard Billy. 'You all right, mate?' she said.

'Yeah, I'm okay. I think it looks worse than it is.'

Kelly tried to look under his fur at the red gashes, but being unable to actually touch anything, she found the task near impossible.

A loud snarling cry came from below.

'Do you think they can handle that thing?' Kelly wondered.

'I –' before Graveyard Billy could finish, Max ran up the stairs and into the back yard, the disgusting, limp creature trailing from his mouth. He dropped it in the centre of the garden, a pool of red instantly drawing into the snow.

The cats all came up the stairs behind him, Mr. Ruffles at the head of the pack.

'You killed him! You killed my master!' Max growled, shaking the creature by the fat that hung from its head where a neck should be. It was a long, bloody wreck, like an elongated tapeworm that had fused with Issac's innards as if they were it's own.

'Come and see, you two,' Mr Ruffles called. 'Come and see the thing that has caused so much havoc and commotion.'

Graveyard Billy hissed in the dying creature's direction, his eyes blazing with anger into the creature's still-twinkling eye. Its spindled arms were gone now – chewed away, its body a meaty, bleeding lump.

'Come on, Graveyard Billy,' Mr. Ruffles said. 'Come and celebrate the creature's death ... come celebrate in the great feast.'

'*The what!*' Kelly gasped, too terrified to go near the awful thing even in its subjugation.

'My pack and I were locked up for a long time ...' Mr. Ruffles smiled,'... and we're hungry ...'

'You must be kidding,' Kelly gasped, her face stuck in perpetual shock.

'Come on, dog,' Mr Ruffles said. 'I can see by those ribs your master neglected to feed you because of this ... *thing.*'

'It's true,' Max growled, never taking his eyes from the creature.

'For one night, we shall dine together in victory!' Mr, Ruffles howled.

Max curled his black lips, gave the cat a smile of white salivating fangs.

The mauled creature on the snow looked up through its one good eye, welling tears of fright swelling in its socket.

'Not such a big scary monster now, are you,' chuckled the Turkish Van. 'Is that what you've been doing? Trying to become human, trying to put meat on your bones inside this lad's master?'

Mr. Ruffles nodded at Max as snarls of drool poured from the dog's mouth.

'I don't like humans,' Mr. Ruffles grinned with a smile that would make the Cheshire Cat from *Alice in Wonderland* pale. 'And I really don't like imposters who want to be human.'

More of the cats began to crowd around now, looming down like carrion birds. A chant began from their hissing lips: *'Bite the hand that feeds us! Bite the hand that feeds us! Bite the hand that feeds us!'*

'Care to join us, Graveyard Billy?' Mr. Ruffles laughed. 'You look a bit hungry yourself, lad.'

'No ...' said Graveyard Billy backing away from the pack.

'I guess our debt has been paid to you,' Mr. Ruffles said. 'An eye for an eye ...' he said with a gleaming look to the quivering creature at their feet.

'Bite the hand that feeds us! Bite the hand that feeds us!

'... A tooth for a tooth...'

The revolting, meaty creature tried to make a final, dying lunge for freedom, squealing as it tried to escape. It didn't have a chance as the other animals pounced. Meaty, ripping sounds quickly tore out.

Graveyard Billy turned, walking to the front of the house as Kelly held her hands over her face and did the same.

'It's over,' Graveyard Billy said to Kelly, closing his eyes and thinking of Piper as the creature's final cry ended as the cats went in, as Max went in, as slobbery meaty strips were torn from the creature. As the killer – the supernatural creature – became nothing more than a meal for the strays.

Graveyard Billy glanced back to see Mr. Ruffles bloodstained mouth before the Turkish Van disappeared from sight. The big cat winked and said, 'I'll see you around, Graveyard Billy,' then laughed and feasted with the others until the creature was nothing more than a big red stain in the falling Christmas snow.

The small black kitten, the youngest of Mr. Ruffles' followers, ran into the bushes with the creature's one good eye it had plucked, chanting muffled peeps of, *'Bite the hand that feeds you! Bite the hand that feeds you!'* as it went.

CHAPTER FIFTY ONE

It was over. Christmas Eve turned to Christmas Day, the black of night was burned away with the rise of the sun at dawn, and Brighton's landscape was sheeted white with snow.

Graveyard Billy's wounds were superficial but ugly; the scratches from the creature would no doubt permanently scar his side. After leaving Max and Mr. Ruffles and the other strays to do the deed, he and Kelly had found the back of a restaurant where scraps of pre-Christmas dinners had been thrown away: Graveyard Bill ate turkey, chicken, pork, and all the trimmings from the insides of a bin. 'After everything you did tonight, you should be eating from a silver plate,' Kelly told him.

They walked aimlessly the following Christmas morning. Kelly's glow was a vibrant spectrum of supernatural blues now she was whole, finally reunited with that part of her essence stolen by the parasite that had possessed Issac.

Graveyard Billy asked her what happened with the blind girl – Jamie – after she escaped. Kelly told him of the man they'd found tied up inside Issac's house.

'He should be glad he wasn't tied up in Aunt Coral's house,' Graveyard Billy said. 'He could have ended up with his bum stuffed with sawdust.'

They both laughed at that; the first time in a while, either had done so.

'How come the blind girl could sense me, Bill?' she asked.

'Maybe it's the same reason some people see ghosts when their emotions are at their peak. Think of how scared she must have been in that place with Issac. Her senses must have been running wild: It's the only reason I can think of.'

They watched cheery people move about the streets, arms loaded with presents.

'Merry Christmas!' they would say to one another, December twenty-fifth the only day that talking to strangers was socially acceptable.

Graveyard Billy asked Kelly what the creature had meant, who exactly the Crowley was it spoke of. She told him, trying to patch everything together verbally, so the story of a parasitic soul-sucking demon that floated around Woodvale Cemetery made sense. Why wouldn't it make sense? Over the past few weeks, Kelly had realized animals transmit, had found out firsthand that ghosts walk the Earth: This was just another addition to these oddities the human eye didn't see, that human instinct didn't pick up on.

The day slipped by as they talked idly. The sun warmed the winter cold, twinkling on the snow-white ground as they wandered towards Dawlish Close.

'Bill,' Kelly asked with suspicious eyes, 'where are we

175

going?'

He stayed silent for a moment, then spoke: 'It's Christmas; everyone should be with their family on Christmas.'

'Bill, I don't think there's any chance you're getting in my house again.'

'You don't need me for that anymore,' he said with a blink.

'Of course, I d–' She had forgotten what had happened in the underground lair, that when she was made whole, the otherworldly bond between her and Graveyard Billy had broken.

'Yeah, but I can't leave you, Bill! You're my ... You're *my* cat,' she said sadly.

A winter wind caught Graveyard Billy's black fur. 'You know, cats pick their people – people don't pick their cats.'

Sadness set into Kelly's face; a deep hurt was visible in her eyes.

'Even though you attached yourself to me ... I would have picked you, you know,' he smiled. 'I did want you as my human.' He blinked a soft, warm blink.

A smile spread across Kelly's face that could have melted the cold winter snow. 'I love you, Bill,' she said. 'I can't leave you alone out here.'

He blinked softly again. 'You're not,' he replied. 'When we released those pieces of trapped souls, I suddenly knew where she was – where I have to go.'

'She?' Kelly asked.

'Piper,' he said, his tail swishing back and forth with the thought of seeing her again.

'How, but ...' Kelly stuttered. 'You didn't tell me!'

'I'm telling you now.'

'You just can't leave me!' she said.

'I'm not,' he replied. 'I'm putting the last bits right that that creature put wrong. Just like you can use the love of your family to pass over to the other side, Piper has to use mine.'

Kelly thought about this, her cul-de-sac coming into view ahead. 'Where is she?' she asked.

'South,' he said. 'Somewhere near the sea.'

'But how are you going to get there?' Kelly cried. 'There's roads, there's cars: all kinds of nutters about, and don't we know it!'

'It's Christmas Day; there's no one about!' he replied.

'Let's go together!' she said. 'We're a team!'

Suddenly, an old Ford Escort pulled around the corner, Uncle Frank the Crank behind the wheel, the car's back seats filled with presents. *'Oh-my-God!'* Kelly exclaimed, 'They've let Uncle Frank round on Christmas Day! He must have spent some money on those kids for Dad to let him in the house; that bloke has some serious making up to do!'

'Kelly,' Graveyard Billy said, 'You belong here.'

176

She sighed, then nodded in agreement.

'And I have to do this alone,' he said.

The smile from seeing her Uncle Frank faded, a knowing in her that he was right.

Graveyard Billy transmitted to Kelly with a smile in his voice, 'You know, when you pass, you can finally get rid of that outfit.'

Kelly had all but forgotten about the Tina Turner getup, the sparkling dress, the enlarged wig. 'We were having such a nice moment, and you have to remind me of that!' she grinned.

'You have to promise me something, Bill,' she said as they neared the front of the house, watching as Uncle Frank, laden with presents, was welcomed in. 'If something goes wrong, if you need help, I'm going to be here waiting for you. I'm not leaving this world until I know you're sorted. That whatever you need to do for Piper is done and … well … you're happy.'

'If I need you, I promise I'll be back,' he replied.

They held a gaze at one another, ghost and cat staring deeply into one another's eyes.

'I never had a pet, but I would be proud to be your owner,' she said with tears in her eyes.

'I think, for a little while – you were,' Graveyard Billy blinked.

Kelly put a hand to her face, wiped away the beginnings of ectoplasmic tears.

'I need to go before it gets dark,' Graveyard Billy said.

'I'm not going anywhere until I know you're happy. I'm going to be around,' she said.

'And If you need me – I'll be around too,' said Graveyard Billy

'This has been –' she sobbed, tried to hold it in, '– it's been something special.'

'It has,' he replied simply, sadness filling his yellow eyes.

Kelly walked away towards her house, sighing deeply. She turned before she vaporized through her living room wall and said. 'I think you're someone very special, Graveyard Billy.'

He blinked.

'You finally said my name,' he projected, watching her turn from him and return to her family, to the place she belonged, knowing in his heart that their adventure was over.

CHAPTER FIFTY TWO

The snow stayed settled; bursts of sun were unable to penetrate the bitter chill that had grasped Brighton. Graveyard Billy made his way down towards Kemptown: Strings of multi-coloured lights lead him to the coast; windows filled with twinkling Christmas trees the only consistency from house to house. Drunks with loud, cheery voices made him cower beneath bushes in front gardens. As he reached the promenade, he saw a few families wrapped in thick winter clothing, walking off their Christmas dinners.

He could sense Piper's presence down near the crashing of the waves. He was at the sea. It was a sight he had never seen before; the vast awesomeness of its unknown depths bristled his black fur.

She was here, somewhere close to the sea. Trotting along next to the green-painted railings, following their length along the pebbled beach, a jolt of knowing hit Graveyard Billy harder than the cold, gusting wind. It stopped him dead in his tracks: It was here where could sense her.

He looked up at the illuminated symbols that Kelly could have read, but he could not – 'BRIGHTON PIER.'

This was where she was; this is where he had to go.

The pier was shut: Huge black gates met in the middle, conjoined with a lock. For humans, there was no entry, but for a cat, slipping between the gate's bars was no problem.

He moved quickly to the pier's end, knowing he was somewhere he shouldn't be. Teddy bears hung from hooks with dead eyes at the window of the amusement arcade; Zoltar, the Fortune-Telling Machine, was unplugged, unable to predict anything without the aid of electricity. The funfair towards the pier's end sat silent, the only cries from the roller coaster being the whistle of wind through its still tracks.

Suddenly, Graveyard Billy had run out of places to go. The black railings that stopped people from falling in the sea on either side now boxed off. He was at the end of the pier, nothing in front of him but rolling waves and the cloud-muted sun as it began its afternoon cycle to dip into darkness.

He lay belly-down on the pier's cold wooden slates, paws stretched out before him and closed his eyes. *Where are you? Where are you? Where are you?*

Something stirred beneath the water under the pier, something that made his eyes pop open. He looked below through the wooden boards, one wide, perplexed eye staring down at the shimmering waves, seeing beneath them as a crackling, sparking electrical storm brewed in the current. Ethereal light forked under the pier; teleplasmic tendrils of spectral life reached from the sea like the tentacles of some great, supernatural sea-beast. They shot up, seeping through the gaps in the boards, and made a cage of shifting light around Graveyard Billy.

Fear gripped him, the shock of what was happening making him cower, his head flicking from side to side as the tendrils reached out and snaked around him, connecting him to an otherworldly power, reuniting him with …

'Graveyard Billy,' a warm voice said, making him jerk upright, embracing the ectoplasmic tendrils that curled around his body.

He looked around, senses going into overload, knowing, understanding that his instincts were correct that – 'Behind you,' she laughed. – Piper was here.

He slowly turned around, and there she stood, exactly how he remembered her, exactly how she was, complete with her old black paint-speckled hoody, her old greyed skinny jeans, and that wonderfully messy blonde hair tied up on her head.

He stayed still, staring at this vision of the person he'd picked. Here she was, his Piper, *his* Piper!

'That's the quietest I've ever heard you!' she smiled.

'Piper … I've missed you *so* much …' was all he could manage.

She opened her eyes as wide as his at the surprise of hearing his projected voice. His voice was exactly how she could have imagined it: warm, just like running a hand through his thick black fur. 'And I've missed you, my Graveyard Billy.' She smiled, tears welling in her eyes.

'I got him Piper, the man – the thing that got you. Me and a girl named Kelly, she was a ghost too – I think you would like her – and the biggest Turkish Van cat you've ever seen, and a dog named Max –'

Piper laughed at his eagerness to tell his story.

'– and we all did it together. Oh, and we saved a girl who that awful thing was going to try and do awful things to –'

'I know!' she said, trying to wipe her eyes with her wispy hands. 'I was there in that underground catacomb that Issac made. I saw some of what was happening before rejoining with my life force, and I became whole here again.'

'But,' Graveyard Billy said with a frown, 'why are you here? Why couldn't we find you in any of the graveyards? I don't understand?'

'When I was at uni a few months ago, me and my friends thought it would be funny to make out our wills – what we would want to happen to us if we died. I didn't think I would need it that soon,' she shrugged. 'I wrote I wanted to be cremated and my ashes scattered here … Brighton pier.' She held her hands out as if to introduce the place. 'I didn't think they would actually do it, but they did.' She shrugged again.

'That's why we couldn't find you.' Graveyard Billy said, understanding why their search had been futile.

'Do you remember your dream?' she asked.

'Dream?' Graveyard Billy asked with puzzlement.

'When you were hit by the car when you were unconscious? There was moment when you almost passed, a moment when you touched death – that's what the dream was. You were here with me; that's why you could sense the part of me that Issac had held in that cylinder. It was an instinct from the dream that echoed back into life, a connection that was somehow made to a part of me. Then, when that part was finally reconnected with my life force, you were able to sense where I was – that's why you were able to resurrect me here.'

Graveyard Billy walked towards her. Piper kneeled to touch him. Her hand passed through him, but the vitality of her soul made him purr in a way he hadn't since her death.

'I've missed you, my Graveyard Billy,' she said.

'You'll never know how much I missed you,' he said. 'You'll never know.'

They stayed like that for almost an hour: Piper sitting on the pier's boards, running her vaporous hands over Graveyard Billy's body, never really touching, but connecting them in the comfort of one another, watching as the sun slowly dipped to the west.

With everything that had been happening, Graveyard Billy hadn't really thought about Christmas, but in a way, he had received the one gift he had always wanted: the human he picked as his own, back together with him.

'What are we going to do now?' Graveyard Billy asked.

'We're going to have one last day together,' she grinned, a slight sadness in her eyes. 'Then you have one final thing to do.'

CHAPTER FIFTY THREE

Graveyard Billy didn't want it to end. They walked slowly around the deserted lanes near the seafront of Brighton, side-by-side, together, just like they used to, just as how they should, always, as darkness infected the sky.

Twinkling lights were strung from buildings; they fought the oncoming gloom of night. The streets in town were snow-free now, salt gritters spraying the settled coldness away.

They walked past a newsagent – the only shop that was open – and the sign outside held a headline that caught Piper's eye. She read it out loud: '"Brighton Killer Finally Revealed." They should have your picture in the paper, Graveyard Billy,'

They looked through the window at the racks of daily rags, all of them featuring Issac's face.

'Do you think he knew what he was doing?' Piper asked. 'Do you think he knew that thing was inside him?'

'I don't think so,' Graveyard Billy said. 'But the only thing that front cover's good for is lining a litter tray.'

Piper burst out laughing, and a warm rush of happiness pushed through his small, furry body. He kept looking up at Piper's face, an uncontrollable purr erupting from within him with each glance. She was back, his Piper, his human.

Everything that had led him to this point he had forgotten: the aching slash marks in his side, the malformed face of the awful parasitic creature; all just distant slices of the past. All that was important was now was that she was here.

They ran together in the Royal Pavilion Gardens, playing a game of hide and seek, Piper laughing as he bolted like a black steak of night. She pounced upon him as he hid in a thicket of bushes, unable to escape too far, as they were now connected by the same supernatural teleplasm as he had been to Kelly.

Graveyard Billy led Piper to the pungent bins Kelly had taken him to the night before, showing off his foraging skills to her. 'I've got used to being out here on my own,' he bragged from the inside of a bin. 'I've had to learn how to be independent, stand on my own four paws.' He emerged from the lid of the old bin with the meaty remnants of a roast dinner, gravy soiling the black fur around his mouth.

'You shouldn't have to be living like this,' Piper said sadly. 'This isn't right.'

'But its fine, now,' he said, biting into an already chewed piece of turkey. 'You're back, and we have each other.'

'But it's not fine,' she sighed. 'If anything happens to you, what good can I do?'

'It's okay; I really can look after myself. I've learnt a lot being on the streets, fending for myself.' He chewed back the mouthful of food, his eyes never leaving hers. 'I was thinking, maybe we could go back to Woodvale. I mean, it's not going to be the same because someone's living in the flat and, well, it's not going to be very warm – for me at least – but you will be fine, you ...'

'Graveyard Billy,' she said with authority, 'There's something we need to remember: You are very much alive and I ... well. I'm very much not.'

'Well ...' he bumbled. 'What does that mean?'

'It means you have to keep on living, and I ... have to move on.'

Graveyard Billy jerked upright, instant worry projecting from his eyes. 'But ... you've only just come back! I've only just found you, and –'

'And you deserve better than a life on the street, hanging around with me.'

'No, that's not true.'

'It is true. You are a very special cat, and I think –' hurt shimmered in her eyes, a reluctance to say the words she had to. 'I think you need someone to show you the love you deserve.'

But you do!' he cried, panicked. 'You are everything I wanted and needed. You're the reason I kept on going until the end, you –'

'Are dead,' she said dully. 'I'm dead, and I'm never going to come back.'

'But you are back; you're here now!' he said, trying with all he had to convince her.

'I'm not here the way I should be,' she replied. 'I can't take care of you the way I want to, the way you deserve.'

'Please don't go,' he begged. 'Please ... I've waited so long ...'

Tears welled at the edges of her eyes. 'You've helped a lot of other people. Now I'm going to help you.'

'You are helping me, being here now!'

She shook her head, tried to fight back her tears. 'No ... I *know* somewhere you will be wanted, somewhere that goodness that's inside of you will be appreciated.'

They walked back towards Florence Place Cemetery almost in silence. Graveyard Billy never took his eyes from Piper, fearing she would cross over and leave him.

The cold night chilled him, his footpads aching in the frosty bite of the snow.

'This is where we first saw Issac,' Graveyard Billy said sombrely. 'This is where he tried to take that girl.'

'I know,' said Piper. 'That's where we're going.'

Piper shifted through the flat's front door: The lights were off, everything was in darkness, and no one was at home. 'How do you know about this?' Graveyard Billy asked, sitting on the snow-covered edge of the flat's balcony.

'When Issac extracted part of my essence – the other girl's essence, too – he was draining our life force bit by bit, using it to power himself. But it was a two-way thing. We could see and understand what he was doing – who the last girl was and where she came from.'

'So what do we do?' asked Graveyard Billy.

'We wait,' Piper said.

'What if I don't want to?' he snapped back petulantly. 'What if I want to be with you and I just leave?'

'You won't do that,' Piper said, shaking her head. 'You want to make me happy, right?'

'Why don't you make me ha –'

'You want to make me happy?' she reiterated angrily.

'Yes,' he said in a peevish tone.

'Then let's just see,' Piper said, leaning against the wall. 'Let's just wait and see.'

They sat on the balcony all night, talking like the old friends they were. Graveyard Billy nuzzled next to Piper's glowing aura, vibrating his loudest purr to show his affection towards her.

Eventually, with his small front paws crossed and his head bowed forward into the fur of his chest, he slept. Piper held a hand towards him, passing through his body, knowing this was the right thing to do. She knew that there is a time to live and a time to die, but she was stuck in this in-between limbo. Now was the time to put the wrongs right; now was the time to make plans to move on to the next life.

Chapter Fifty Four

The sun began to rise and at the bottom of the flat's stairwell, footsteps echoed, started marching up the stairs. Two female voices drew nearer.

'I really don't think you should stay here alone,'

'It's like the police said – it's over, and that's exactly how I should treat it.'

'But it's Christmas! Surely you could come and stay at the home with us ...'

'I just want to get on with things. I just want my routine back.'

'You shouldn't be alone, especially after that blow to the head,'

'The doctors said I'm fine, Harley – they should know.'

Graveyard Billy opened his eyes at the sound of the voices, looked at the top of the stairs as the blind girl – Jamie – walked around the corner, a huge bandage on her head from Issac's handy work. Her care worker, Harley, a smartly dressed woman in a suit jacket and matching skirt, led her to the flat's door.

'I just want to sit down and have a cup of tea,' Jamie said. 'I think going home is the best place you could ever want to be going.'

Harley had her arm linked with Jamie's. Fumbling with her keys, she noticed Graveyard Billy looking up at her with pie eyes. He stared at Piper next to him, then stared at Jamie. 'How could anyone hurt her?' he transmitted, seeing the sad vulnerability in her forward-staring eyes.

'There's a cat here, next to your door,' Harley said. 'A black one.'

'A cat?' Jamie said, puzzled.

'Yeah,' Harley said, turning her head like the others in the past had, reading his name written on his collar.

'Graveyard ... Billy ...'

Jamie let out a gasp. She had neglected to tell the police about the 'other girl' who had helped her escape, her instincts telling her that something ... odd had happened as she fled to freedom. She remembered the girl's final words – 'Go with him! I need to go back and help Graveyard Billy!' – and even then, she somehow knew she was talking about the cat that had come in to save her; the cat she'd heard keep that awful man back as she made her escape.

Harley finally managed to get the door open, tried to shoo off Graveyard Billy.

'No, don't do that,' Jamie said, wanting to meet the creature that had saved her.

'You don't want him in your flat,' Harley said. 'I thought

you were allergic to animals?'

'No, just dogs,' Jamie quickly replied, trying to reach down to find Graveyard Billy.

'Go to her,' Piper whispered, standing back, a bittersweet expression on her face.

Slowly, Graveyard Billy moved forward towards Jamie.

'It's okay,' Piper smiled.

Graveyard Billy shifted up on his back paws to touch Jamie's outstretched hand, rubbing his face into it, enjoying her warm touch as she rubbed behind his ear.

'Look, I don't think you need that cat hanging around he –'

'He's my cat,' Jamie replied, in a tone that really meant it.

'Since when?' Harley asked in a disgruntled tone.

'One of the neighbours moved out and asked if I wanted him. They couldn't take him with them.'

'When did this happen?' Harley said.

'A few days ago,' Jamie lied, reaching down and picking up Graveyard Billy, putting him over her shoulder and holding him tight. Graveyard Billy closed his eyes, enjoyed her touch through his black fur, enjoyed the warmth they shared pressed against one another.

'You should have told me,' Harley said, her nose put out of joint. 'It's a lot of responsibility looking after a cat.'

'It's a lot of responsibility looking after a blind girl. I should know.' Jamie replied.

Harley smiled, 'You've always got a smart reply, Jamie, I'll give you that.'

'If that's my only Christmas gift, you can keep it,' Jamie said.

They walked in, Piper following behind as Harley shut the door. Jamie carried Graveyard Billy to the front room, sat on the sofa, and placed Graveyard Billy on her knees as Harley went to the kitchen. She began to feel around Graveyard Billy's face, held his head in her hands and whispered into his ears: *'You were there, weren't you.'*

Graveyard Billy blinked once.

She felt the slight movement under her touch. *'The other girl … was she …'*

Graveyard Billy blinked again.

'You don't have any bowls or cat food!' Harley called from the kitchen.

'I was going to pick some up the night …' Everything hit her like a concrete slab of reality: It had all happened, all of it. Graveyard Billy jumped up and placed his front paws on her shoulders and rubbed into her face, and purred, Jamie's expression instantly changing.

'I'll pop to the shop, pick you some bits up,' Harley called. 'Are you going to be all right for ten minutes?'

'Yeah, I'll be fine!' Jamie called back.

Harley let herself out of the flat, calling, 'I'll be back soon,' as the door clicked shut.

Jamie sat in silence for a moment, then spoke to Graveyard Billy again. 'Did you come back to find me? To look after me?'

Graveyard Billy turned to Piper, who stood near the corner of the room and nodded at him, ectoplasmic tears streaming down her face. He turned towards her, rubbing into Piper's face, and let out a long mew, making the blind girl laugh.

'I think I need to go now,' Piper said.

Graveyard Billy looked at her sadly, knowing he would be needed here with Jamie, knowing that the girl who held him would give him the physical love Piper would never be able to.

It is a known trait in the world of the cat that they pick their humans – humans never pick them. Even though he had fought for the honour of Kelly and the memory of Piper, Graveyard Billy had also fought to keep Jamie alive. In a way, inadvertently, he had picked her as the human he had to keep safe, and now, together, they could look after each other.

A pang of guilt spurted through him, watching as Piper slowly moved towards the flat's hallway. 'I'm sorry,' he said.

'You have nothing to feel sorry for. You were the best friend I ever had, my Graveyard Billy, and I'll never forget you.'

He jumped from Jamie's lap, headed towards Piper.

'Billy? Billy?' Jamie called, worry in her tone.

'Go to her, please.' Piper said warmly. 'You have a lot of important things to do in life; I've got … something else to explore now. I'm ready to go.'

A supernatural rip opened in the hallway, a bright, pale aura illuminating from a faraway place. 'Don't worry,' Piper said, blowing Graveyard Billy a long, slow kiss. 'We'll meet again one day.' She turned and walked into the light, and as quickly as it had come, the tunnel and its ethereal light vanished.

'Billy? Graveyard Billy?' Jamie called, reaching down to the floor, clicking her fingers to get his attention. He turned back to her and ran to her touch, a deep sadness in his bones that Piper had crossed over, but a knowing in him that he would look after Jamie, that his place was here, that now, they would be together. She picked him up, held him tight, and he held her back. Everything truly was over, and as the sun rose in the sky, a new day begun for both of them.

CHAPTER FIFTY FIVE

The snow had melted, winter had passed, and slowly, as February rolled in, as it did every year, everything began to green up. 'Hi!' said the manager of the Oxfam charity shop on London Road as Jamie came through the door. He looked down at the taut lead that pulled in front of her. 'Oh – I didn't realize you had a guide dog? Is he trained?' He instantly felt stupid at the question.

'He's trained to do lots of things,' Jamie smiled. 'But I'm not sure how good he is at being a dog.'

Graveyard Billy leapt up onto the counter with a chirping purr, making the man jump. 'Guide Cat is what he prefers to go by.'

The man laughed and introduced himself. 'I'm James – James Harrison – the manager.'

'I remember,' Jamie said. 'So, what do you want me to do?'

She worked behind the till, dealt with the public, became known as 'the girl with the cat,' a nickname she preferred to 'the blind girl,' which she'd had all her life.

Graveyard Billy would either sit proudly on the counter or would drape himself around her neck – always with her as her loyal companion. He would often think of Piper, would think of that day on the other side when they would meet again when he could tell her of all the things he had learnt to be Jamie's guide.

One day while in the shop, he heard a voice no one else could hear, one he knew well.

'Oi, Bill!' Kelly stood there with her mother, the spectral Tina Turner outfit finally gone, the all-black attire of her corpse now worn in life after death as the older woman thumbed through a rail of clothes.

'What are you doing here!' he asked.

'Thought I'd pop down the town with my mum. She's getting over things now; it's taken a while. It's weird being about with her. I think she knows I'm here, like.'

'I'm sure she does,' he grinned.

'I've heard about you, Mr. Guide Cat,' she grinned back. 'I'm proud of you, mate.'

'We were a good team,' Graveyard Billy purred.

'We were the best,' she replied. 'I'm thinking of passing over soon: I think my time down here is done.'

'If you do ... if you see Piper, tell her you saw me, will you.'

'Of course, I will,' Kelly replied. Her mum picked up the

bags of shopping she had dropped at her feet and began to walk towards the door, the supernatural trail connecting Kelly to the woman pulling tight.

'I better go! See you later Bi –' and just like that, she was gone, shifting through the shop's front windows.

Jamie looked up: She had heard Kelly the first time when her emotions were at their peak. Now, an expression pulled on her face suggesting she somehow heard the voice of the girl who had led her to safety.

Life went on, and Graveyard Billy and Jamie lived in peace together, found happiness together. Any confidence she had lost with the attack from Issac, Graveyard Billy helped her find.

He was her Guide Cat; it was his job to help her.

Jamie went to the Day-to-Day shop for the things she needed, Mo Shaan's dad now running it again, deciding to hand it down this time to Mo's younger brother.

'Mo's off to uni to do a graphics course or something,' he told Jamie. 'Life's too short to be trapped in here if it's not for you, I suppose.' He shrugged.

'It would have been a lot shorter if you hadn't found him,' Mo's mum added as she stocked shelves.

'Thank you,' Mo's dad said, squeezing Jamie's hand. He always gave her as much free cat food as she wanted for saving his son.

In the summer, Jamie and Graveyard Billy sat out the back of the flats in the long grass of the graveyard, enjoying its peace and silence, enjoying each other. She ran her hand over Graveyard Billy's furry head, rubbed behind his ears, and said,' I love you, Graveyard Billy.'

'And I love you too,' he purred. 'I love you too.'

The End.

David Irons is an award-winning filmmaker and writer living in West Sussex. His films, colourful and stylish in design, have won awards at the Cambridge Film festival, Las Vegas VIFF festival, and LA Independent Festival for cinematography, editing, writing and directing. '7 Winters Alone' a sci-fi, horror short was a winner in David Lynch's Short Film Competition in 2014.
In 2019 David's first novel Night Waves published by Cosmic Egg books, followed by Night Creepers and Polybius in 2020 from Severed Press and Hard Copy Games.

Read more of David's work here:
https://www.davidironswriter.com/books

Join my mailing list for news on all new releases:
www.davidironswriter.com/contact

OTHER TITLES FROM THE AUTHOR:

NIGHTWAVES

POLYBIUS

NIGHT CREEPERS

WOLF MOON

7 WINTERS ALONE

THE BLOODY TRACKS OF BIGFOOT

MOONLIGHT FLIP

MY OUIJA BOYFRIEND

THE SKIN ON THE SKELETON

DON'T GO TO WHEELCHAIR CAMP